ROGUES HOCKEY ONE

COACH SULLY

SLOANE ST. JAMES

Copyright © 2024 by Sloane St. James
All rights reserved.

No part of this publication may be reproduced, distributed, or transmitted in any form or by any means, including photocopying, recording, or other electronic or mechanical methods, without the prior written permission of the publisher, except for the use of brief quotations in a book review as permitted by U.S. copyright law. For permission requests, contact SloaneStJamesWrites@gmail.com.

The story, all names, characters, and incidents portrayed in this production are fictitious. No identification with actual persons (living or deceased), places, buildings, and products is intended or should be inferred.

Line Editing by Dee Houpt | www.DeesNoteEditingServices.com
Developmental Editing by Bri | DevEditingWithBri@gmail.com
Formatting by Cathryn | FormatByCC@gmail.com

1st Edition 2024

MINNESOTA ROGUES TEAM ROSTER

Left Wingers
#7 Cori Kapowski
#16 Ebony Renaud
#89 Viviane Colbert
#80 Gabby O'Hara

Centers
#20 Kiana Jackson
#71 Becca Walters
#28 Leslie Stewart
#65 Zara Iko

Right Wingers
#95 Delta Makkonen
#18 Marine Chaput
#21 Theresa Roy
#48 Justine Bollinger

Left Defense
#58 Joanna "Joey" Breck
#63 Carrie Thomas
#49 Jennifer Skarbakka

Right Defense
#31 Amalia Werner
#52 Brittany Grattle
#41 Isabelle Duval

Goaltenders
#34 Timber Healy
#29 Manon Beaulieu

For all the readers who asked me if Sully was getting his own book.

Here you go, baby girl.

PREFACE

I want to start out by saying that my intention when writing Kendra was to add representation for BIPOC readers. As a white woman, I can pretty much pick up any romance book and know that when I open those pages, I'll be able to imagine myself as the female main character. I won't ever have to overlook the male character waxing poetic about the FMCs creamy, porcelain skin or her pink goddamn nipples. I don't even have to think about it—how convenient it is to be the "standard". This is part of my white privilege that I was born into and whole-heartedly acknowledge.

I'm not going to pretend like I'm some white author on the crusade against racism with this book, though some may see it that way, because let's be honest, nobody is more performative when it comes to anti-racism work than white women—we run that shit. This book will have imperfections. After all, Kendra is a Black woman written by a white woman. There is no amount of research I can do, or sensitivity readers I can involve, that will ever allow me to understand what that is like.

By publishing this book, I'm opening myself up for a lot of criticism, but for the sake of adding a little melanin to the romance world, which we desperately need, I'm going for it. I am not an expert on what is or isn't racist because I've never been on the receiving end. Therefore, I had two amazing

Black sensitivity readers comb through this manuscript to ensure accuracy and remove any harmful language. I readily took every suggestion and made changes.

Still, there will be readers who take issue with how this story is told. Some will argue Kendra's not Black enough, yet others will say writing about a white man falling in love with a WOC is fetishizing Black women in general. That was never my intention. I am a smut author, and this is a smut book.

I will get some things wrong, and that is a discomfort that I'll sit with when it comes. You can always email me: SloaneStJamesWrites@gmail.com I will listen to your criticism, learn, and do better next time. Just please know it was never my intent to hurt or misrepresent the BIPOC community.

I want to extend a special thank you to my incredible sensitivity readers, Tione and Teri, for all their insight, knowledge, and advice. I appreciate the time and mental energy you sacrificed to educate me on how to be a better writer and human.

—Sloane

CHAPTER ONE

SULLY

Why do I keep subjecting myself to blind dates and online matches? Maybe because I can't just go out to a bar. I've tried. The women are too young. Too desperate. Too ... opportunistic. And that's if I'm not swarmed by bros who want to discuss my NHL stats or my time with the Minnesota Lakes hockey team—especially since they just won the Stanley Cup a week ago. Holding that cup with Barrett was everything.

"So, what do you like to do on the weekends?" I ask.

"Saturdays are usually reserved for my yoga classes, and sometimes, I'll meet up with friends in the evening to see live music or something. On Sundays, I attend church and have dinner with my parents. It's sort of a weekly tradition, a nice wind down before starting the work week."

"That's cool. You must be close with your family."

Katherine offers a forced smile. She's a beautiful woman with brown hair and blue eyes. Her wardrobe is appropriate and put together. She seems like she has her shit together. "Yeah, we've always been really tight. What about you?"

"My brother lives a few states away, so we don't see each other as often as we'd like. We both have busy schedules."

This is the third time I've had this conversation this week. How do people handle having the same conversations day after day? Reciting the same boring, rote bullshit over and over again. It's madness. *What are your hobbies? What music genres do you enjoy? Where did you grow up? Do you have a big family? Do you have kids? Pets?*

We sit opposite each other at a small table while dining on Italian cuisine. My eyes are drawn to the dancing flame from the candle on the table. The food is terrific, the wine is excellent. The woman across from me is lovely ... She's nice and pretty and says the right things, but there's no spark. I can't imagine staring at her the way my best friend, Barrett, stares at his wife, Raleigh.

One thing's for sure, the dating pool is a lot smaller the older you get. My career was my focus for most of my life—I have zero regrets; I love hockey. It's in my blood and my bones. Plays and strategies haunt my dreams at night. Even now, on a date, my mind slips to the game when I find myself staring at that damn candle for too long.

Retiring was one of the hardest things I ever did, but my body was ready, and I didn't want to be the player who didn't know when it was time to hang up his skates. Do I miss hockey? More than anything. I'd never admit it out loud, but there's been a hole in my life since leaving. I tried traveling, golf, knocking things off my bucket list, and hoped a partner would provide me with some closure the way it did for Barrett. But I've yet to find someone to calm that storm inside me, the one that drags me out of bed every morning and has me lacing up my skates and heading to the arena.

Last year, I was offered a full-time commentary spot on a television panel, but that's not for me, I want to be in front of the action. I want to feel the bite of cool air on my face and breathe in the fresh scent of ozone right after the Zamboni turns the ice to glass.

I'd love to find someone who's more interested in the sport than in the fact I played it professionally. I've only ever desired simplicity, someone who fits with my life and vice versa. I want to find my person. A friend. An equal partner. For life.

Barrett loves to give me shit because I want to meet someone but don't want to meet people to do it. Maybe it's me? Am I dull? I'd like someone who prefers staying in and binging Netflix to going to a nightclub. Enjoys letting me cook for them rather than being seen on my arm at the new opening of some trendy restaurant. A woman who'll bring me a cold beer when I'm done mowing the lawn. Normalcy.

I could have that with Katherine, across from me. Nothing's wrong with her, she's lovely, she's just not *my* person.

Dating is hard, even when the woman looks like a sure thing on paper, if the connection isn't there, it doesn't matter how perfect we'd be. The whole endeavor is frustrating as fuck. Maybe it's time to put this whole dating thing on hold.

After our plates are taken away and the wine is gone, I pay the bill and we head our separate ways.

I'm not hers either.

―――

"Man, I told you, I'm taking a break from dating."

I open the fridge and grab a beer, then an opener from a drawer and pop the top off.

"Look, I get it, but—" Rhys says.

"Actually, you don't ... Sorry, bud. I'm retired and almost twice your age. You have no idea how hard it is out here.

Dating sucks." I pace the floor as Rhys tries to convince me to meet up with one of his wife's friends.

He sighs. "Yeah, okay. You're right about—" There's shuffling in the background before his wife, Micky, cuts in. "Sully?"

Here we go. "Hey Mick," I say, sighing. "Gotta give you props for turning Rhys into your errand boy."

"Who knew he was so good at begging, right?"

A sharp crack echoes through the phone, and she shrieks.

I roll my eyes. "I'm hanging up now—" I don't need to hear this.

"No, wait! Just give me a second!" Micky shouts.

My fingers pinch the bridge of my nose. "You've got a minute."

"I need you to have dinner with Kendra—"

"Already told Rhys I'm taking a break from dating."

"Do I get my minute or not?"

My head falls back, and I stare at the ceiling and shut my mouth, giving her a chance to plead her case. After a beat, she continues. "It's not a date. Well, the dinner with Kendra isn't, at least. She's producing a new dating show. But hear me out, it uses AI to find your perfect match. It's based on real-life compatibility instead of just interests and shit. They had a guy, but he backed out last minute. I told her you would sit down with her. You don't have to agree to anything! All I'm asking is for you to get a free drink and listen to her pitch. If you still aren't interested by the end of the meeting, just say no. It's not a big deal. But please, she needs this. It's her show, and it's going to get scrapped if they can't get a solid replacement. She's worked really hard for this and deserves to see it through."

I blow out an exasperated breath. "Micky, this is the first

and last time you ever agree to anything on my behalf without running it by me."

"I promise! Never again!" Her voice rises as the excitement shows through. "Does that mean you'll do it?"

"I'll meet with her," I grumble. "But that's it."

"I knew I could count on you! You're the best. Okay, she's expecting you tomorrow night at Urban Elixir. Seven o' clock."

"Got it. Your minute's up. Bye, Mick."

I take a long pull from the beer. There's no way in hell I'm doing a fucking television show.

CHAPTER TWO

KENDRA

My foot bounces under the high-top table. Almost seven o'clock. I'm not nervous to meet Lee Sullivan, but there's a lot riding on this. If we can't license this show to the network, the production company will pitch something new. Which would make it the third time a show has slipped through my fingers.

The first time, funding got pulled. After that, the schedules couldn't align. And now my lead for *Love Algorithm*, the dating show I created, has dropped out last minute. It's a great concept, and I sold it to the production company as a package deal, one that locks me in as the producer. Do I care about the show? Not entirely, but I know it will work, and all I care about is getting the experience it offers.

Women's hockey and the professional teams being formed across the United States are being discussed on the TVs mounted on the walls. Maybe this is a sign, considering I'm meeting with Lee Sullivan, former captain of the Minnesota Lakes NHL team. I need him for my show. Sipping my cocktail, I roll my shoulders. It's fine. Everything is fine.

COACH SULLY

It's not like I've spent the last four months working tirelessly with engineers to perfect the AI algorithm. I've busted my ass and trust the system we've created to match singles based on artificial intelligence. However, starting with a new love interest means we have to move fast, because we've got to open another casting call for matches, plus run their background reports, carry out psychological interviews, and perform screen checks to make sure it's not some fifteen-minute-Felicity looking to boost her Instagram following.

My racing thoughts are interrupted by a tall blue-eyed Norwegian drink of water ducking under the doorframe when he walks in the bar. Sully. Damn ... He's gorgeous. Even better looking than the headshots I pitched to casting ... and those headshots were pretty great.

Raising my hand, I grab his attention, and he smiles. *Oh shit, he's perfect.* I'm certain that smile is pouring butterflies into the stomach of every woman in his vicinity. Even my stomach did a little flip-flop. I *need* him for *Love Algorithm*.

"Kendra?"

Game time. "Hi, Lee! Thank you so much for meeting with me tonight."

"It's no problem. I actually go by Sully—or Sullivan, whichever you prefer," he says while taking a seat across from me.

God, he smells good too. We shake hands, and his palm engulfs mine. It's huge. I steel my expression, slipping on my professional mask, to keep from nervously laughing. All I can think about is the damage those fingers could do to me—I mean, a different woman. A woman who isn't me. Because this isn't a date, this is a business meeting—and I never mix business with pleasure. Never. Especially not when everything I've worked for is riding on this show.

"Can I get you something to drink?" I offer.

"What are you having?"

"A Tom Collins."

He raises his eyebrows. "Old school."

"I prefer *classic*."

The corner of his mouth tips up. "Just surprising for somebody so …"

Young. The word he's looking for is young. I raise a brow back to him, daring for him to finish his sentence. "Somebody so …?"

I have a love-hate relationship with my age. I'm proud of what I've already accomplished at age twenty-three, but that number often gets me overlooked. They tell me it takes time to make it in the industry. I know that, but let's face it, this industry is based around youth. As a young Black woman, the cards are stacked against me. I gotta make a name for myself early if I want to get somewhere.

Sully clears his throat. "I was just expecting you to order something like …"

He's struggling, and I can't help but enjoy watching him squirm, trying not to offend me. It's cute. Why did he feel the need to even comment on my age? It's a pet peeve of mine.

I take a sip from my straw as he stumbles over his words.

"Hennessy?" I suggest. That was probably a little much, but he had it coming. Don't come for my age like that. If you make me feel uncomfortable, I will make you feel uncomfortable right back.

His eyes lock onto my brown skin and grow wide. "What? No. I didn't mean—I just meant because you're more Gen-Z, you know?"

When he notices my smirk, the realization I'm kidding sets in and his broad shoulders relax as he shakes his head. "Do you know how Hennessy became popular in Black culture?" he asks. *Is he serious right now?*

I actually do know why, but I want to see if he does. "Because Tupac rhymed Hennessy with enemies and we ain't been the same since?" I snark.

He laughs. "Hennessy was one of the first warehouses to employ Black workers and pay them equal wages. They also used Black models in advertisements and gave leadership positions to people of color."

Guess he does know. Well done, Norway. "Some people argue that Hennessy exploited Black communities for profit, but I'm still impressed you know your history." A slow smile creeps across my face as we call this bizarre truce. "Sorry, I didn't mean to fuck with you like that … You just looked like someone who's …" My eyes rove up and down his body.

"An easy target?" He finishes with a raised eyebrow.

I raise my eyebrows and grin. "I was going to say *old*, but …"

He gives me the full mega-watt Sully smile. His acute gaze flickers with mischief. Damn, he's attractive, and I stare back with equal intensity. Thankfully, we're interrupted by a bubbly server who asks for his drink order.

His eyes continue to drink me in for a beat before he peers at the petite server.

"What's your *oldest* whiskey?" he says.

Grinning around my straw, I take a sip of my Tom Collins.

"Oh. Um … I-I don't know. I'm sorry. Let me go check —"

"Nah, that's okay." He holds the drink menu between us and scans it, then peeks over the top of the black book to glance at me. "Age doesn't matter, anyway." He winks at me, then returns his attention to the server. "Actually, I'll have whatever stout you have on tap."

"We have Black Beauty on nitro?" she suggests.

I laugh, and the corners of his lips tip up, and he slides his hands together. *Those hands.*

"Yeah. I really want that," he says, looking at me.

Is he flirting? Wait, am I blushing? Shit. This is unprofessional. I avert my gaze. The server strides away to fetch his drink. He crosses his arms, sits back, and grins.

I'm here with one goal in mind: get him to do the show.

"Speaking of segue …" I say, clearing my throat and severing the heady connection forming between us. "Did Micky tell you why I wanted to meet?"

His smile falters now that I've killed our playful banter. He sighs and uncrosses his arms. "Something about a dating show."

"It's different from most other shows. It's not like *The Bachelor*, where people are simply signing up and hoping to 'win' you. We do an in-depth analysis of what you're looking for, we look at your lifestyle and values and use artificial intelligence to find the most fitting matches out of thousands of applicants also searching for love. They don't know your identity prior to applying. We will narrow it down to ten women. As long as you're honest in your answers, you'll leave the show in love."

He sighs. "And then what?" He's already skeptical. I can't totally blame him, with his level of popularity.

"We film your dates with the different women, evaluate your progress, and let America fall in love with you and one of the ten matches." The server returns with his drink, and he takes a big swig of the obsidian beer topped with a creamy head. *Creamy head?* Goddamn, I can't seem to pull my mind out of the gutter tonight.

"I'm burned out from dating. I'm tired of having the same conversations over and over. This sounds like all of that but doing it on camera. Respectfully, I'd rather rawdog a garbage disposal."

Well, there's a visual. "Except you'll already have chemistry with these people. We've tested the system, it's solid. By the time it's been thinned down to ten women, the challenge is picking only one, because you'll likely want all of them. I can guarantee you'll depart satisfied."

"If this works so well, how come you're not starting your own online dating app or something? Monetizing the technology?" He nods to me. "Tell me what *you* get out of it, then I'll consider."

"What I get out of it doesn't matter. This is about you finding love. You said you're burned out from dating, so you've obviously been trying to meet people, and since you're still single—"

"Kendra." The way he says my name in that deep voice gives me chills and disarms me. "What's *your* reason?"

I swallow, glancing down at my hands before sighing and coming clean. "I'm passionate about cinematography. It's my greatest love. I'm the youngest Black woman to get a shot at producing her own show. Sure, I could sell the technology and make money, but let's be honest, dating companies are already working the AI angle, it won't be long before I'll be competing with them, anyway. This is my ticket to do what I love. It gets me closer to production and network executives." The sparkle in his eye tells me he's satisfied with my answer. "This is dating on the next level; every date is a good date. Dating in the wild sucks. It's a lot of work. But I promise, the hardest part of this show will be having to choose which one is *the* one."

He drags a hand down his face. "I'm not a fan of being in the spotlight. Especially a dating show. This sounds messy and complicated. People's feelings will get hurt publicly. Also, I hate reality television ... No offense."

Shit. I've worked alongside casting and have interviewed people more times than I can count. Sully is easy to read; he's candid with his words and body language. He doesn't seem like the type to change his mind once he's made a decision, and it's obvious he's not comfortable with the show. This is where I should end the night.

Brushing off the rejection, I give him a tight smile and hold up my hands. "None taken. Also, it's *unscripted* television," I say, the same way car salespeople say *pre-owned* rather than used.

"Right."

Maybe another shot. "It's only a three-month commitment."

"For you!" He laughs. "Sounds like it's a lifetime for me." He takes another sip of his beer.

"I mean, why are you dating? Just to get laid?"

He cocks an eyebrow. "No."

"Well? You're sick of dating. Don't you want to skip to the good part?"

CHAPTER THREE

SULLY

By now, I'm two and a half beers in and have no clue how to let this woman down easy. No way in hell I'm doing her show ... It sounds like my worst nightmare. Besides, I don't like the idea of her setting me up with someone. Mostly because I'm attracted to her and want to run with it. This "business meeting" is ten times better than any date I've had in the last year. She keeps me on my toes. She's funny and driven and knows how to hold a conversation. I like that she throws a little sass my way. On top of that, she's fucking gorgeous with her rich warm skin, curly hair, and light-gray eyes I could get lost in for a week. Don't send a search party.

I find myself forgetting to breathe, and instead of telling her no, I've been stalling, redirecting our conversation. I'll do anything to draw this out.

"Do you miss hockey?" Kendra asks.

"I do, actually. I miss it a lot. I've tried other sports, but nothing has been able to fill that void that hockey left."

"I mean, not to talk you out of being on my show or state

the obvious, but why don't you do something hockey related?"

The half-full pint glass in front of me slides as I pass it from one hand to the other. I nod because it *is* what I want to do. "I was offered a commentary spot with MNSports, but it's not the same as being on the ice. I don't want to sit in a studio and talk about hockey, I want to be out there again," I explain. "Barrett Conway is my best friend, we played together on the Lakes. He recently retired and has a hockey charity called Camp Conway, so I volunteer with that on the side, working with some of the kids. I love it, but it's only during the summer."

"What about coaching?"

"I'd love to coach. Honestly, that would probably make me happiest, but the university just got a new coach last year. If they ever asked me, I'd say yes in a heartbeat … Until then, I'm happy spending my mornings at the arena skating or volunteering with kids. I share the ice with a couple young figure skaters. I was a figure skater before hockey, so I've been able to do a little bit of coaching with them. It's nice, but obviously very different from a hockey team."

"Wait, you were a figure skater before a hockey player?" She stares at me wide-eyed. A lot of guys started with figure skating. They're usually the more graceful players.

I nod after taking a sip of beer.

"Like triple Salchows and shit?"

Her beaming smile is contagious. "More like a double, at best. That was a long time ago. You know, because I'm *old*."

"When did you find out you were better with a stick?"

"When I was tired of being the only guy in a class full of girls." I chuckle. "But as it turns out, the guys were all jealous that I got to touch Amber Tolefson during our partner routines."

"Oooh. Did you and Amber Tolefson ever ... ya know ..." She bounces her eyebrows.

I smile and shake my head. "No, Amber was not my type. Also, we were nine."

She laughs. "You had a type at nine?"

"Oh yeah, I had a type. My English teacher, Mrs. Wilbur. Every time she turned around at the board, her ass was covered in chalk marks."

She parts her lips in faux shock. "What a tease."

I take another sip and chuckle. "Right? What about you, who was your childhood crush?"

"Hmm ..." She narrows her eyes toward the ceiling, and a big smile splits her face. "Oh, I know! Corbin Bleu."

I laugh. "Isn't that a food?"

"No, Greatest Generation, that's *cordon* bleu."

"Excuse me, I'm a millennial." Barely, but I made the cutoff. She can't be that young. She's drinking, so she's at least twenty-one. And I don't feel forty-two.

She raises her eyebrow.

"Okay, fine. *Elder* millennial. On the line of Gen X, but that's the cool generation. How old are you?" I ask.

"Just turned twenty-three." She takes a sip of her drink. Shit, I'm almost twice her age. *I could be her fucking dad.* "How old are you?"

She knows how old I am. It was obvious she did her homework when she brought up my sponsorships and career highlights earlier.

"Does it matter?" I ask. That's the important question.

She looks down and straightens her cocktail napkin, pausing before she answers. "No."

The tension between us is building. I've dated on and off for almost a year and not once have I experienced the attraction I share with her. Maybe it's true what they say: you find someone when you're not looking. I've all but given up on dating, and she practically falls into my lap. I file that image away for later. How do I say *No, I don't want to do your show, but would you like to go out to dinner with me?* without sounding like a complete asshole? Like I'm haggling for a lower price, handing over a hundred, and asking for change.

It's a dick move. Man, my luck sucks.

Other than the fact that she's trying to set me up with other women, there's not one thing I dislike. I'm not doing Kendra's show ... *I could do Kendra, though.* She's gorgeous, funny, and sweet. She's fun and easy to talk to. The past few months of dating have taught me there's a difference between nice and kind, Kendra is the latter. Those captivating silver eyes are difficult to turn down. And she's right, I want to find love, but not in front of a camera.

I like this girl. I like her a lot. I like that her clothes are vibrant and she wears too many bracelets. I like the way she tells a story, her voice, how she occasionally touches my arm when I make her laugh. I love the look and feel of her hand when it lands next to mine. Hell, I like that she does her research before going to a business meeting. She's motivated and on top of her game and can still have fun. She's got a brain full of big ideas and plans for her future and is determined to see them through. It's sexy as hell.

She peeks at her phone. "Whoa, we've been here over three hours!"

No wonder the wait staff has been checking on us so often.

Feels like twenty minutes. We've got that lose-track-of-time connection. The one I've been looking for.

"Time flies."

"So ..." she says. "What do you think about the show?

How about you take a couple days to think about it?" She bites the corner of her lower lip. *Fuck me.*

I lean back in my chair and rub both hands down my face. *Just bite the bullet and get it over with.*

"Kendra, I'm sorry. I can't do the show. It's not for me."

She pauses for a moment, lets her head fall forward, then nods. She's not happy, but I suspect she knew it would never happen. Still, seeing her bright eyes turn disappointed is harder than I imagined it would be.

"I get it," she says. "No worries. Thanks for coming out tonight."

She gives a tight wave to the server to let her know we're ready for the check. Damn, I'm losing her. Maybe I should have tried to prolong my answer. I don't want tonight to end like this. I'm still gonna shoot my shot.

"Hey, I'm starving, have you eaten yet?"

She takes the last sip of her drink. "I'm good. I had a protein bar on the way over."

"That's not a meal. Come on, let me get you dinner. I mean, it's the least I can do after turning down the show."

Her eyes narrow as she seems to consider my invite. It's more playful than scrutinizing. It's a good sign. "It really is the *least* you can do."

"Then let's start with dinner and go from there."

CHAPTER FOUR

SULLY

We drive around for a little while, but there's not a lot open.

"What's your favorite late-night food?" I ask.

"Breakfast."

A woman after my heart.

"You know …" *I'm going out on a limb here.* "I like to cook. If you want, I could whip up something at my place? No pressure … I'm just not seeing anything open." I duck to get a better glance of the street up ahead. Most of the restaurants have the lights off.

She smiles and cuts her eyes at me.

I shrug. *Guilty.*

"Can you make omelets?" she asks.

"I make the best omelets."

———

"What do you want in yours?" I ask, selecting a frying pan and setting it on the stove. She sits at one of the barstools, watching me. "I've got ricotta, cheddar, gouda, spinach, mushrooms, ham, bacon, onions, potatoes …"

"Hashbrowns?"

"Sure."

"I'm a little particular about my breakfast food."

"Let's hear it." I enjoy a challenge.

"I want an omelet with bacon, mushrooms, and spinach. *But* here's how I want you to cook it … ready?"

"Lay it on me."

"Fry the bacon in the pan first, when it's cooked, set it aside and use the grease to cook the hashbrowns. Add gouda to the hashbrowns until it gets all nice and melty, then shove the whole thing inside the omelet with the mushrooms and spinach."

The smile on my lips grows with each word. I love that she knows exactly what she wants and how she wants it. "Damn, Kendra. Yeah, I can do that." In fact, I'm making one for myself. She had me at bacon grease.

She removes her bright-pink blazer and drapes it over one of the barstools next to her, then rests her elbows on the kitchen island, propping her chin on her fists to enjoy the show. What is it about grown-ass women getting excited for food that I find so appealing? Maybe I like seeing the hunger in their eyes.

Kendra appeals to a nurturing side I didn't know I had. I want to feed her. A woman who knows exactly how she likes her omelet shouldn't eat energy bars for dinner. That's not to say I've never cared about previous partners, but the need is stronger with her. I have the urge to protect and provide for her. It's bizarre. Maybe it's the age gap?

I plate our food, and she seems pleased with it as I slide it across the counter. When I take a bite, everything melts on my tongue, so I groan while pulling the fork from my lips.

"Told ya." She laughs next to me, then takes a bite. "Perfect. God, this is my favorite comfort food."

I nod. "Might be my favorite too." It's delicious, but I can already tell I will want to sleep after this, and I'm not ready to be done with her yet. We've been making glances at each other since we arrived. It's been a long time since I've brought a woman home. The first ever to step foot in this house.

She looks around, taking in her surroundings. "You have a nice house. Is it new?"

"Yeah, I moved in last fall."

"Did you design it?"

I nod.

"Can I have a tour?"

I bring the napkin to my mouth before answering, struggling to hide my grin. "Right now?"

I feel like we just sat down, but she wipes her hands and hops off her barstool. "Yeah."

As soon as she turns to face the living room, my eyes drop to the brightly colored embroidery on her high-rise jeans. The flared bottoms are covered in flowers, every color of the rainbow, with stems and petals climbing her legs like ivy, up to where the denim hugs her ass as if they're custom made. I'm jealous of pants. I want to delve into her back pockets and fill my hands with her. I've always been an ass man. The crop top reveals a sliver of her stomach, and I resist the temptation to touch her.

"Sure." I clear my throat and stand.

We start at the lower level. I show her the theater, then to my "mini rink" which is essentially a twenty-by-twenty room with synthetic ice flooring.

"Whoa. Can I step on it?"

"Sure. It's slick, though. Let me go first." I pass her

covers for her feet, then pop on my skates and tuck in the laces.

I step on and extend a hand, and she takes it. I can't help but appreciate how convenient the extra physical contact is. She takes tiny steps and almost loses her balance, but I've got my arms around her before she can fall. I had no idea this floor would be such a great wingman when I had it installed. *I'm a genius.*

"This is so cool!"

The only people who have been down here are other hockey players. I use it for training, but to someone who doesn't skate, I suppose walking on synthetic ice is a novelty. "It's about ten percent less slippery than real ice."

I skate backward and pull her into me. She smells so good. I don't know if it's perfume or something she puts in her hair or just her, but I like it.

"I want one of these."

"A hockey player?"

She rolls her eyes and pushes back from me, glancing down at her feet. "One of these floors."

"You need a pair of skates first."

"Want to teach me?" she asks with a laugh, as if she's only joking, but I wouldn't mind giving her private lessons down here. I wouldn't mind that *at all.*

"Yeah, I do," I answer seriously.

"If I didn't know better, I'd say that's an attempt to see me again."

I drag her close again, and she smiles, clutching my sides harder. I stare into her light-gray eyes, and her gaze drops to my lips. Fuck. I lean down, brushing my mouth over hers. Covering her hands with mine, I take her wrists in one hand and pin them over her head in the air. Then I pause and lean in close, biting her earlobe.

"This okay?"

She sucks in a small breath. "Mm-hm … Maybe we should continue the tour."

I withdraw slightly, searching her eyes. She bites her lip again.

"Do you want to see my bedroom?"

"Is there any chance you would reconsider the show contract—"

"None," I answer firmly.

"Then… yes."

I waste no time getting off the synthetic ice with her and tossing my skates in the corner of the room. She follows me back upstairs and not-so-subtly smiles as we cross the threshold to my bedroom. The large king bed is the focal point of the room, but her fingers trail across the foot of the bed as she saunters toward the wall of picture windows. I stare at her silhouette against the night sky and watch her reflection in the mirror. Her gaze wanders as she overlooks the illuminated pool and forest surrounding the property. The full moon makes the lazy river that winds through the corner of the property sparkle.

I take the opportunity to admire her ass before I walk up behind her and place my hands on her hips. She leans her back against my chest, and I bring my palms up to her revealed stomach between her jeans and crop top. Her sweet sigh makes me blow out a breath. Even in the reflection, I see her nipples peak. It's not the first time I've caught a glimpse tonight. The free-the-nipple movement is a beautiful thing. Rotating her head to face me is easy. Her chest rises and falls against my sturdy one. First woman to christen this new bed, and it feels right.

My thumb swipes over her lower lip, and I relish watching her cool demeanor slip as she becomes a needy puddle in my hands. A small whimper escapes, and instantly, I have to hear every other noise she can make.

"I knew the second I laid eyes on you I could never be a part of your show. It was never going to happen."

"Why?"

"And miss out on this? I'd never forgive myself." I wink.

She bites the corner of her lip and brings her arms up, linking her fingers behind my neck. The desire to taste her is overwhelming. I drop my mouth to hers, and she sucks in a breath. Her lips are so fucking sweet. Our mouths fit perfectly together. It's heated and hungry. She's still holding her breath, though…

I pull away and smile at the way she blinks open her eyes. "You good?"

She smiles and chuckles, and the deep-red blush fades from her skin. I'm relieved when she exhales and takes in air again. She eagerly nods but still appears slightly timid. "Sorry, it's just been a while."

How long is a while? I get the impression she lives for her career, and it probably leaves little room for a social life. Kendra's been take-charge all night, but kissing me now, she's giving a softer, shy side of her, which is playing right into my desire to fulfill and take care of her every need.

My hands find her ass and grip her, picking her up and holding her against me. Our lips don't leave one another as I walk her toward the bed. My tongue skates across the seam of her mouth before nipping at her pouty bottom lip. She sighs and I grin. I could kiss her forever. I want every inch of her, but if she's not ready tonight, I'll be happy doing this until the sun rises. I'll wait until next time or the time after that. As long as it takes. This isn't the normal progression of my dates, but I find her irresistible, and I'm desperate for her.

Settling on the side of the bed, I let her straddle me. The

way she gyrates her pussy over my cock makes me groan. *Fuck.*

"Sully …" she breathes. Goddamn.

"What do you need, baby girl?"

"More."

I unhook the top button on her jeans, then push the colorful denim down her legs. She stands, and I shove them to the floor, then she steps out. I unbutton and remove my jeans. Pulling her back, she straddles me once again, this time wearing only a lace thong and that damn crop top. Grabbing my shirt at the back of my neck, I tug over my head.

She toys with the thin gold chain at my neck while my fingertips skim up her thighs, over her waist, and to her attention-seeking nipples. As she leans into my hands, I glide my palms over her ribs, then raise her shirt and drop my mouth to her dark peaks. Her nails scratch the back of my neck as she cradles me tighter to her chest.

I continue to work the shirt over her head, and she releases me to let it slide off her arms. Lying back, I peruse her body. You couldn't find a more perfect human form than Kendra's. There's muscle under those curves of hers, yet she's soft in all the right places. And that face? Fucking hell. She's gorgeous. She's got it all.

She leans forward, and her lips find mine again. I love the feel of her nipples scraping over my bare chest. Her G-string doesn't cover much, and my boxers are getting tighter by the second. I want to flip her over and fuck her senseless. The way she rolls her soft hips has me hypnotized. She fists my cock, making me groan. "This is going to hurt, isn't it?" she mumbles against my smiling lips.

I sit up. She's so cute, trembling as I trace up the inside of her thigh. Peeling her thong down, I run my knuckles over her clit, and she moans. She's slick as fuck. Her knees part, and I sink my middle finger inside, then add my ring finger, slowly stroking as she rocks on my hand. "I'm going to get you there. This tight pussy"—I pump in and out of her, and she grips my shoulders, hanging on as her muscles tighten around my fingers—"is going to take every inch I feed it. Isn't it?"

Her darkened eyes lock onto mine, filled with equal trust and lust. "Yes, Daddy."

I almost choke.

Holy fuck.

That's a new one for me, but I like it ... a lot. I want her to call me daddy all night long.

I smack her ass, the loud clap echoing in the room. "Good fucking girl," I growl. She has no idea what she's doing to me, but I'm feral for her.

She sighs against my neck, and my dick throbs. I know for a fact I won't last, so I've got to get her off ahead of time. It's been way too long, and when you add an emotional connection to the physical attraction, sex just hits different. *Everything* hits different with her.

"You say stop, we stop. Okay? We aren't doing anything you're uncomfortable with."

She nods.

"Say, *yes, daddy.*" I need to hear it again.

"Yes, Daddy."

Fucking hell. It's like a livewire straight to my cock every time she says that word. My thumb presses against her clit, and her legs shake. Her nails pierce my shoulder blades and her breath hitches as she comes. Her rasp is so sexy. Kendra's eyes glaze over, and the corner of my mouth tips up.

"Oh, baby girl, that's so good. I can't wait to feel you strangle my cock with that tight little pussy of yours." She rides my hand, and I don't give her a chance to come down from her orgasm before I'm flipping her on her back and ripping her thong the rest of the way off in one smooth motion. Dropping to my knees, I throw her legs over my shoulders. I want to devour my prize.

With one lick and her taste on my tongue, I know I'll never get enough. My eyes dart to her watching me intently as I draw my tongue over her. Kendra's mouth drops open, and we stare at each other. Eye contact has never gotten me this hard, but seeing her eyes gleam and lashes flutter as I feast is everything. Goddamn. I close my eyes to keep from climbing on top and fucking her bare.

I tear off my boxers, spit on her pussy, and stuff two fingers inside as I lick. My tongue plays everywhere except where she needs it. She writhes, seeking more.

"Tell me."

She pants. "Are you seriously going to make me say it?"

I grin. "Yes."

"Suck my clit, Sully."

I love her saying my name, but now that she's called me something else, that's all I want.

"Sully? Try again."

"Suck my clit, Daddy."

Growling into her lips, I latch onto her and fuck her with my fingers. Her hand threads through my hair and grips as she grinds against my face, crying out those sweet sounds. Her body gives up the orgasm so easily. I keep my gaze on her as my tongue fits inside, her taste flooding my mouth and intoxicating me. I groan. This woman is wild. I go back to sucking and drive my fingers deeper. I love the way she squeezes.

She moans, rocking against me. Fuck. I don't dare let up on her juicy, twitching clit as her pussy thrums around my middle and ring fingers.

As soon as her muscles ease and she lets go, I drop my head and kiss her inner thighs. "You did so well, baby girl. Such a good job taking my hand." I stroke her pussy, stretching her until I'm satisfied I won't hurt her. "You ready?"

She nods, her eyes are eager, but there's still a hint of nervousness in them. It's flattering. I drop another kiss and sit up, reaching over into my nightstand for a condom.

"I've been tested," she says.

"So have I, but you're the only one I want calling me *daddy*. Are you on birth control?"

"I can't have kids. My tubes are tied."

Her tubes are tied? She's kind of young for that, isn't she? But whatever. I'm not about to tell a woman what to do with her body.

"Okay."

She scoots farther back on the bed and rests against the pillows on the side opposite of the one I sleep on. Seeing her there sends a rush of adrenaline through me. A familiar feeling, as if she knows it's hers.

I climb over her, and she parts her legs, giving me an eyeful of where my tongue was. Her taste lingers on my tongue. The way she looks at me makes my chest tight. Looking at her almost hurts. "You're painfully beautiful, baby girl."

She bites the corner of her mouth again—a shy habit I hope she never loses. Leaning forward, I coat my length in her, rubbing soft circles against her clit until she loosens up some of her tight, overzealous muscles. Notched against her opening, the head of my cock is already being constricted. I blow out a breath and watch her face as I push inside. Her chest rises and falls faster. "Relax, baby."

"It's a lot ... Please, don't stop."

"A few more inches ... I told you you're going to take all of them."

She nods, and I sink deeper until all of me is snug inside her.

"Goddamn, Kendra."

I'm seeing stars, so I drop my head to draw her nipple into my mouth while I adjust to how good this woman feels. It's intense, but it's more than just physical. Is this what the guys are always going on about?

Years ago, my best friend had a one-night stand with a woman named Raleigh. They lost contact, and he spent years looking for her. I couldn't understand this obsession he had with her. But now ... I've only known Kendra for a few hours, but if I lost her, I'd be searching every crowded bar for her face too. No question.

Kendra is not a one-night stand. She's not a ten-night stand. She's not someone you give up without a fight. I slide out and plunge back in, and she digs her hands into my ass and forces me deeper. "Fuck, baby. That's my girl ..."

She pulls me down, and I kiss her with everything I have. A small laugh slips out; I'm so happy to be in this moment with her. Where the fuck did this woman come from? Shit, we click so well. Best nondate I've ever been on.

"I'm going to see you again," I tell her.

"Yeah?" she asks, panting, and her wide eyes take me in.

"You have no idea. I'm going to see you again so fucking hard." I nip at her bottom lip, and she laughs. I sit up on my heels, admiring how well we look together. I love it.

"Pretty," she comments out loud, reading my mind.

I grip her waist and slowly fuck her sweet little body as she adjusts to my size. "Yeah, baby girl. We're pretty." I can only imagine the number of suitors' hearts she has broken—I'm willing to risk being the next one.

Reaching up, she braces against the headboard, adding resistance to fuck herself on me. With pleasure written all over her face, I love seeing her stretched beneath my much larger body.

I match her rhythm. "Oh my god," she whines. She bites her lip, biting back curses as she lets me take over. My hand finds her clit, and I tug it between my fingers and let go. I repeat the action twice more, and each time, she squeezes my cock harder, and it's a struggle to hold out. Her legs shake, and hearing her cry for me is so rewarding. Her involuntary movements are pure gold as she loses control.

I pull out. "Get on your hands and knees, baby girl." I'm desperate to watch her ass bounce as I pound into her. "Show me how good you look being fucked from behind."

"Yes, Daddy." She gets up and does as she's told.

"Fuck me," I groan, rubbing the back of my neck. "You have no idea what that does to me."

She gets in position and has the nerve to look back at me with a mischievous gleam in her eye; she knows exactly what she's doing. I slap her ass twice, and it jiggles under my palm. "Dirty fucking girl." She wiggles side to side, as if daring me to do it again. I rub her backside, then crack an open palm across it. She jolts and drops to her elbows as I grab her hips and bury my length inside. She gasps, panting at the sudden fullness. "Be a sweet girl while I fuck you, hm?"

I lean over her back and whisper in her ear, "I'm going to be a little rough with you, baby girl. Can you handle that?"

"Yes, Daddy." There it is. I caress the welt on her ass from my earlier punishment. She rocks against me, impaling herself on my dick.

"That's better."

My hands spread her cheeks, and I admire the view as I push and pull. I give her one more swat before I skate fingers from the base of her spine to her neck and pin her to the bed while I work her over. She fists the pillows while she makes the sexiest moans. Someday, I'll fuck this tight ass too. *I wonder what noises she'll make then.*

I lift up long enough to turn her head to face the windows. The night sky has turned them into the perfect black mirror to capture our reflection, and I want her to see what I see. How beautiful she is like this. "You look so fucking good taking my fat cock. Don't you, baby girl?"

She nods, and our size difference is even more apparent this way. It's impressive. I hold her steady while I drive into her, loving the way she trembles. She mumbles something.

"What is it, baby?"

"Choke me again," she begs.

"No *please*?"

"Please, Daddy." She adds, desperate.

I drop to one elbow, covering her body with mine, wanting to see how much she can take. My index finger and thumb on each side of her neck, enjoying the ricochet of her pulse as I urge her into a vulnerable head space.

"Give in to me," I whisper. "Close your eyes when you start to float." My other hand snakes between her legs, and I play with her clit while thrusting into her, then watch her face carefully for her fade out.

The moment she turns to mush, those eyes drift shut. I release her neck and grab her shoulders, forcing her down on me harder.

"Show me what a pretty girl you are when you come on my cock." She does that thing where she forgets to exhale. It only spurs me on. When I'm about to remind her, her pussy clenches and I rise to my knees, then shove her hips down to the mattress. Her ass spreads for me, and I strike her on each cheek three times, fucking her through her orgasm. Her sounds are ragged and rough around every "Thank you, Daddy."

My dam is about to break. I withdraw and flip her so she's facing me.

"Hold onto me." She seizes my forearms, and I do the same to her, stabilizing her body while I pull each whimper from her lips with my cock. "One more, baby." She groans loudly at the thought of having to give me another orgasm. Her body is wrung out, but she nods.

I'm beyond impressed by her strength. I'm not going easy on her, yet she's taking every inch like a fucking pro. She's been tossed around, spanked, choked, and roughly fucked—her body is nearly limp. The grip she has on me loosens as another part of her takes hold.

"That's it, almost there. Can I come inside you?"
I didn't realize I wanted to so badly until I said it. I'll be disappointed if she says no, but I hide that from my face. I'm relieved when she nods.

"Fill me with your cum." She bites her lip. "Please, Daddy?"

"Goddamn it, Kendra."

I bring my palm to her throat and watch the smile slowly spread; she's got my number and knows it. Her enthusiasm is incredible. My pale hand against her warm skin feels like home. Her slender fingers wrap around my wrist, bright-pink nails peeking out as she perseveres, taking all of me and relinquishing control. Glancing into her eyes is my undoing. This beautiful woman has me under her spell, and the flutter of her pussy right before I come is divine.

"Here you go, baby girl. All this is yours." With every stroke, more cum spurts from me as I pound into her, spilling myself until it gushes out around my length and her pussy glistens with me. It's so fucking hot.

I pull out, enjoying the view of her pulsing cunt as it leaks my climax. It takes my breath away. I collapse onto my elbows, pressing my forehead to hers.

"Holy shit, Kendra." *What the fuck was that?*

She chuckles under me, still heaving, and her nipples graze my bare chest again. "That was insane." Her voice is rough.

I nod, catching my breath, then burrow my hand into her hair while kissing her. "You did so fucking well, baby." I flop onto my side and haul her into my chest, needing her closer. "How are you doing?"

"Sleepy."

I nod and laugh. "Same." I groan, hoisting myself up and stepping into the bathroom to wash up and prepare a warm washcloth. Her body is spent and relaxed when I return. *Perfect.* I drop a knee on the mattress and spread her knees apart, then take a mental picture before gently bringing the damp cloth across her body and cleaning up the mess I made.

We've got an emotional, physical, sexual connection that has me questioning if she's even real. I pray this isn't a dream. If it is, fuck it, let me sleep forever.

When I'm done, I head back to the bathroom and toss the washcloth in the sink. I give her a couple painkillers and a full glass of water. "Drink this."

She takes a small sip, downs the acetaminophen, and holds the glass out to me.

I push it back toward her chest. "All of it." Goose bumps rise on her arms, so I find one of my Lakes shirts for her to wear. She puts it on, and I fail miserably at hiding my smile. It's practically down to her knees.

"I'll give it back tomorrow," she says, yawning.

"Keep it, it gives me another excuse to get you back here."

"For real? Thought that was just a line because you were in the moment."

I laugh. "Hell no. I meant it then, I mean it now." She's already ruined me; I'll probably hang on her every word from now until forever.

"Okay … Um, do you want to exchange numbers?"

"Yes." I dig my phone from my pants on the floor and unlock it, noticing a missed call.

Whit Moreau. Damn, I haven't heard from that guy in forever. He and I played in the minors before I was drafted by the Lakes. I heard he retired about five years ago, but he's been keeping busy with the NHL as a consultant. The call must have come through when I was driving to meet her. I close out of my calls and focus on the task at hand.

I open a new contact for Kendra. "I realize I don't even know your last name," I say, slightly embarrassed.

"Ames."

"Kendra Ames," I say, typing it in. I save her number and send her a text, pleased when I hear the notification ding from in the kitchen.

"What time is it?" she asks.

"Almost one."

"Shit. I have to be up early." She grimaces. "Can you get me to my car by six?"

After the sex we just had, I'd walk over hot coals for her. Six a.m. won't be a problem. "I'll set an alarm."

CHAPTER FIVE

KENDRA

Even though we were exhausted, he woke up early and brought me to my car. However, based on how late we stayed up, I'm guessing he went back home to crash, but I'm on my second cup of coffee. It wasn't easy leaving his place this morning. I like his house; the design is well thought out. It's big but not obnoxiously so. It's practical. Very *Sully*. The setting suits him, with lots of trees and landscaping out back. He probably mows his own lawn. Great, now I'm picturing him mowing shirtless and dripping in sweat.

"Get it together, Kendra. Game face," I tell myself. My body might be at work, but my mind is still in bed with him. Sully and I had chemistry from the start. I'd never sleep with anyone who I wasn't one-hundred-percent sure isn't a conflict of interest. Sully isn't doing the show, so why shouldn't I pursue him? I shove off my overactive mind and fish through my bag for my beeping phone. When I feel it in my grasp, I pull it up and smile at the text from Sully, more memories of our night together replaying in my mind.

SULLY

Good morning. Again.

> It's almost noon.

SULLY

Hard to get out of bed when my sheets still smell like you.

> What a bum. I've already been working for six hours.

SULLY

I'm retired, sweetheart. I can do whatever I want. And I want you to get some lunch. Nothing that comes in a wrapper.

I look down at the energy bar peeking out of my purse—my lunch, if I remember to actually eat it.

> 😊 Yes daddy.

SULLY

Goddamn girl...

> I've gotta step into a meeting. Talk later.

Right on time, Pierce Haldermann, one of the production company executives—my boss—enters my office, and I tuck my phone aside. He sits down in front of me and breaks the news. News I don't want to hear. Apparently, this show was riding on Lee Sullivan's cooperation more than I anticipated.

"If he won't do the show, the network doesn't want it. You told us you could get him."

I may have implied he was an easy get when I thought I could talk him into it.

"Pierce. I sat with him for three hours. I tried. He's hard set on not doing it."

There's a strict no-fraternization policy. For once, I'm

okay with the roadblock. It means I get to keep him all to myself. I'm careful not to share any of that information.

"I'm sorry, the intel I had told me he was in. I've got a backup, though. I spoke with Paul Heitz's agent this morning, and he seems enthusiastic and wants to sit down for a meeting. He was last year's MVP, he's attractive, women love him. We can make it work."

Pierce shakes his head. "The network wants Lee Sullivan. Here's the thing, women's hockey is becoming a thing—a big thing—and the local sports network has chosen to sponsor one of the teams. This is confidential, but we're going to be partnering with the Minnesota PWHL team, and they want him to help boost viewership—"

Are they serious?

"I'm sorry ..." I shake my head and flail my arms, trying to make sense of this. "The network wants to promote women's hockey—a historic moment for women's sports, mind you—with a fucking *dating show*?" My voice is a little screechy, but I'm pissed on principle. "Not only a dating show, but a dating show where *women* compete for a *man's* attention?" This has to be a joke. I can look past a lot of shit in the television industry, but this is insulting.

"I know, the irony isn't lost on us either. But I don't need to explain to you that television isn't about dating or women's history, it's about advertising. There's a big opportunity for crossover between female viewership of dating shows and women's sports. When Taylor Swift started dating Travis Kelce, she generated an additional 331.5 million dollars in brand value for the NFL."

"Yeah, because she's *Taylor-fucking-Swift*. We're talking about Lee Sullivan." The guy's a catch, but let's be realistic, there's no comparison.

"The research they've done is positive." *Research?* How

long has this been underway? "We're looking at a large increase in revenue for the PWHL, primarily, the Minnesota team. As their sponsor, they want to see it succeed. Lee Sullivan was born and raised here. He has ties to the Lakes NHL team. The network wants him. He's their golden boy."

"And what makes them think they can get him to agree? I told you, he's not going to give in."

Pierce looks around and gently closes my office door.

"They're willing to offer him the head coach position."

Oh my God.

My heart drops to the floor. It's selfish, I know it is, but I'm not ready to give him up so easily, not while I'm still sore from our night together. Sully and I just met, but, damn, last night was incredible. If they offer him the coaching spot, he's got to take it. I *want* him to take it, he told me himself how much he missed the sport. This is great for him ... but filming him date women—women who aren't me—isn't my idea of fun. I don't look forward to filming his confessionals, don't want to ask him which women he's most attracted to and who he can see himself with for the rest of his life. I'd rather perform my own root canal.

"So this is their answer?! Dangle a hot hockey coach so women buy tickets? You think women won't be supporting women's hockey without a man?" The narrative is disgusting.

"Sports fans will be buying tickets, they want to capitalize on a larger fan base, viewers who don't watch sports. They have chosen to convert the show into a docuseries. Covering him coaching and navigating the dating world. They're calling it *Scoring with Sully*."

What a stupid name. I can't believe this is happening.

Well, there goes all the progress I've made. *Love Algorithm* is just another show to slip through my fingers. "So we're just cutting the AI and losing our investment?" I take a deep breath. Whining will not help. "So, what do you want me to do, Pierce?" I snap.

"Look, I know you're upset. I don't blame you. It's not the first time you've been given a show only to have it pulled last minute."

"Yeah, it's the third time." That's not the only reason I'm irritated. I've been possessive over career opportunities, but my current possessiveness is personal. But this is good for him. He's been wanting to coach hockey. Our relationship isn't even a relationship yet, it's a morning-after. I'd never stand in the way of such a great opportunity; it wouldn't be fair to either of us.

"I'm sorry, Kendra. It's bullshit, I get it. But we both know how fast things change. It's part of being a producer. This is something you'll have to adapt to if you plan to make it. Your time will come, I promise. We're meeting with Lee and his agent tomorrow afternoon to drop the offer and make negotiations. Would you like to attend?"

"Wait, he doesn't even know yet?"

"I haven't been given all the details, it's still confidential." He gathers his coffee. "Cross your fingers!" he calls out, stepping out of my office.

I pick up my phone to text him … and then I stop.

This is his dream.

One night is not a reason to give up an opportunity like this. Even talking about it to him makes me look pathetic. I understand how important those dreams are. As much as I want to see what could become of us, perhaps we were only destined for one night. Our night together was unforgettable, and I'm glad I got the opportunity to know Sully in that way. Let's face it, he's a fucking catch. I want him to be happy. This way he can find love and get his dream job. Lucky man. Like Pierce said, my time will come.

I drop the phone into my pocket and swallow the bittersweet loss, hoping it will drown the butterflies he put there only moments ago with his text.

I'm twenty-three. We're in different places in our lives. It never would have worked out ... but it was fun.

CHAPTER SIX

SULLY

I call her again. No answer. We've texted back and forth, but she's been silent since yesterday afternoon. My last text from her said she was going into a meeting. I'm hoping she's simply heads-down in her work. She's probably swamped because I turned down the show, so I shouldn't blow up her phone and cause a bigger disruption.

When I returned the missed call from Whit Moreau, he told me he's the new GM for the Minnesota Rogues, the new PWHL team, which is awesome. Even better, he called to discuss an opportunity; I've been in the sport long enough to know *opportunity* is code for coaching.

"I want to offer you the position of head coach." The words have played on a loop in my head since he spoke them. His pitch had my hands shaking. As soon as I ended the call, I dialed my best friend, Barrett Conway, to shout out my adrenaline. I want this so bad. After that, I called my lawyer. I need someone to help me go through contracts. Whit mentioned there were some goofy stipulations, and we're meeting to discuss them today.

My life is coming together for the first time since retirement. I met a great girl and might have a shot at the head coach spot of a pro team? Things are good. I was eager to tell Kendra about it. Thought maybe we could go out and celebrate. If anybody understands career wins, it's her.

We're meeting at the Lakes arena offices, where the Minnesota women's team will also play. I'm pleased the Lakes are sharing the space instead of some bullshit like having them play at the university arena. Professional hockey is professional hockey, regardless of gender, and they deserve to be on this ice as much as the NHL. And to coach a team on the same ice I used to play on? It doesn't get much better than that.

Standing at the mouth of the locker room tunnel, I observe the Zamboni smooth the ice for tomorrow morning's practice. *My own professional team.* Holy shit. I will do whatever it takes to get the head coach spot.

My phone dings with a text from my lawyer letting me know he's heading toward the conference room. I stuff my phone back in my pocket and give the arena one last look over before straightening my tie and heading upstairs.

When I find him in the conference room, I smile. "Nick."

"Sully!" he says with a big smile. "How are you feeling?"

"Fucking amazing. I want this, man." My gut tells me this position is meant for me. I just need the PWHL to see it. Voices from outside the conference room draw closer. I assume that's who we're meeting with, and I straighten. Nick slaps my back. "Let's go, Coach."

We stand together as staff members filter into the room. I freeze when the name of the production company Kendra works for, Vault Productions, is on one of the visitor badges. *What are they doing here?*

It doesn't make sense for them to be in this meeting. I'm trying to pay attention to everyone's names during introductions, but it's distracting. There are a few familiar faces from the Lakes administrative staff, but I've never met them before today.

A hand is thrust in my direction.

"I'm Pierce Haldermann, from Vault. I believe you already met one of our producers, Kendra Ames. Unfortunately, she couldn't be here today."

Hearing her name snaps me out of the fog. *What is going on?*

I accept the handshake and nod slowly. "Nice to meet you."

Eyeing my lawyer, he gives me a trusting nod.

We take our seats, and one of the executives jokes about ambushing my meeting with the PWHL rep. I'm still trying to decipher what a television production company has in common with me coaching a hockey team.

Whit Moreau hurries through the door. "Sorry I'm late."

I shoot him a glance, and he looks away. Something's up. Why do I feel like I'm the odd man out?

I can't deal with the unknowing a second longer. "Sorry, I'm confused here. Why is a production company present for this meeting?"

My lawyer nudges me with his leg, then they explain how the job I want most is now wrapped up in my own fucking nightmare. Apparently, the Minnesota women's team is being sponsored by the MNSports network. The same network Kendra's production company is contracted with.

"I already met with Kendra and told her I wasn't interested in *Love Algorithm*."

COACH SULLY

One of the PWHL reps speaks up. "Part of our sponsorship agreement is that you'll agree to filming a new show. It's no longer called *Love Algorithm*. We'd like to film a docuseries following your position as the head coach of a women's team, going from NHL to PWHL. In addition, we'd like to have access to your personal life. You know, dating, bachelorhood, et cetera. This would be a six-month commitment. In exchange, you'll receive a two-year contract as head coach of the Minnesota Rogues hockey team. At the end of those two years, you may reevaluate your contract for an extension if you choose."

"So, what, you only want me as the coach if I do the show?"

"We want you as coach regardless," Whit interrupts. He seems as annoyed as I am about this whole ordeal. "However, we need to align with the prospective sponsor. Which means you'll have to commit to the show."

Someone from the Lakes staff speaks up. "The PWHL will be receiving some help from the NHL. We'll assist with the start-up, but the Rogues need their own funding."

A PWHL staffer adds, "MNSports is the highest sponsor, and we want to keep it that way."

Of course. It always comes down to money. The more money a team has, the more resources they have. The more resources, the better odds of a team's success and a higher return on investment for owners and shareholders. It's not about whether they want me.

I'm a bargaining chip. If I say yes, I get my dream job and earn the team a sponsor with a lot of money. If I say no, I'm not only giving up my dream, I'll be costing the women's team their highest paid sponsor. I'll fuck over an entire PWHL organization.

"I'm here because I want to coach. I'm not the next *Bachelor* reality star."

The Vault Productions bro in the corner sighs as if he's annoyed with me. "Actually, you are. You're not just a player. You're the retired captain that women fall over. You've got a good record, you're likable. You're intriguing because you stay under the radar, but you've thrown enough punches on the ice to show you don't fuck around. It's a winning combination for viewership. You check all the boxes." He leans back in his chair and pulls out his phone as if he's bored. Guy's a dick.

"We want you as the coach, Sully. That's why I called," Whit adds. It makes me feel a little better that I'm not the only one who thinks this is asinine.

"And if I say no to the show?"

The jerk in the corner opens his mouth. "Then we will consider different candidates. Someone who can handle the show and being head coach." Whit glares at the guy from across the room. *Is this legal?*

"Just to be clear, we all know this is bullshit, right?" I say. The room responds with silence. Unreal. "Surely there's another hockey player out there that would be better for the show?"

"Perhaps a former Lakes player?" my lawyer suggests.

Douche-bro speaks up without glancing up from his phone. "There are better options, unfortunately, they're all married. We prefer to have someone single who can add more interest for our female viewership. It's not just some hockey team documentary." I don't like this guy.

Shit.

"Was this the plan all along? Kendra never mentioned any of this." Was this her backup plan? What the fuck, Kendra? How could you not tell me?

"This is a new development. Kendra wasn't informed of the network's involvement as a sponsor until yesterday." Her text … *I've got to step into a meeting. Talk later.* She was just as blindsided as me. That's why she stopped communicating with me. I feel like a dick for blaming her.

Fuck. I want this coaching position. The first pro women's team in Minnesota. This is huge. It's history. I also want Kendra, but Kendra isn't guaranteed. *This job is.*

"Let's negotiate the terms."

My lawyer interrupts. "The salary request we submitted is now void, and we'll be resubmitting a new number based on the information learned today."

I nod. Then I point at the guy in the corner with a smug look on his face. "Is he the producer?"

One of the executives nod back. So Kendra also got fucked out of the job she wanted. "No. I want Kendra to stay on as the producer."

The guy in the corner sits up. "With all due respect, she's not experienced enough for a docuseries."

I lean forward in my chair in his direction and look him in the eye. "I don't like you."

Next to me, Nick clears his throat. "… Respectfully," he tacks on.

"She's the only one I'm willing to work with," I say.

The producer opens his mouth to retort, but one of the executives—I think his name is Pierce—cuts him off before he can get a word out. "We can reinstate Kendra as a coproducer. She can be the only producer that you have to interact with, but Jeremy will remain on as the senior producer."

Right. Jeremy Bowers. What a dick.

She's still my endgame, even if I have to do this stupid six-month song and dance with the network first. The managers and execs look at each other before returning their gazes to me. Nick makes notes in my peripheral.

I glance over to Whit; we've had parallel careers with similar goals. I respect him and know he'll make a terrific GM. Everything is perfect ... except for the show.

"Put all of that in the contract and send it to my lawyer for review."

Whit drops his head and lifts it again. *Thank you*, he mouths to me.

We shake hands, and they throw an NDA in front of me to sign to make sure I keep my mouth shut until a formal announcement is made. I sign and initial, then get the fuck out of there without sparing the executives another glance.

It's just six months. We can wait six months.

CHAPTER SEVEN

SULLY

"Ready?" I ask Whit as we sit down and situate ourselves in front of the webcam. We've got a morning news segment we're calling in for. Neither of us wanted to fly to New York to do it live, but the Rogues's publicist told us that meant we'd have to do it over video call instead. Better get used to it, there's going to be a camera in my face for the next six months, anyway.

"Yeah, let's get it over with," he grumbles.

I'm glad we're on the same page. The interviewer on the other end pops up on the screen of the laptop sitting in front of us, and we do quick introductions before they give us the rundown.

As if neither of us have ever done a press box in our lives.

Once we're live, the host pastes on a big smile. "We're sitting with Minnesota Rogues's newly appointed head coach, Coach Sullivan, and general manager, Whit Moreau," the news reporter says.

"Sully." I correct. "Thanks for having us."

I am glad Whit's by my side. We work well together. Not just because we both played in the minors and NHL and had great careers, but we're also bachelors who dedicated every minute of our lives to the game. Neither of us have ever settled down, and that's what our team needs. Both of us are switching from NHL to PWHL, and we're in the next stage of our lives—coaching the Minnesota Rogues.

"You both are coming from the NHL, what kind of support is the National Hockey League offering the women's league? If any?"

I clear my throat, willing to take this question. "Our goal is to work collaboratively with them, they've got decades of knowledge and experience operating a successful hockey league, and we hope to be able to do the same for our women's league."

"Is the PWHL receiving financial assistance from the NHL?"

"Some. But that's probably a question for the financial team. Sully and I are really focused on the team, scouting players, and making the state of hockey proud," Whit answers. We haven't been cleared to publicly discuss the funding beyond "some."

We've got the draft coming up and have been spending our nights pouring over data with the owner, scouts, and Rogues's staff. We know who we want, and it's likely the same players the other nine PWHL teams want.

"Sully, you were a captain of the Minnesota Lakes for many years. How do you feel about coaching a professional team in your home state?"

"It feels incredible. I was thrilled and honored when Whit called me to discuss a coaching position. Like you said, this is my home state, I love it here and am so excited to be back on the ice again. This time coaching a team of talented athletes who live for the sport as much as I do."

I don't mention the personal life docuseries, that information won't be released until tomorrow, and I'm thankful I don't have to answer questions regarding that portion of my contract. There's nothing exciting about having women vying for my attention and their fifteen minutes of fame. That's nothing new to me, and as it stands, there's only one woman I'm interested in ... and she hasn't said one word to me since the text message the day after.

"And Whit, you've spent most of your career in Canada, but you were born in Minnesota, as I understand it. How does it feel to be back?"

"It's great, a big adjustment, like any move, but it's nice to reconnect with old friends and family. It makes holidays easier." He chuckles. "Since I've been back, I've been able to fall in love with the state of hockey all over again. See the lakes I grew up playing on, that sort of thing. Returning to my roots has been energizing."

"That's wonderful."

My eyes drop to the corner of the screen to check the time, the minutes crawling by like molasses. I haven't spoken with Kendra since our text, but I'll see her tonight at the party Micky is hosting to celebrate the announcement of my new coaching position and *Scoring with Sully*—what a stupid name.

The floor at Sugar and Ice vibrates as the bass travels through it. Micky's cocktail lounge has essentially been transformed into a nightclub for the private event. *Super*.

Thankfully, this is an invite-only event. Most of the guys from the Lakes hockey team, the players' wives and girlfriends, some people from the network, based on the credentials around their necks, and Rogues's staff are here. My eyes scan the crowd for Kendra. I haven't seen her yet. I need to get my head right. After grabbing a whiskey from the bar, I find a dark corner to hide in. It's not long before Conway finds me.

"The man of the hour ... How are you holding up?"

"Never better."

"Hey, you've been wanting to meet somebody, and now you've got women lining up ... You've been missing hockey, and now you're head coach of the Rogues ... Shit, man. Sorry about this string of bad luck."

I smirk and take a sip of the amber liquid as I survey the throng of guests mingling and dancing. I don't know half these people. Even a bunch of the Lakes's rookies are here. They're just here for the party. I don't blame them. It's a pretty good soiree by Lakes's standards. Micky is a natural when it comes to hosting these promotional events.

I haven't told Conway about Kendra yet. I don't even know what we are. As of now, we aren't even talking. It doesn't bode well for us working together, but I'm hoping I can change that tonight. She should know my intentions.

"I'm psyched about the coaching spot. It's the show I'm not looking forward to. Trying to find love on camera? Seriously? I mean, can you imagine a worse person to do this?"

"It might not be so bad," he says, pulling at the silver lining.

"It'll be fine. It's only six months of filming," I say, trying to lighten the mood.

"Filming is six months. But the woman you meet might be forever." He gestures with his beer bottle.

Huh? He's right. There's a chance that could happen. "Holy shit."

As if I manifested her from my thoughts, Kendra breezes through the front door with Pierce Haldermann, one of the other executive producers. Seems like a stand-up guy, being the one who was on board with letting Kendra be my point of contact during production. Following behind him is a handful of whom I assume are the camera crew. I forgot they were attending. Something about getting a few shots for promo material and asking my old teammates what they think of me coaching and being on a dating show.

She assists them in setting up in one of the back corners, then circulates the room, socializing with guests. Her long-sleeved dress is short and tight, showing off each curve. My fingers itch to dig into those curves again. It's fascinating to watch her work. She makes it look effortless. She's a boss.

I can't take my eyes off her. When she seems pleased with what she and the crew are accomplishing, she retreats and visits with Micky, who's with Raleigh, Birdie, and Jordan— the WAGs of my former teammates. Kendra fits in like they've been lifelong friends.

Jesus, all I want to do is talk to her, but I'm in a fishbowl here. Everyone's eyes are on me, hence me hiding in this dark corner sipping whiskey ... and keeping my eyes on her and that body that continues to punish me from across the room.

CHAPTER EIGHT

KENDRA

After arriving at Sugar and Ice with a few of our camera operators and getting our team set up, I delegate tasks to ensure we capture the shots we need. I want it to look like a party and get clips of Sully interacting with his closest friends. He's not doing me any favors by sitting in the corner and cutting his eyes ... mostly at me.

Thankfully, the rest of the guests are loosened up. It helps to arrive after they have a few drinks in them. Sometimes, people perform in front of the camera, especially one-on-one, and forget how to act normal, but when you put them in a room full of their friends first, you can usually get more candid takes. This is an important night for Sully, celebrating his new position as head coach as well as his new role of most-eligible bachelor.

Once we've got most of our shots, I chat with Micky and some of the girls. I've previously been introduced to them, but this time I actually have time to get to know them. Raleigh is the wife of Barrett Conway, who's sitting with Sully. Barrett and Sully are best friends. They spent most of their hockey careers playing together and retired only a year apart. Sully is the godfather of their children. Their kids call him Uncle Sully. When she pulls out her phone to show me pictures with him, my heart melts into a puddle. He looks like a fun uncle.

I resist the temptation to turn around and look at him. I need to go over there and rip off the Band-Aid. It's not like we can ignore each other. After all, I owe it to him for letting me keep my producer spot, even if I have to share the role with Jeremy. I haven't decided if being coproducer is a blessing or a curse. In some ways, it feels like a punishment. If it were up to me, I'd be casting anyone but him, but my hands are tied and so are his. We're both trying to do what's best for our careers.

The soundbites we captured from his former teammates were all positive, and naturally, everyone is excited for him. There isn't a bad thing about this guy—other than the fact that I can't have him. I risk a peek over my shoulder, and he's laughing with Barrett. One of the camera operators has the shot. They're definitely getting his good side. Granted, every side is his good side. His gaze meets mine, and I turn my back to him again but still feel his eyes on me. Every time I look at his face, I'm reminded of the way he stared at me while his tongue was between my thighs. I can still feel the way he held me in his arms all night after fucking me within an inch of my life.

The room feels smaller and heat licks up my spine as I sense his presence growing closer. The women are talking about the Lakes and the recent Stanley Cup win. I smile and nod, playing my part, but can't help but think about the fact that we're in the same room, yet couldn't be farther apart. Seconds later, a hand brushes my back, and his deep voice booms in my ear.

"Can we talk?"

My knees nearly buckle, but I turn around with a fake smile pasted to my face. "Of course!" I tell the women I'll catch up with them later, and he leads me to the dark corner booth he was sitting at with Barrett Conway moments ago.

We sit down and stare at each other for a moment. I wonder if he's feeling the same thing I am, unsure of how to speak to me. Where do we even stand now that everything's changed?

"So …" I say, needing to fill the air.

He laughs, but it's devoid of any humor. "What the fuck, Kendra?"

I exhale, wanting to avoid his eyes but unable to look away.

"I'm sorry for not answering your calls," I say. "I wasn't allowed to say anything, and I didn't know how to talk to you without unloading … and honestly, I needed a couple days to work through the realization that you and I weren't happening. I mean, it was just one night—" I'm rambling.

"You couldn't have given me a little heads-up?"

"I wasn't even supposed to know it was happening, it was confidential. Pierce only told me so that I wasn't blindsided by losing another show. I would have been fired if it came back that I told you."

He exhales, looking down and nodding while rubbing the back of his neck. "I understand." His arm drops, and he raps the table with his knuckles. Finally glancing up at me again, he says what we're both thinking. "This sucks."

I nod. "Bad timing." It ended before it even began.

"I really did like you, and hope you'll give me another shot in six months when it's over."

What?

"What do you mean *when it's over*?" I ask with a raised brow. This isn't just some promotional stunt. Well, it is, but the women he'll meet are real, and there's a solid chance he could meet his future wife. That's the goal of the show, the love he develops has to be genuine, or the audience won't buy it.

"I'd like to pick up where we left off."

I stretch my hands out in front of me, unsure how to answer. "The possibility of that happening is very slim. I'd prefer not to hold onto hope. You haven't even met anyone yet, you have no idea how you might feel afterward. You're a really great guy, and I hope you connect with someone casting selects."

Lie.

Yes, I want him to connect with someone, but I'm salty it won't be me.

"I heard our production assistant Rachel helped you get your first date lined up. All of the consent forms are signed, so we should be good to begin."

The premise is that he'll go out on a date with a woman. After the date is over, he can choose to either see that woman for a second date or start dating someone new. Sort of like a Monty Hall Problem, except instead of prizes, it's women—considering this is being used to promote women's hockey, the metaphor is astounding. God, I can't wait to get out of unscripted television.

"Super … Have you met them? My *dates*?" He says the last word as if it tastes bitter on his tongue.

I nod. "I've seen a few screen tests from casting."

"It would have been better if you chose them." The corner of his mouth tips up, and he locks his eyes on me. "You know what I like."

My melanin can't hide the blush on my face.

"I'm happy to report that they all seem really great. They're very excited and eager to meet you."

He hums, then changes the subject. "Have you eaten yet?"

"I'm good, thank you, though." Birdie, one of the women I met earlier, is the head chef of the restaurant that catered. The food looks delicious, but at this moment, I couldn't eat even if I wanted to.

"When was the last time you had a meal?"

"Earlier." It's the truth.

"Another protein-bar lunch, was it?"

I roll my eyes. I don't always have time for lunch. My energy bars are just fine.

"You have to eat actual food, Kendra. You work too hard to be running around on caffeine and garbage bars. And drink more water."

I widen my eyes at him. "Gee, thanks. Anything else, Dad?" Easy for him to say, he's a retired hockey player. He was probably scarfing down calories all damn day to make up for the deficit.

"Dad*dy*." He corrects. "And yeah, you could sleep more."

"With you?" I sass. I don't like being bossed around. The bedroom is one thing, but that road is closed off.

He laughs. "I wish."

I smile, checking out some of the camera operators to see how they're doing. "I'll sleep when I'm dead."

"Don't run to the point of exhaustion. That was supposed to be my job, and I'll get jealous."

I bite the inside of my cheek, wishing this could have been us. "It was fun while it lasted."

He nods and clicks his tongue. "That it was."

"We have to look at the bright side."

"What about you? Are you gonna let somebody snatch you up while I honor my contract? Do you have parents breathing down your neck to settle down?"

I bark out a laugh. "Ha! No, that will never be a problem for me."

"What do you mean?"

I curse myself for not keeping the conversation light. "My mom passed away when I was young."

"Shit, I'm sorry. That was insensitive … What about your dad?"

"You didn't know." I shrug with a smile. "My dad served in the Army and died during a tour in Afghanistan when I was young. I lived with my grandmother until college. Mom passed away my senior year. So I'm ridin' solo."

"That must have been tough." He's giving me his full attention. His gaze is trained on me, but I refuse to return it. If I have to look into those blue eyes, it'll break my put-together facade.

I roll my lips together and nod. I'd love to not talk about this. "Thanks …" I chuckle. "Sorry for bringing down the room. What a buzzkill."

"Pretty sure the party didn't start until you walked through the door," he says, and I glance at him in time to see his wink. I will miss those winks.

For the first time, the silence between us feels a little awkward. I don't know what to say. We're both victims of bad timing and unfortunate circumstances.

Sully looks down into his glass. "Do you think I should have turned down the show?"

My head cocks back. "And give up a head coaching position with the Rogues? No. *Hell no*. You have to go after something like this."

He nods but doesn't seem pleased.

"And hey, now I don't have to keep trying to make a deal with that basketball player and his agent. So really, you've made my job a little easier. Which reminds me, thank you for bargaining to keep me on as a producer."

"Sorry you don't get to take the lead."

I shrug. "Maybe next time, but for now, it's pretty good. Jeremy Bowers is a great producer. I'm looking forward to working with him. I'll learn a lot. This could open many doors. There aren't many young Black female producers who get this kind of opportunity. Don't get me wrong, I would have loved to see what happened between us, but I think we would both always regret not taking the leap in our careers."

He gives a shake of his head. "Damn, you're driven," he says before taking a sip of his whiskey.

"I have to be." There are no handouts. If I want this, it's up to me to get it.

"Can we still be friends?" he asks.

"That's cold, Sully." I feign surprise. "Are you really dumping me at a party?"

He chuckles.

I smile and tap my elbow against his. "Yeah, we can still be friends."

He drops his arm and wraps it around my back. His caress sets fire to my skin, and I opt to clear my throat rather than suck in a breath.

"Can I still teach you how to skate?"

The memory of being in his arms on that slippery fake ice warms me from the inside. I wrinkle my nose and scoot away from him. I love his touch, but it burns too hot. "That's probably not a good idea."

He drops his gaze to his lap with the rejection, then stares out to the crowd. "Yeah," he mutters before taking a sip from his water. My drink sits untasted in front of me. I need to keep my wits about me when Sully's near.

We look on as a few of the A/V guys pack up their gear.

The show is really happening, this was only a warm-up. Soon, I'll be sitting in the front row, watching his possible love story unfold. One hell of a spectator sport. One of our cameramen, Lance, heads toward our table. He nods to Sully before speaking with me. "We got some great shots. I'm going to head home, but I'll upload everything tonight and will put together some highlights tomorrow morning. Is there anything else you need from us before we take off?"

"Nope, all good. Great work tonight. Be sure to take some leftovers from the dessert table home to Maria."

He nods. "Will do. See you tomorrow, Kendra." He holds his hand out to me, and we do our secret handshake. He looks back to the giant sitting next to me. "Have a good night, man. Congratulations."

He nods and gives his thanks. Lance heads toward the dessert table, and Sully chuckles. "Hmm. That'll be a different dynamic for us."

"What will?" I take the first sip of my drink and gently place it on the cocktail napkin.

"You bossing me around on set."

My cheeks heat as I recall all the ways he bossed me around. Every dirty thing whispered in my ear. He was in control, which allowed me to release all of mine. It was so freeing and grounding. A break from the directing and decision fatigue.

I elbow his side, and he laughs. We stay in our little corner, laughing and chatting with each other while the rest of the party continues on without us. Eventually, people filter out, and Sully's PR manager, Kailey, finds us to say goodbye. I've been in contact with her on and off this last week now that we've got the ball rolling.

"Am I good to head out?" Sully asks.

"It's your party, you can do whatever you want," she says.

His heated gaze falls on me briefly. He can't be this flirty when we're working together, or I'll end up flustered. I ignore his smile. "KTBW wants to do a radio interview. I sent you an email, give me a call tomorrow and I'll go over the talking points."

"Thanks, Kailey."

"You bet." Her bright eyes transfer to me. "Great seeing you again, Kendra, let's get drinks sometime soon."

"Absolutely!" I say, even though we both know we're too busy for that kind of thing. It's still fun to pretend like I have a life outside of work.

We wave goodbye, and I finish my drink in one gulp. Fuck it.

"Did you drive?"

"No, I carpooled with the crew."

Sully taps the table twice. "Want a ride?"

"In a car?"

He chuckles. "I'm heading out, I can give you a lift."

"How much have you had to drink?"

"Not enough," he says under his breath.

Same.

"Nah. I'll Uber." I need more alcohol.

"Come on, Kendra. I'll drive you home."

CHAPTER NINE

SULLY

The hum of my car's engine hangs between us as it idles in the driveway, and I survey the exterior of her house—most of it is cloaked in shadows, but it's a small craftsman-style bungalow with a large stained-glass window on the gable. I want to know what the inside looks like. We sit in silence, each of us waiting for the other to make the first move ... My time is running out.

I'm not leaving with regrets.

"You know ... I'm not America's most-eligible bachelor yet."

We regard each other, and she swallows. I could get lost in her eyes forever. I can't tell if minutes or hours have passed. She bites the corner of her lip. "Do you ..." After a long pause, she continues. "Do you want to come in for a drink?"

I've never been so thirsty. "Yes." We need closure. Maybe it's selfish, but I need one more night with her. I wasn't ready for the last time to be the last time. Turning off the engine, I step out and walk around the car to open her door.

She steps out, and my hand is on her lower back when she

unlocks her front door and I follow her inside. There's not a lot of twenty-three-year-olds who own their own home. The dark space, filled with monotone shadows, is transformed into a vibrant, colorful dwelling when she flicks the light switch. Yeah, this is hers.

Emerald-green living room walls match the art deco sofa in the same hue. Throw pillows, flowers, and artwork make the room come alive with pops of color. I like it. It's a lot, but it's not overwhelming. It's invigorating and creative. Built-in floor-to-ceiling shelves along the east wall hold hundreds of vinyl records.

"Wow."

"My mom was really into music. Most of my memories are of us laying on the floor and listening to records together. I kept them when she passed … and then added a lot more." She chuckles.

Kendra steps out of sight after walking through the dining room into what must be the kitchen. I stand in the living room, taking in the space. It's neat and organized, but she's definitely a maximalist when it comes to color. The floral arrangement off to the side is even coordinated to the room. Impressive.

"Those are nice," I say, pointing to the bouquet.

"I love having fresh flowers in the house. They make me happy."

Personal touches are everywhere, and my brain attempts to catalog everything, to further understand who she is. It's bright, colorful, and just so damn … *happy*.

Ice clinks against glasses as I peruse her shelves while she fixes us drinks. She returns with two tumblers of amber liquid, then I sip the smokey whiskey she hands me.

"Do you have a favorite?" I ask, flipping through some records.

She takes a sip and swallows. "Hmm, that's a tough one. I'm a mood listener, but if the house went up in flames and I could only save one ... probably Tina Turner."

Tonight was supposed to be one last fuck before I'm forced to push her away, but seeing this side of her, who she is when no one's around, only makes me like her more. Kendra's the cake I want to have and eat too. Whatever we are, expires tonight, and the passing seconds piss me off.

"Put something on for us."

She has a broad range of artists to choose from, and I'm curious what album she'll select. Out of the corner of my eye, I watch her take another drink while she looks on to the wall of records before us. After a beat, she steps in front of me and pulls out a cardboard sleeve of *Zero 7*. I'm starting to think Kendra is from an earlier generation than her own. I chuckle as she drops the needle onto the record.

She smiles. "What?"

I shake my head. "Nothing."

Professionally, she's driven and authoritative. She flitted around Sugar and Ice calling shots and making decisions while quietly commanding the team she showed up with. No question, they respect her.

But when it's just us ... she's more vulnerable and free. I hope she doesn't give every man she takes home the same treatment—it's a gift I'd like to pretend is mine alone.

Sitting down on the green sofa, I make myself comfortable. I tilt my head as she sways to the music.

She moves toward the spot next to me on the sofa, and I don't hesitate. I grab her waist and firmly drop her sideways into my lap. Her body tenses, and she takes a deep breath.

I furrow my brow. "What's wrong?"

She shakes her head, looking down into her glass.

"Kendra ..." I say as a warning. "Talk to me."

"I feel like we shouldn't be doing this."

"Why not?"

"Because you're not mine." She glances down to her fidgeting fingers. "I mean, you're not anyone's, but … Do you know what I'm doing on Monday?" she asks.

"What?"

"I'm sitting down and interviewing a woman who is committed to finding love … finding love with *you*. She's probably thinking about you right now, and I'm sitting on your lap. I have to look her in the eye on Monday and discuss her becoming the next Mrs. Sullivan while I'll still be sore from you fucking me two nights prior." I hate the longing in her voice but love that she anticipates being sore. It's an admittal that we both need this and plan to take it.

"How about I come back tomorrow and we practice your poker face?"

"Sully, it's not funny. What I'm engaging in is beyond unethical."

After peeling the glass from her grip and setting it aside, my other hand travels from the nape of her neck to the base of her spine. She arches her back and adjusts against my hardening cock. I bracket her sides in my palms and sit her up, then readjust her so she's straddling me. My hands land on her bare knees and glide upward until I'm hiking the skirt up around her waist and showing off the royal-blue lace underwear she's rocking. "Very cute." Her short dress never stood a chance. We've been dancing around this all night, and now the only things between us are my clothes and her underwear.

"I don't want to get into trouble."

Aww. "You're a terrible liar, baby."

"I'm not lying."

"Do you have any idea how warm your pussy is on my leg?"

Cupping behind each of her thighs, I yank her forward, grinding her over my cock. My lips cover her small gasp at how hard I am for her. We're so close. It's right here. I want her more than my next breath.

After we tease each other with our proximity, she whispers, "I never said I didn't want it. I just don't want to get in trouble."

I smile against her lips. "I won't tell if you won't."
Burying my hands under the stretchy fabric of her dress, I grip her thighs, loving the feel of her against me.

Her fingers work the buttons down my chest before she pulls the shirt tails from my pants. "This is the last time." There's sadness in her tone. *Fuck* ... If this is it, then I will make it worth remembering.

"Then you better get down on your knees, baby girl, because there's no way in hell I'm walking away before I've seen how pretty you are with that mouth wrapped around my cock."

She drops to the floor like the sweetheart she is, and I shove my pants and boxers down. Then she reaches for me, and I shake my head.

"Take your dress off, baby."

As she peels her arms from the sleeves, I fist my dick and admire how gorgeous she is. The strapless black satin bra underneath makes her look like my own personal pinup model. There's a sophistication to it, which makes the depraved act she's about to perform even sexier. She pushes the dress over her hips, and I love that I can see how wet she is. I hook my finger around the soaked scrap of fabric. The pad of my thumb finds her hot clit, and she pulses against me. "That's my troublemaker. Show me what a bad girl you can be."

Her thong snaps back into place, and she drops between my legs, spreading me wider for her.

"Will you come down my throat?" she asks. Her mouth dips to my inner thigh, where she drags her pouty red lips over my skin. My jaw tics and my mind races with all the ways I can smudge her lipstick. I relax my arms over the back of the couch to watch her work. Last time we were together she asked for my cum too.

"Do you have a cum kink, Kendra?"

She smiles, bites her lip, and nods. Her fingers grip my length, but instead of wrapping her lips around me, her head tilts to the side and she sucks one of my balls into her pretty fucking mouth while she tightens her fist around my length and lazily strokes me. It's hot as hell, but what really gets me is the way her eyes sparkle as she does it. Yeah, she's a cum princess.

"Goddamn, Kendra." I groan. "I'm a sucker for those gorgeous gray eyes of yours."

I throw my head back and look at the ceiling to collect myself. When I've reined in the threatening orgasm, my eyes find hers again. She flicks her tongue over my sack once more before sitting up and spitting on my cock and covering it with her mouth.

My hands slide into her hair and set the pace, then I thrust deeper. She hums around me, and I smile down at her. "So beautiful …" I mumble, marveling at the sight of her. "I bet you'd look even prettier fucking your fingers while you suck me off … Do it, Kendra."

She skates one hand down her body until it disappears under her thong.

"Now the other one …"

She releases me, and I relish the sexy way she writhes against her fingers.

"Fuck, just like that ... I'm going to take your mouth, tap my leg if you need me to stop." I sink my other hand into her curls, cupping her head on both sides while I work those lips up and down my dick. She moans and rocks harder, and her hips snap eagerly to get more friction. My eyes bounce between watching her getting herself off to seeing her mouth take more of me. I push her down on my cock, and her throat opens up. All my muscles engage, staving off my climax. I growl through clenched teeth. I'm playing a dangerous game right now.

She bucks against her clit. "Look at me when you come." When she glances up, her eyes well as she struggles to take the extra inches. I pull her off me and give her a quick breath, a string of saliva still connecting her mouth to my length. Then I fist her hair and force her to take me again. It's not enough to give her a chance to relax her throat, so she gags. "Shh ... you're doing so well, baby. Make that pussy come for me, and I'll give you a breath."

Her body clenches and shakes, then sweet tears stream down her face when her climax erupts.

I wrench her mouth off me, pick her up, and toss her onto the couch where I was sitting so I can take her spot on the floor. Ripping her underwear from her legs, I shove my face between her thighs as she continues to come. She takes a deep breath, then exhales a cry of pleasure. Her fingertips dig into my scalp as she grinds against my face. I devour her with my tongue and practically drink. "Good, good girl," I drawl, "giving me so much cum."

Her legs relax, and she starts to retreat. Hell no. I suck her clit hard, and she screams, trying to kick me away as I tug on the oversensitive bundle of nerves. She breathes like she can't get enough air.

I grip her thighs and lock her tighter against my face. She

twists and shrieks before another orgasm builds. Now she welcomes the torture, pushing back against the sofa and lifting her hips. I focus on staying latched to her, trying not to smile. Her nails rake through my hair, and she scratches the back of my neck, clutching me as the second orgasm hits her.

I love how sultry her voice becomes when she's getting off. I lift my head away and slap her clit—hard.

"Fuck, Sully!"

"Nuh-uh. You don't call me Sully when my face is covered with you." I slap it again. "Who am I, Kendra?"

"Daddy," she whines.

Sitting up, I pull her onto me again, this time stuffing my length inside, feeling the steady roll of her last orgasm around my cock while she straddles me. I grasp her chin. "That's right, baby girl." It's a test of my patience to remain still inside her while she throbs around my dick. Letting the involuntary movements of her pussy work me over while I lick up her neck, claiming her. She's the one I want. I'll do her stupid fucking show, but it will be her I take home when it's over.

She slows. Our eyes meet, and it's as if everything else fades away. Her gaze matches mine. We both know this situation is fucked. "I don't want to give you up," I say.

Her sad smile is torture when she nods. "I know."

She kisses me, and it drips with sensual longing. I move my lips with hers, needing Kendra to recognize the hope I have. We're not done yet, but I can't tell her that. She'd try and stop me, and I'm not fighting her on this. Not tonight. I cradle her against my chest as she rides me. Her body is so soft and pliable in my large hands. When her thighs tremble and her knees knock against my sides, I grip her ass and help her keep the rhythm she's struggling to follow.

As soon as she comes, she calls me daddy one last time and I pull her down, burrowing deep as I spill inside. I growl into her flesh. It will be six long months before I hear that word again, so I commit it to memory, along with her smell, touch, and taste.

She throws her arms around my neck and holds me. I can't see her face, but a tear rolls down my back.

"It's going to be okay" is all I can tell her. She nods into my shoulder.

Tired and spent, I lie on the sofa, taking her with me. The tips of my fingers graze up and down her back as she rests her head on my chest. When she shivers, I wrap her in my warm arms and enjoy the sound of her content sighs as we relax without sharing another word. I'll be here until she kicks me out. After cleaning us up, I take my spot next to her again. Grabbing the blanket off the back of the couch, I throw it over us. It doesn't take long before our heartbeats are in sync and we drift into a deep sleep.

CHAPTER TEN

SULLY

Approximately 10 weeks later

Player drafts are anxiety inducing on their own, but it didn't help that my flight was delayed and I barely made it in time. I had to put my suit on in the airport bathroom, grab my rental car, and haul ass to the arena. The cold sweat is finally dissipating. Luckily, the only thing I missed was recognition of team scouts, red carpet photo ops, and watching interviews with athletes and staffers.

In the past, I've always been on the player end, but now I'm on the floor. Standing next to me is Whit Moreau. Behind us, the hum of exuberant chatter fills the stands and echoes through the arena. Families, friends, and fans are settling in while we take our seats at the designated Rogues table on the drained floor of Colorado's NHL arena.

I sense Kendra's presence even though I haven't seen her yet. She and the camera crew are hidden in the throng of media attendees. I keep my head down and try not to look for her. It's been weeks since we've seen each other. She's kept me at a distance and has stayed professional. It's almost as if our last night together never happened. I've been respectful of her boundaries, but despite her efforts, my attraction for her has only grown.

Barrett and Raleigh are in the stands somewhere. Not only for me but for the athletes who spent time with his organization, Camp Conway, and are now up for the draft. Including Timber Healy, a goaltender we have our eye on. I can't imagine the pride he feels. Probably similar to the loved ones of the players wringing their hands right now. Their children, siblings, spouses, and significant others are about to be the first hockey players of the inaugural PWHL season. They're making history. The anticipation is palpable.

Everyone at the Minnesota Rogues's table has been hand-picked by Whit. It's mostly executives and team scouts—those who are important to help with on-the-fly decision-making. A couple seats are reserved for members of the organization with higher status, like the owner. We try to keep the table neat, which isn't easy between all the laptops, tablets, papers, water bottles, and snacks.

I've made small talk saying hi to past colleagues, but now people are settling into their spaces. Next to me sits Jeanine Vance, the assistant coach, and we discuss the players and our plans to work with our athletes once it's established today. We're eager to get our roster filled and begin their training.

Once the emcee goes through the fanfare of this being the first PWHL draft in history, things are ready to begin. The order of picks is determined by a computer, and when we see the results, Minnesota is picking first.

Fuck.

The order goes in snake format, so once we get through the list, the order is reversed, meaning we don't get to pick again until the end of the second round. It drops our odds on the elite players since most will be picked through by the time we choose again. However, winning teams aren't composed of the best players, they're made of the *right* players. We have three minutes to submit our pick.

"Cori Kapowski," Whit mutters next to me. It's a no-brainer. Cori is a power forward and was born to play this game. She's played internationally on women's teams, and we planned to pull her first. Fans call her Celly Kapowski. We all nod, we've already figured most of our choices and the order we would take them in, but going first means this pick is easy. Going forward though, we'll need to make sure we stay the course.

We submit our decision, and once the name is announced, Cori stands and takes the stage along with Margaret Baylor, chairwoman of the board for the PWHL. Our runner supplies the jersey she receives. She holds it up for photos. We'll shake hands later. Much of the fanfare is saved for after the draft when everyone gets together for photo ops during contract signings.

From our table, we watch as the remaining nine teams pick off players. We cross them off our list as we go. A few grumbles can be heard among staffers, and even Whit let out a sigh a time or two. We decide our best bet is to get our top goalie lined up next. Goaltenders are critical and can make or break a team. Our defenders are important, but when it comes to shots on goal, we need to make damn sure the person we put in our net is the best. And the best is Timber Healy.

She's a tremendous athlete. Focused and dedicated. Oftentimes, goaltenders get away with more shit because they know how important they are to a team and organizations will let that shit slide as long as pucks are staying out of nets, but she's solid.

We put forward our pick for Timber Healy, and as soon as her name is called, I glance up to the crowd and catch Barrett standing alongside Timber's parents and clapping like it's his daughter presenting that Rogues jersey.

We have back-to-back picks this round and have to focus. "Okay we've got a powerhouse in Kapowski. Let's add Delta Makkonen, she'd be a great winger. They would be great together."

Whit pulls up her profile for what seems like the hundredth time. It's like he's getting cold feet when it comes to her. I can't figure out why.

"We need to cover our defense," he says. "Joanna Breck."

Joey is damn good defense. Unfortunately, she's also got a reputation for being a wild card off the ice. Even the media calls her "Trainwreck Breck." When it's our turn to submit our pick, the scouts are all in for her; they know how talented she is. The rest of the staff, including me, exchange looks, knowing she's a liability.

"We need Makkonen now," I argue. Timber is great on defense, but we need to grab up one of the best wingers before she's snapped up by another team.

"Timber Healy has a rapport with Breck. We must establish our defense."

"Whit, I'm with Sully on this one. Delta Makkonen should be priority," Jeanine says, backing me up.

The scouts waffle between themselves too. I duck my head next to Whit's shoulder. "Delta won't be available after another eighteen rounds ... Last night, we were solid on choosing a winger third. Makkonen is it. What the hell changed overnight?"

He closes the tab on his laptop with her face and stats and reopens the submittal window. "I'm pulling rank on this one. If she's available next round, we'll get her then."

I clear my throat and swallow down my frustration. *What the fuck?* There's nothing I can do here, and I'm not about to make a scene. When I played for the Lakes, we had a player named Banksy who was the biggest pain in the ass as far as liabilities go, and after I left, he replaced me as captain, turning everything around. I've seen miracles happen. I just hope Joey can hack it.

I nod. We'll figure out a way to get the other shit under control later on. Whit blows out a breath and taps the enter key to submit her name.

"Do you think our PR team will be submitting their resignation or requesting raises?" Jeanine mutters and I chuckle.

As soon as Joey jogs up to the stage on her sky-high heels, she accepts the jersey and hollers out a boisterous "Hell yeah!" Shaking my head, I hope we didn't make a mistake.

Whit chuckles next to me before answering, "Resignation."

"She's worth it," Tanya, one of our player scouts, chimes in. "Promise."

"I'll remind you of that when our Christmas bonuses are spent on PWHL fines," one of the staffers, Jonathan, adds.

"Enough," I say, ending the jokes.

Waiting through the next eighteen rounds is fucking anxiety-inducing. Picking first sucks.

The emcee announces Yasmin Nielson for Toronto's pick. I cross her name off our list. Next is Renata Lacroix, and she goes to Vancouver. Shit. Leah Pendergast, New York. Fifteen more rounds of picking and it's our turn again. Somehow Delta's name hasn't been chosen yet. Remember how I said I believed in miracles? I exhale relief.

"Delta. Makkonen." I say it more firmly than necessary.

He nods, but his voice conveys he's conceding rather than

being thrilled we were able to grab her. *The fuck is up with him?*

We submit her name for our fourth round, and I cross my arms. As soon as the emcee announces her name, I return to our next choice now that we're back on track. Our next pick was supposed to be Lacroix, but now that Vancouver has her, I throw out the next best thing. I pull up Kiana Jackson's stats, and we go back and forth with some scouts on whether to pick her or Jamie Paulson. We submit our choice: Kiana. Afterward, we settle in our chairs, waiting out the next fifteen rounds before we can choose again.

"You may not want to hear this, but I think we should consider Delta for captain."

He nods without looking at me, and I raise my eyebrows.

"She works hard. Has a good attitude and personality. She'll be a solid leader," he agrees.

Jonathan, one of the male staffers getting on my nerves as the night goes on, decides to open his mouth and join our conversation. "And she's hot, which means she's pretty enough to charm the refs and officials will have a hard time saying no to her."

Next to me, Whit's back stiffens.

I glare at him. "How many NHL players have you said that about?" I counter. Delta hasn't gotten to this point because she's attractive, she's here because she works her ass off.

Jonathan rolls his eyes at me. "I'm just being real here. Come on, Sullivan, I know you know what I'm talking about. She's a good player, all I'm saying is she's got other qualities that'll be beneficial to the team."

I raise an eyebrow. Fuck this guy. Jeanine scoffs next to me and mumbles something about him being an asshole. Justified. Before I can respond to him, Whit leans forward and stabs a finger in Jonathan's direction, whose face has gone pale at the attention he's garnered from the Rogues's general manager, not to mention the rest of us. Whit drops his voice to a low growl. "Don't ever talk about her—or any other player—like that again. When we get back to the office on Monday, you can pack your shit."

"You're firing me?"

"Yeah. You're dismissed." Whit doesn't spare him another glance.

Jonathan looks around at our faces, seeking support but gets none. Eventually, he shoves his chair back from the table and walks off. Everybody stares at Whit with wide eyes after witnessing his normally calm demeanor shift into overdrive. He adjusts his tie and rolls his shoulders back. "I'm implementing a zero-tolerance policy for sexual harassment, that goes for not only our players but every other member in our organization ... Can we finish picking our fucking roster?"

Jeanine grins.

"Let's get back to work," I announce, hoping to remind everyone what needs to be priority. "Who's our next forward? Paulson or Baylor?"

CHAPTER ELEVEN

SULLY

After we meet all the players, shake hands, and sign contracts, the coaches and general managers usher us to the private box for a cocktail after-party. I'd rather get checked into my hotel, but Whit insists I attend. Neither of us brought plus ones; we're the old bachelors who were always married to the game.

I grab a whiskey and find a seat next to Whit. We look down at the arena, surveying the players and guests still carrying on, it's their party. Hockey families catching up with other hockey families and congratulating each other on their recent signings. Hockey can be a small world, especially at the top. Probably more so for female players. Scanning for Barrett and Raleigh, I pause when Kendra comes into view. Her back is to me, but that body is unforgettable. She's chatting with people wearing media badges, and I'm pretty sure I recognize one of them as Lance, the camera operator I met the other night. She points toward some of the new Rogues players, likely directing to get a specific shot or candid interview.

When she turns around, I blow out a breath. She's a showstopper in that off-the-shoulder dress. It's damn near cruel. Dressed to the nines with everyone else, but she's here to work. I smirk, enjoying watching her in her element ... Until some asshole comes up and gives her a too-long-for-my-liking hug. I quirk a brow and scrutinize their body language. His touch lingers while she tries to put space between them. He doesn't take the hint and sways with a drink in his hand before settling his palm on her lower back.

Who is that guy? Do I know him?

He looks familiar, but it takes a minute to realize he's one of the guys who plays for Toronto. Or at least he did last time I checked. She reaches behind her and removes his hand from her body, then turns her back to me again and points across the room as if telling him she's got to get going. I grind my teeth when he returns, steps in front of her, and puts an arm around her lower back for the second time, but this time it drops to her ass. *Motherfucker.*

A tap on my shoulder pulls me away from my glaring.

"What?" I snap. When I realize it's a catering staff member, I take a deep breath and blink a few times. "Sorry." I shake my head. "What's up?"

"Just wanted to know if I can bring you a drink or grab you something to eat ..." Their voice is barely above a squeak.

I shake my head. "No, I'm fine, thank you." When I glance back down, Kendra is storming away from the guy. *Shit.*

"Wait!" When I spin, the catering staffer is practically at my feet, eager to earn a tip. I wave her closer to me and point down toward the arena at Kendra. "Do you see that woman in the long orange dress, one shoulder, curly black hair, all done up?"

"Yeah?"

"She's my producer," I explain. "I'm supposed to be meeting with her, but …" I glance over and snatch up one of the VIP lanyards someone ditched in the seat next to me. "She forgot her credentials." I lie. "Could you bring this to her and make sure she finds her way up to the box?"

"I'm really not supposed to leave …"

I dig out my wallet, grab a couple of bills, and stuff them into her hand.

She looks around, then scurries off, and I turn back to the view below. Kendra's helping some of the camera crew pack up their gear. I pray she stays there long enough for my little catering friend to find her. I shoot off a text to Kendra, telling her to come find me, but with as loud as it probably is down there, I'm sure she can't hear her phone.

So I plop down in my seat and wait.

Whit side-eyes me. "Wanna tell me what that's all about?"

"I really was supposed to meet with her." I shrug.

"You gave that kid my VIP lanyard," he says, calling me out.

"Saw some guy bothering her."

He huffs. "These events are always full of assholes."

I nod. "Speaking of assholes, what the hell happened with Jonathan earlier? I know we haven't worked together long, but we've shared the ice before, and I've never seen you jump on somebody that quick." I don't mention it seemed personal.

He raises his shoulders. "He was a dick. Jonathan needed to be made an example of."

"Well, I think your point got across."

"Good." His answer is short and sweet before he stands. "I'm gonna get another drink."

Seconds later, Kendra takes the open seat, and her

normally bright, bubbly, and outgoing personality is detached.

While taking her in, all I can muster is "Hey."

She looks stunning tonight. I feel like a prick when she catches me checking her out. I summoned her, but now that she's next to me, I'm too dumbfounded by her beauty to string a sentence together. Instead, I turn around and offer an appreciative wave to the helpful catering staff member who tracked her down.

"Hey yourself," she mutters. "Thanks for … this." She waves the VIP lanyard and sets it down on the table. "Were you spying on me?"

I narrow my eyes. "Does it really constitute spying if I'm not secretive about it?"

"I suppose not … Well, congratulations on a fantastic player roster. How are you feeling about everything?"

Her hands are still slightly trembling. "When was the last time you ate?"

"I had a protein—"

Always with the protein bars. She probably forgot to eat with everything going on. I stand. "I'll be right back."

I stray over to the catering tables with way too much food and fill a couple plates with a smattering of everything. I'm not sure what she likes or doesn't like. When I return, I set it in front of her.

"I'm not hungry."

I sigh. "Don't argue with me." I know she probably hasn't eaten anything that doesn't come in a wrapper or fast-food bag.

She rolls her eyes at me with a half-cocked smile. "*Yes, Daddy*," she mocks.

The smirk on her face calling me daddy? Holy fuck. I

never thought I'd be into the whole "daddy" thing, but with Kendra, I can't get enough.

Raising an eyebrow, I respond with "Easy, baby girl" and watch as her neck reddens slightly. Two can play this game. I need to stop flirting with her, but it's so easy to fall into without thinking.

She picks at her food but doesn't eat much. Says her stomach is in knots, which she attributes to nerves from covering the draft. It's unlike her. I can't imagine her flustered in any work environment. Every time I've watched her work, she looks like she's done it a thousand times before.

We hang out in the box talking among ourselves until people begin filtering out. I check my watch and realize it's time to go. "I'm having a great time, but I should probably look at heading out. Did you drive?"

"I'll grab an Uber."

"I've got a rental car. I can take you back to your hotel. Where are you staying?"

"The Grand."

She opens her mouth like she's about to brush me off, but I don't give her the chance.

"Me too."

Funny how things just work out.

When we arrive, I pop the trunk to grab my bag. I can't believe my delayed flight was only this morning, it feels like a week ago. *What a day.*

She pauses. "You haven't checked in yet?"

"No, my flight got delayed. I barely made it to the arena in time for the opening ceremony."

I close the trunk and roll the luggage at my side as we walk toward the hotel entrance.

"Yikes. Well, the hotel bar is fabulous in case you get thirsty. They make a mean Negroni."

I smirk. Of course she ordered that. "Do you ever drink anything that was invented in the last century?"

She laughs, digging through her purse for her room key. "Classics never die."

We walk through the revolving doors into the, well, *grand*, lobby. It looks like it came out of the 1920s. No wonder she loves the hotel bar.

"Oh good. I've been jonesing for a good *Sidecar*," I say with a bite of sarcasm.

She scrunches her nose and gives me a small shove. "Suit yourself. I think I'm going to grab a nightcap before bed. You know, for spite. Feel free to join me when you realize I have great taste."

I walk toward the desk as she saunters past me toward the bar. "Stay out of trouble," I call to her. "And eat something with that Old Fashioned!" She didn't have enough to eat earlier.

She spins around and winks. I smile, shaking my head. When I face the desk attendant, he greets me with a wide smile, but I notice his eyes dart to the suitcase handle extended at my side.

"Good evening, sir. How can I help you?"

"Evening. Just checking in. Lee Sullivan."

His eyes move the computer screen in front of him, and he taps away.

"Are you staying with someone?"

"Nope. Just me."

"Do you have a confirmation number?"

I furrow my brow. "No, the reservation was set up by someone else."

"Who booked the reservation?"

"Umm …" I grab my phone and open my emails, searching for the admin in charge of booking my room. "Jessica Boelter? Or it might be under Whitney … Olson." I haven't actually met these people, but those are the only contacts I have. "Is there a problem?"

"I see that we had a reservation for you …" He continues clacking away at the keyboard.

Had. Don't like the sound of that.

He nods at the computer. "I see what happened. We had you checking in yesterday with the rest of your party." Everybody else got here a day early, just in case—they were smart. I was hoping to avoid all the partying the night before. "Unfortunately, when you didn't check in within twenty-four hours, we were forced to give your room to someone else. We tried calling you earlier."

Probably while I was on a plane.

"Yeah, I think there must have been some miscommunication on my arrival dates when the rooms were booked. That's fine. Can you hook me up with a new room? I'm fine with whatever you have available." I don't give a shit what happened with my original reservation, just give me a bed so I can crash.

The man grits his teeth, cringing. *Shit.* "I'm so sorry, we are fully booked for the night. With the hockey draft going on, we're at max capacity. I truly apologize for the mix-up."

I nod and sigh. "Not your fault. Mind if I hang out in the lobby while I find a new hotel?"

"Not at all. And we'd be happy to shuttle you to any nearby lodging. Can I get you something to drink while you wait?"

"I'm good. Thanks."

Damn it.

I roll my suitcase over to a gold-colored upholstered chair off to the side, then unbutton my suit jacket and open the search bar for any available accommodations. Dropping into the chair, I scrub a hand down my face. This is bad. I've been to enough drafts to know that there's probably not anything available. I rest my elbows on my knees while scrolling for hotel vacancies on my phone. It's not going well. After five minutes, it's clear to see there's not a room in the whole fucking city. Everybody is here for the draft.

I can get a room at a hotel outside of the city in the suburbs, but I don't feel like commuting that far out. Especially if I'm supposed to be meeting with my team for breakfast tomorrow. I contemplate driving back to the airport and seeing if I can catch a red-eye home. Brunch be damned.

"Do you need help finding your room?" she says on a giggle, and my frustration eases at the sight of her smile.

I chuckle. "I don't have a room. Whoever booked my travel accommodations had me checking in yesterday. So when I didn't show up, they thought I was a no-show and gave the room away."

"What! Well, have them give you a different room."

"They're fully booked." I glance back down to my phone and scroll. "Every hotel is full. Happens at every draft ... Anyway, did you enjoy your bourbon neat or whatever?"

She extracts her phone and taps the screen. "I did. You look like you could use one too ... Let's see if I can find something for you." She yawns.

"Don't worry about it. Go up to your room, Kendra. I'll be fine."

She shakes her head, still tapping around. "Damn, you weren't kidding, there's nothing available ..." She locks her phone and slips it into her purse. "I can't leave you. You're important to me—I mean, to the show—I need to make sure you get settled. It's part of my job."

"Kendra."

"Come with me to my room. I gotta get out of these shoes and then we'll figure everything out."

"You don't have to—"

"I'm serious, it's part of my job. Fighting me on this only makes you a bigger pain in my ass. Please don't."

I show my palms in surrender. "Whatever you say, Boss." I'm honestly too tired to argue.

We get in the elevator, and she presses the button for the eighth floor. She pulls out her phone again, as if somehow in the last couple minutes the hotels nearby had vacancies magically appear. "Okay. Here's what we're going to do," she says, yawning again. "I'm going to give you my room—"

"I'm not taking your hotel room."

"Yes you are. I'm going to see if someone from my team has an extra bed I can have."

"Just give me your sofa, and I'll be fine."

Stepping off the elevator, she walks with purpose to her door.

"This is a boutique hotel, there is no sofa in my room. Even if there was, you're, what, six-four?"

She unlocks it and enters, holding the door open for me to pass by.

"Six-five."

"Exactly. There's not even a sofa in the lobby big enough for you. Take my room, I'll find a bed, and we'll reconvene tomorrow." The room lights up, and it's smaller than I thought it would be, but the bed is big enough.

"Kendra. It's fine. It's a king-size bed, we can share. Let's stop making it more awkward than it has to be."

"Are you sure?"

"We're both adults, I think we can handle it. Are you comfortable with me sleeping next to you?" I shouldn't assume just because we've slept together that she'll be okay with sharing a bed tonight.

She furrows her brow and looks at me like I'm being ridiculous. "Of course! I just, you know ... we can't—"

"I'm not going to try anything. I know where you stand."

She nods, then grabs clothes from her suitcase and enters the bathroom, locking the door behind her. "What time is it? Are they still doing room service?" Her voice is muffled through the wall.

"Uhh ..." I turn around and scan every surface until my eyes catch on a menu. I check my phone. "Yeah, you've got thirty-five more minutes. Want me to order you something?" *Finally.* I'm pleased she's getting something else to eat.

"Yeah."

I wait for her to give me more information, but she seems to be done with that sentence.

"What do you want?" I spin around.

"I like everything. Surprise me."

"Allergies?"

"No."

I pick up the hotel phone, press the button with a server icon, then sit on the edge of the bed waiting for someone to answer. When Kendra exits the bathroom, she somehow looks as beautiful in her baggy T-shirt and boxers as she did in the gown and stilettos from earlier.

I vaguely register someone talking on the other end of the phone.

We're supposed to be just friends ... but friends don't look at each other the way I'm looking at her.

"Hello ..." the hotel staff repeats, for the second time. *Focus.*

"Uh, shit. Yeah, um. Can I put in an order for room service?" I order a calamari pizza, remembering the way she was eyeing it at Micky's launch party. Next a grilled pineapple cucumber salad with a peanut dressing, a couple bags of kettle chips, a side of tzatziki sauce, a slice of chocolate cake, and a slice of cheesecake. Hell, I could eat.

Kendra listens with bright eyes, dancing more enthusiastically with each item I rattle off to the person on the phone. By the end, she's waving an invisible lasso around her head. I chuckle through the last of the order. It's so ridiculous I'm tempted to read off the rest of the menu.

"Room number?" the person asks. I was too busy staring at her ass in that dress to remember what number was outside the door when we arrived.

I tilt the phone away and confirm with Kendra, still grinning at her antics. "Room number?"

"844," she says, doing the cabbage patch. I chuckle. She wasn't even alive when that dance was invented, which is exactly what I'd expect from her. At this point, I wouldn't even blink if she jumps up and does the foxtrot when the food arrives.

"844 ... Yes ..." I refocus my attention back to the caller. "... No, I'll pay over the phone."

She waves her hands in front of my face to get my attention. "Bill it to the room!" she stage-whispers. "Sully!"

I shake my head and pull out my wallet. She tries to snatch it away from me, but I hold the credit card above her head as I finish reading off the numbers. They give me a time estimate, and I hang up the phone.

"Why didn't you bill it to the room?"

"The least I can do is feed you." It comes out more sexual

than intended, so I quickly tack on, "Thanks for letting me crash here."

"It's not coming out of my pocket, the company is paying for it."

I stand and walk over to the mini bar. "Well, in that case ..." I pour myself a couple fingers of whiskey and kick my shoes off. "Thank you, Vault Productions ... Besides, if I didn't buy you dinner, I'd have to pay you back another way, and you've already established that there will be no funny business tonight." I waggle my eyebrows at her over my tumbler as I take a sip.

She laughs. "Is it too late to cancel the order?"

"It's never too late."

That earns me one of her eyerolls. "I'm only teasing."

Yeah, no shit.

"Uh-huh." I smirk, then shrug off my shirt jacket and remove a pair of sweatpants and an undershirt from my suitcase. I take one more sip and set my drink down. "Don't try to drug me," I say.

She scoffs. "You're six-five ... Besides, I left my elephant tranquilizers in my other pants." Her other pants. My eyes fall to her ass without thinking as I walk past her. A sliver of cheek can be seen. Damn it.

I lock the bathroom door and drop my clothes on the counter, then splash my face with cold water and stare at myself in the mirror. *You cannot fuck her tonight.* What we did can't happen again. The show is happening, and as much as I would love a repeat, she'd be disappointed if she acted on impulse. Especially since she's been drinking, and I have no idea how much she's had to drink. If I ever get a chance with her again, it'll be because it's our time.

I strip off my button-down shirt and pants, swapping them with gray sweats and a white shirt that's probably too tight across my chest. Whatever. I give myself one more glance in the mirror. *Keep it in your pants.*

I open the door and hang up my shirt, jacket, and pants in the small closet. She's sitting cross-legged on the bed, clutching the television remote and scrolling through the TV guide. "I'm trying to find something to watch while we wait," she says, keeping her eyes on the screen. I close the closet doors and hop on the bed, making her bounce. She smiles and chooses a channel. I'm not sure what she chose. So far, it's just commercials. It's not long before the food arrives.

"Food!" she announces, hopping up and grabbing the door. Two people in black attire enter the room with two trays and a pizza box. Each tray has two silver domes covering the dishes. They place the food on the short dresser, and we bid them farewell.

I carry the trays over to the bed, and she grabs the pizza box. "I love it when the food has the silver lids," she says, peeking under them. "Makes me feel like I'm in *Pretty Woman*."

The corner of my mouth tilts up as I lift the lid of the pizza box and grab a slice. I scoot back, resting my back against the headboard. She plates her food along with some of the salad. I hold the half-eaten slice of pizza between my teeth and open the bag of kettle chips, then hand it to her. We work together in silence.

Once she's settled, I finish eating my slice and go in for another. That's when I notice what we're watching. I glance down at the calamari pizza and back at the television, where the narrator is speaking in a relaxed cadence. "And there it is, the mighty Humboldt squid. Its whiplike tentacles and rhombic fins make this beautiful creature a sight to behold. With a length up to twelve feet, these large squids have come up from a great depth to hunt and feed on mackerel."

"Squids? Really?"

She winks at me, plucking off a piece of calamari and popping it in her mouth. *Weirdo.* I expect her to change the channel, but no, we sit and watch as the narrator describes the creature's hooklike grips and how water propels through its mantle, whatever the hell that is. Then they explain how these huge fuckers can actually pull divers down to the deep.

"Well, that's terrifying."

"Right? The rest of the world fears being eaten by squids, meanwhile, Japan makes porn out of it."

"Seriously?"

"Yeah." She chuckles, like it's the most obvious thing in the world. "You didn't know about tentacle porn?"

"Is that what you kids are into these days? Tentacle porn and eating ass?"

She shrugs. "The rumors are true."

We continue watching, and she's absolutely fascinated by the show while she eats. "Swimming in the ocean is like soaring over a dangerous forest filled with flying lions, tigers, and bears—and you're just a fucking pigeon."

"And half of them are hungry," I add, nodding.

"And the other half would kill you just to learn what pigeon tastes like."

I chuckle and open the other bag of chips to snack on.

"God, this footage is incredible," she says.

"Would you ever want to produce a documentary?"

"Yeah."

Her response surprises me. "Wait, really? Like this one? Animals and stuff?"

She shakes her head. "Music."

That, I can picture, she's clearly passionate about music.

I listen to her go off about her plans for future documentaries and the different musical genres she finds interesting.

She relays how subjects such as language and sociology affect certain subgenres and talks to me about the artists she wants to cover. The more I learn about her, the more I like her.

She asks me about hockey, not just what it was like or my favorite memories, but about the arena and traveling details, how people become Zamboni drivers, if the uniforms are itchy, and the thickness of ice we skate on. Some of her questions I don't even have answers to. I never thought to ask. Her brain operates so differently than mine. It's as if she wants to learn all she can about how the sport functions, not just my experience. It's refreshing after years of: *"What do you plan to do differently next time to win the game? How do you feel after scoring that last goal? Do you regret retiring a year before the Lakes won the Stanley Cup?"*

When she asks questions about me, it's things about me as a person. She asks about my family, what makes me anxious, what my favorite sandwich is, what songs are currently stuck in my head. We flirt, both of us walking the line of professionalism and joking. It's hard to avoid it when I enjoy her company so much.

"Can we talk about the show for a minute?" I ask.

"Sure, what would you like to know?"

"What's the point of it?"

She furrows her brow. "Entertainment, baby."

"No, really though, like what is the show about?"

She nods, understanding what I'm asking. "The main story arc is you becoming a coach and your dating life, but as we film, little things will happen, and we'll develop mini stories that branch out from that. This could be a few good or bad dates, your struggles between people you work with, team wins and losses, all the little drama bits."

I hum, not loving the sound of that. "Do you make drama out of nothing?"

She finishes swallowing a bite of food. "Some producers are really into that, you'll see it on a lot of competition shows, but I've always believed that it's psychological abuse."

"Wait, so the fighting you see on reality shows, it's real?"

"A lot of times, yes. But it's often created by producers."

"How?"

She shrugs. "It's easier than you'd think. It would be like if I handed you a piece of candy and said, 'Don't let anyone take this candy from you or I'll kick you off the show.' And then I walked up to your adversary and said, 'We need you to steal that piece of candy from Sully, or we'll kick you off the show.'"

"But instead of candy, it's infidelity, greed, jealousy."

She nods. "It's sad. I believe you can still have reality TV without fabricating drama and traumatizing people, but maybe that's just because I haven't had my spirit broken yet. There are organizations out there, like the UCAN Foundation, that ensure production companies are following regulations and not abusing or exploiting cast members. But your show is mainly about you and the team. Your new career, the team you're coaching, and how you're balancing all of that with love. You're dating one person at a time, so there won't be competition between any of your love interests."

"Are you going to edit what I say and take things out of context?"

"I mean, there's always a chance that's what they're going to do, so just don't say anything stupid. We won't ever force you to say something you don't want to. Occasionally, we'll give you direction on what we want you to talk about, but everything you say is going to be unscripted. Your conversations are your own."

I take a calming breath. This is all so bizarre.

"I know it sounds awkward now, and it might feel a little uncomfortable in the beginning, but after a while, you won't notice the cameras as much, and it will become natural."

"Do you think things will be weird between us?"

"Things are already weird between us." She chuckles. "We'll get over it. Producers work closely with talent—you're the talent—because it helps foster mutual respect, which makes the whole production more successful and more fun. We're a team. So, if you need to talk on the side or you're feeling uncomfortable, let me know right away. We can figure things out."

I smirk. "I'd say you've worked very closely with my talent."

She gives me a shove and laughs. "Gross."

"Those goddamn noises you were making weren't gross." I smile. Six months from now, I'll be hearing them again.

She cuts her eyes at me, and I drop the subject. Our conversation picks up again, and time melts away. I could talk to her for hours on end and never run out of things to say. The plan was to ask her about that Toronto player grabbing her, but seeing her face so brightly lit while we discuss a wide plethora of topics, share our favorite things, and compare our values, I don't want to dampen the mood. I'm enjoying our little bubble.

"Holy shit, it's three a.m.!" She shrieks.

"I wasn't going to say anything," I confess, standing up and stretching. "Guess I'm having too much fun with you, Kendra."

"This was nice." She hops off the bed, and we brush our teeth side by side. My hand falls to her lower back as I move around her to spit in the sink. Every time I touch her, it's not enough. The tension is palpable, but admitting it is pointless. There's nothing we can do about it right now. Not without hurting the other professionally or making it worse. Somehow, pretending it doesn't exist is easier.

She wraps up her curls, and I grin.

"Don't make fun of my bonnet."

I smile and pinch her side. "I'm not. I think you look cute."

She flips the bathroom light off and clears off the bed, then pulls back the top bedding. "Oh, do you care what side you're on?"

If I thought the no-fraternization policy was hard to abide by earlier, my will is really about to be put to the test.

"I'm usually on the left," I reply.

"Perfect. I'm a right sider."

I remember from the night she slept in my bed. "Easy enough," I say, peeling off my shirt next to the bed. She looks away from me like I'm about to strip naked. "Do you want me to …" I raise the shirt, and she waves me off. "No, it's no problem. I'm on this side, you're on that side. We're adults, right? Doesn't bother me! Are you okay with it? I mean, it's not like—" We've literally seen each other naked before, but now there's this barrier between us we don't know how to put up. I'd be fine taking it down, but I'll respect her wishes.

"You good?" I bite back my laughter.

"What?"

"What?" I echo, climbing under the sheet.

She does the same and taps the lamp to turn it off. The silence between us is deafening. Every little sound of the hotel settling is amplified. Each of us stare at the ceiling. I hear her swallow and open her mouth, inhaling, like she's about to say something. Then more silence.

"What were you going to say?" I ask. I turn my head in

her direction, and the streetlamps outside barely illuminate her face.

Eventually, she turns her head to face me. "If things were different ..." she whispers.

My hand covers her small one, and I weave our fingers together. "If things were different, things would be different." A melancholy longing falls between us.

Kendra's someone I'll never forget, regardless of how my future plays out. Decades from now, whether I'm married to another woman or not, I know, without a shadow of a doubt, my thoughts will drift to her from time to time. The luckiest night of my life, when the hotel gave away my room and I stayed up until 3:00 a.m. with Kendra Ames discussing anything and everything. I'll likely wonder what could have been if I had chosen her over my career, because it's natural to regret the things you don't do, but if I had chosen Kendra, I'd probably regret not accepting a head coach position.

My fingers twitch to pull her into my side, cover her body with mine, and hold her close, but until I can give her all of me, I won't hurt her by dragging out the fling we had. I release her hand. She will be watching me date other women, women I'm not even excited to meet, and she deserves better than that. The longer my mind ruminates on this show and being intimate with women right in front of her, the more frustrated I become, until my thoughts formulate into a plan ... *this is only temporary.*

I'll go on the dates. I'll do what they ask. I'll finish this stupid contract with the production company ... but I'm coming back for her.

CHAPTER TWELVE

SULLY

I tried to focus on the woman I was introduced to, but all the show prep I had with Kendra over the last couple weeks has closed me off to anyone else. The less I'm allowed to have her, the more I want to say fuck the rules and do it anyway. Especially after that night we stayed up talking for hours at the hotel.

I was reminded twice today to not look into the camera, which I wasn't, I was looking at Kendra standing next to it. Luckily, now that she's interviewing me, I'm supposed to keep my eyes on her. That's easy. Trying to separate myself from her, for her sake? Not so much.

I'm in the back studio where the questioning takes place, or as they call them, "confessionals." Since I'm only meeting one woman at a time, they want to practice filming my first impressions so I know what I should be noticing. They asked me for feedback after my first date, and apparently, I need to say more than "Fine." I'm set up in a chair under bright lights. A paper napkin thing is folded and stuffed in the collar of my shirt by one of the makeup artists as they apply some product to my face, what that is, I have no idea. I can't tell a difference.

Before long, Kendra hustles through the door wearing one of those headsets everyone and their uncle is wearing, along with walkie-talkies. She appears to be in the middle of a conversation.

Everyone at the studio loves her. I've watched her do at least six unique handshakes with staff members. She's alive in this place. They should be doing a show about her, not me. She's way more entertaining to watch. Like a ball of light brightening the faces of everyone she's put in front of. Myself included.

"Thanks Curtis," she says, then her eyes lock onto mine and that bright smile appears on her face. "Ready?"

I nod. Her demeanor is friendly, but she's focused. They snatch the paper from under my collar, and the director I met earlier—James—checks the shot through the camera lens. "Levels are good," he says to Kendra. They do a countdown and just like that, we're filming again.

"Tell me what you think about Kia."

"Seems nice," I answer.

"Remember, we need you to use full sentences in your confessionals or the viewers won't know who you're talking about ... These will be used as footage in between the candid shots. Most of the confessionals will be filmed at the end, but this is a good warm-up."

I resist groaning. "*Kia* seems nice ... she volunteers with kids, so that's cool ..." I chuckle nervously. "Is it weird that all my dates have been marketing managers?" I've been in front of the camera a thousand times, it's not the filming that has me uncomfortable, it's that I'm discussing dating other women with Kendra—the woman I *actually* want to date.

She moves onto another question. "Is there anyone here you felt you had a natural chemistry with?"

"One."

CHAPTER THIRTEEN

KENDRA

Death has come for me. I woke up this morning nauseous and tired ... Fuck, I don't have time to be sick. Shit, I hope it's not burnout. *Perhaps I need to be better about following Sully's advice when it comes to eating healthier*, I tell myself as I stuff a couple of energy bars in my bag for later.

On the way to the arena to film Sully's first official day coaching, I go through my mental checklist. All the player consent forms have been signed. Walkie batteries are charged. Headsets are charged. Lance is already on-site with our PA Rachel.

Despite feeling like a moldy meatsack, I'm looking forward to today. We already met them at the draft, but this is the first time meeting them as an official team. Once we arrive at the arena, we find the Rogues women's locker room and are given clearance. The room smells of fresh paint and appears to be new construction. The floor and a wall have been painted with the team logo, a fierce rogue wave behind the letters.

We take our places in the back so as not to disturb the

players while we gather candid footage of them chatting and building a team bond while we wait for Sully to arrive. When he does, his eyes find mine briefly before returning to his team. He doesn't look nervous and fully embodies a confident head coach. The conversations die down when he enters.

"It's nice to see you all again. Before we head out on the ice, I want to say a few things. First is that I'm thrilled to have you as part of this team, and I'm honored to be your coach. As your coach, I have three expectations of you. The first one is to respect me and respect your teammates. We are a team, these are your sisters. You may not get along all the time, but you better have their back when they need it," Sully announces with authority.

"Two, work hard. Game or practice, you give your all. Do that and you will be successful. Hockey legends aren't born with talent, they're legends because they play a lot and they play hard.

"Three. Never lose your love for this game. You're all here because you're some of the most dedicated and passionate players in the league. We picked you. Each and every one of you were specifically selected to build this team. Love this sport, and show your fans how much you love it ... We good?"

"Yes, Coach."

"Good. Oh, and one more thing." He points at me. "Everybody, this is Kendra. You are to ignore her." He winks at me but doesn't smile. "She's the producer for ... the docuseries about the team. As you know by now, they'll be here for the next few months. You've all signed your consent forms. Pretend it's any other game-day film crew. It might be a little weird at first, but you've all performed on camera before—"

"I didn't really perform, mostly just laid there," Joey

Breck interrupts, and I can already tell she's the sassy one. The corner of my mouth tips up, and I roll my lips together to keep from laughing.

Sully inhales a dose of patience and forges on. "Occasionally, there will be times where they ask to pull you aside for a couple questions. You can always say no. But please remember you're not just representing yourself, you're also representing our team and Minnesota, so keep it short and be *professional*." He faces Joey Breck when he says the word, then aims his gaze at me. "You." He points a finger in my direction. "Don't turn my players into clowns."

"Yes, Coach," I respond.

Sully tucks his tongue into his cheek. "Do you want to add anything?"

I step forward. "We really appreciate all of you welcoming us into your space, we'll do our best to stay out of your way. I speak for all of us when I say we're delighted to be a part of this journey with you. Best of luck this season."

"Any questions?" Sully asks the team.

"What's the name of the show, Coach?" Joey Breck asks, leaning back and chewing her gum with a shit-eating grin.

"The name doesn't matter. Okay, time to—"

"Maybe Kendra knows," Cori Kapowski suggests. He rolls his eyes, and I hang my head between my shoulders.

"It's called Scoring with Sully," I answer.

"Catchy," Cori Kapowski adds with a grin.

A few women snicker. I don't blame them, the name is ridiculous.

Overall, the players and staff are accommodating of our crew intruding on them.

The captain of the team, Delta Makkonen, laughs softly while wrapping tape around her stick. Another player, Timber

Healy, stretches in the corner. She's flexible in ways no human ought to be. I'm guessing she's the goalie.

I grab the bag of gear at my feet and another wave of nausea tries to creep in, but I hold it back. We wave goodbye to the team and head toward the door. "It was nice to meet everyone, we're going to get set up in the arena. See you out there."

I was not prepared for watching Sully on the ice. It's been the best distraction from my nausea. I knew he was hot on skates after our night together, but I didn't see this. Seeing *Coach* Sully? Lord help me. He's hot. Like, really hot. This man is more stable on two knives on the ice than I am on two feet on land. I'm supposed to be capturing everything happening in front of me, but I cannot tear my eyes away from him. He's hypnotizing. I could watch that man cut up a rink for days. Hell, maybe I'll hang out in the editing room and do just that.

The practice consists mostly of passing drills, a few plays, and Sully passing pucks to each player while they take shots on goal. What I would give to be the whistle in his mouth. Feeling dizzy, I sit down and dig around in my bag for one of my energy bars, but as soon as I unwrap it, the nausea is back and I want to throw up. "I'm gonna grab some water."

I head back to the locker room and throw away what was supposed to be my lunch, then splash some water on my face and sit for a second. I need to pull myself together. What is up with my body today? After a few minutes, the sound of stomping is heard in the hallway, and the women flood back into the locker room, followed by Sully.

He gives a summary on what he wants the players to work

on and what they're doing well. The girls stay in their gear until he leaves, then they undress.

"First practice, we gotta celebrate!" Joey says, grabbing a can of beer, smashing it on the back of her skate, and shotgunning it. *Did she bring that from home?* Uff. That sounds absolutely awful.

"Girl, you better not let staff see you," Timber says.

Delta turns her back. "I didn't see anything, but Joey, you better wait for the fucking bar next time. I'm not getting fined because of your wily ass."

"Whoa, Kendra. You okay?" Cori asks.

Shit. "I'm great! Sorry, just a little tired. I was up too late getting prepped for today. I'm going to grab some coffee after this. I need to get on Joey's level." I laugh it off. "It was awesome watching you all practice today, thanks for letting us film."

"You bet. See you at the next one?"

"Definitely." I wave goodbye, then grab my bag and head out. A nap is on my agenda. I can't be coming down with something right as filming begins. All in all, I feel positive after today. We captured some great content, and the players are fun and entertaining and will be great to splice into the show.

CHAPTER FOURTEEN

KENDRA

The day at the arena was great, we captured excellent footage. Even though I was fighting off a stomach bug, I still had fun. It was one of those days that reminded me why I love this job so much. But now, while watching him stare into another woman's eyes, I'd rather take a cooking class from Jeffrey Dahmer. *Dissociate from the subject matter.* I cloak the jealousy with my producer mask and shut down my attraction to him. I'm here to do a job. The time he and I had is over. Focusing on my goals should be my only priority. I'm young, and now's the time to grind and prove I've got what it takes to get my own show. My love story will come, but for now, his is more important.

Today's shoot isn't going well. He's uncomfortable, and it makes me feel terrible. It's rare to film someone so uninterested in being in the spotlight. Most unscripted cast members can't wait to get their fifteen minutes. Sully continues to look in our direction. We need to get out of his line of sight and away from their table.

"Let's pull the camera's back," I say into my headset. His body language tells me he's feeling cramped. We've got both of them mic'd up. We can add subtitles later and get a zoom shot from a distance. "They're too stiff, let's give them a little privacy."

"Thanks, Kendra," he says. His eyes are apologetic, but I give him an encouraging smile. "You're doing great!"

The beautiful brunette across from him smiles in our direction. "Sorry, I'm not doing a good enough job at distracting him." She laughs. "I think we might need more wine." She holds up the bottle in my direction. One of the production assistants, Rachel, hustles over to the bar and gets a new one sent to their table.

Should have had her grab me a bottle too.

"It takes a little getting used to. Totally normal to have some first-date awkwardness. No worries. Just focus on each other." I try to hype them up. This is his *third* first date. I thought that last one would get a second date, but maybe third time's the charm.

Staying in the hotel with him that night was a bad idea. I think Rachel had a spare bed, I could have crashed with her. But *no*, I had to stay up almost all night with him talking and joking and discovering how great we are together. We bonded, and it was more intimate than any sex could have been. It went so much deeper than physical attraction. It laid a fucking foundation.

But, ugh, the sex. The sex is so good too.

My thighs clench at the memories. Before Sully, I'd only ever slept with guys my age. The only time I'd get off—*if* I got off—was during foreplay and usually after a lot of instruction. When it was time to have sex, it consisted of them rutting into me at the same pace for five minutes, or however long it took them to blow their load. Hands were shaky, every touch was cautious. It's not their fault, they simply don't have the experience yet. They're boys.

Not Sully.

He knows exactly what he wants and doesn't hesitate to take it. *Hard*. He goes after it like a predator stalks their prey. He earns the *Daddy* title. When I'm with him, he dominates me, tosses me around like I weigh as much as a loaf of bread, and whispers dirty things in my ear until my mind goes blank. I've been sleeping with boys all these years, but what I needed was to be fucked by a man, by Sully.

Having sex with that man altered my brain chemistry. I don't know if I'll be able to date in my own age bracket ever again. Maybe it's time to find my own date, someone older and more experienced. Maybe it's not Sully, maybe it's older men.

Shaking the thought from my head, I focus on our shot. I wonder if we'll be filming him taking a date home. Candace is funny, sweet, and intelligent. The other men in the restaurant haven't taken their eyes off her. She's beautiful. However, I can tell he's got a wall up. He's friendly with her. Laughs and makes jokes when he's supposed to. But it's all surface level, like he's going through the motions. That doesn't stop my mind from imagining him with her. Him grabbing her body the way he grabbed mine. Kissing her the way he kissed me. My thoughts are interrupted by Candace's laughter.

She whispers something to him, and the mic didn't pick it up well. The editing team will decipher it later. I'm not sure what she said, but the way she's looking at him with fuck-me eyes tells me it was suggestive.

He chuckles and looks down to his food, nodding and slicing into his steak. He pops the bite into his mouth and leans back in his chair while he chews. They aren't saying anything, just staring at each other. It's exactly the footage we want and full of sexual tension. They're having a conversation with each other without even saying a word. We've reached the point where he's forgotten about the cameras.

Forgotten about me.

I swallow, immediately feeling sick to my stomach, then ask Rachel if she can run out to the van and grab me the antacids from my bag. She nods and heads toward the exit. All of the food aromas are blending together. I'm not sure what it is, but I find the smell offensive and overpowering. I don't know if we're under some vent or something, but the scent is repulsive, and I need to find a bathroom.

"Be right back."

I hurry to the restroom and immediately heave. Despite not eating today, my body is determined to empty its contents. What the hell is wrong with me? I lean against the wall and take a few deep breaths.

When I feel well enough to move, I rinse the taste of bile out of my mouth at the sink. Fuck. It's a strange feeling between hunger and nausea. Do I eat something and risk it coming back up? Sully would chastise me if he knew how many meals I've been skipping. It's not intentional, nothing appeals to me lately. I think it's this stomach bug. The only thing that sounds appetizing is a long nap. I'm not a person who naps, but lately, the idea of stretching out like a cat all afternoon and sleeping sounds fantastic.

When I exit the bathroom, I startle at the massive, unexpected wall of Sully blocking my path.

"Are you okay?" he asks, looking down at me.

"I'm fine. Why aren't you with Candace? Do you need something?" *Shit, what did I miss because of this stupid nausea?* My salty feelings breed jealous, impulsive thoughts. It's unfair to both of the cast members. *Grow up, Kendra.*

"You're ashen."

"Uh, thanks?" I say, brushing past him back to my post in

the corner of the restaurant. Then I spot Lance at the end of the hallway with his camera trained on us. It doesn't look good with the way Sully was standing so close to me.

"When was the last time you ate something?"

It pisses me off. I've already been kicking my own ass about it, I don't need his help. He has to stop checking in on me, it's none of his business. I grit my teeth and spin to face him. "Sully, I need you to sit down at your table so I can do my job. Do you understand me?" My voice is stern.

He glares at me. His jaw tics, and the anger comes off him in waves. I'm acutely aware of the camera fifteen feet behind me. Sully rubs the back of his neck, and his shoulders relax. His gaze drops to the floor when he realizes this isn't something we're going to argue about.

"Yeah. I understand," he says.

"Good. Is the date going okay?"

His eyes find mine again. "Well, she's not you."

The words make me want to throw up all over again. I'm well aware that woman is not me. The reminder is cruel. I scoff and turn around, putting on a tight smile for the camera as I find my place next to the crew, not looking back.

After a few seconds, he strides back to his seat. Rachel hands me the antacids, and I pop them in my mouth. It takes the edge off some of the nausea.

"He's good now," I say to Rachel. "Growing pains, ya know?" I want Rachel and Lance to believe our close conversation was simply a pep talk from me, rather than the awkward confrontation it was.

CHAPTER FIFTEEN

SULLY

"Three-on-twos!" I shout to my players.

Three play offense against two defense to protect the net. I want them to push harder. "Where's your grit? Take up space!"

They run the drill, and after each shot on goal, a new set of offense and defense jump in to run it.

"New puck, new puck!" I shoot another one out to center ice for the next set of players. "Let's go!"

On the ice, the cameras don't bother me. I'm used to being on camera on the ice. It's a relief from the other night with that shitshow of a date. *What even was that?* And the way she looked at me when she told me to get back to my table … Shit. Those eyes were empty, like I was nothing to her. Like we were strangers.

If we're to survive these upcoming months, I will have to place some distance between us. She clearly has. This show is her priority; she's young and career focused. I understand that mentality and respect it. When I was younger, that was me too. I can't hinder what she's working toward. We can get along and wrap up this contract.

Jeanine, the assistant coach, who's been covering defense, positions herself next to me. "We have a weak corner. Let's swap out Grattle for Skarbakka."

I nod. "Affirm."

"Out of play! New puck!" I yell, shooting another one across the ice. I need to be as focused on my team as Kendra is on this show. These players didn't fight like hell to get here so I could give them less than one hundred percent of my attention. I run the three-on-two drill over and over until they're getting a little sloppy.

"Go hydrate!"

The speed skating stops, and they turn on the edge of their skates back to the bench. While they take a break and grab water, I collect the pucks. I encourage them to bond with each other as much as possible, which happens best if I'm not around. I've even set mandatory nights they go out together so they can connect off the ice. By game one, they should be thick as thieves. I smile when I hear mostly laughter from the bench. That's a good sign. I let them have a few more minutes while I set up the drill again. Giving them a demo will help them visualize the issue we're trying to correct.

"Okay, everybody back to the net. Skarbakka, you're on D with Breck."

"Let's go, Trainwreck!" one of the girls hollers, and Joey laughs, finding her spot on the ice.

"Here's what's happening." I skate to center ice, then toward them as a demonstration. "Here comes offense, it's coming in hot." I navigate between my players who are standing still. Joey gets into position along with Skarbakka. "Right there! Stop!" I move to the open area, where we're having a problem. "Right here, there is no presence. We have a huge open pocket. Delta, I want you making sure these

COACH SULLY

holes are getting plugged up. You should all be taking up space. Everybody got it?"

"Yes, Coach."

"Great. Run it again."

Their technique improves this time. It's progress.

Kendra's wearing the Rogues jacket the players gave her. The team already likes her, because of course they do. It's impossible not to. Her hair is up, showcasing the thick curls I loved digging my fingers into when I kissed her. She holds up a mittened hand behind the glass and waves. I haven't spoken to her since the restaurant. Her smiles range between big and fake, and pained. I crave the real one, so I skate closer to her.

"How am I doing?" I ask, half-joking.

She gives me a thumbs-up. "Really great."

Cool.

I head back toward my team covering the open pockets like I showed them. "Beauty! Okay, let's move into corner one-on-ones, and then we'll finish with edgework drills." I slap pucks out to the players, and they snatch them up. "Yes, Coach!"

Pretty sure Joey said something about edging; thank God she's not mic'd up today.

I meet Whit in his office after practice to discuss our progress. The more we learn about the players and how they operate, the better we can coach them. Some of the old-school coaches think there's only two methods: hard-ass or buddy-buddy. I disagree. We're a team. I will not rip them down and hope they build themselves up, but I'm also not going to pass out participation ribbons.

I've come to learn that Whit is very hands-on. He's

observed every practice from the stands. Something I never saw the Lakes GM do. I wonder if Whit should have had this job, so for now, I will treat him as another coach to learn from. Two heads are better than one and all that.

"So, what are you thinking?" he asks.

"Our defense is good, but we have to get our offense focused on where they lack coverage ... Speed could be better too, I'd like to see them dig in more. But they're hungry."

"That's all we need." He nods. "How's Delta doing as captain? Is the rest of the team receiving her well?"

I nod. "Yeah, all good. She's dedicated and focused, but, ya know, not a dick about it. Overall, the players are getting along well from what I can see. I've got them going out together on Friday to Top Shelf. Hope they can strengthen that team bond a little more."

"They don't seem distracted by the camera crew, so that's good."

"Yup."

"What about you?" he asks.

I don't understand the question. "What do you mean?"

"Are you distracted by the camera crew?" His eyes laser-focus on me. Guess my subtlety needs some work when it comes to my producer.

"Not at all."

In the parking lot, Kendra is helping Lance load some of the equipment into a van. I adjust my hockey bag, hoisting it on my shoulder.

"Hey you," I announce.

"Hi." She spins around. "Great work today."

"Do you have a second?" I want to make sure she's okay after the weird interaction we had at the restaurant.

Lance shuts the van doors and gives me a small wave.

"Hey, man," I say, wanting to acknowledge him.

Lance nods and climbs into the driver's seat. He's a quiet guy.

"Is it about the show?" she asks. *Why does she look so ashen?*

"Kind of."

She nods. "Look, I'm really sorry, but do you mind if it waits until later? I don't mean to brush you off, but I'm absolutely beat. I gotta grab some dinner or something before I collapse." Her hands tremble, then she quickly tucks them into her jacket pockets.

"Mind if I join you?" Might be a good way to talk some of this tension out, but she's definitely got to eat.

"I'm just going to make something at home. I've got some reports to go over, then I'm going to crash." We hold each other's gaze for a moment, and she lowers her voice. "We can't be more than friends."

We've been more than friends since that first night together.

I nod. "Understood. Have a good night, Kendra."

"You too."

———

Hours later, I lie in bed, flipping through the TV channels. I'm trying to focus on sports highlights, but it's not doing it for me tonight. She didn't look great, so I wonder if she's sick. I open up the messages on my phone and click her name. I should make sure she got home okay. Hopefully she ate something healthy instead of one of those bars.

My fingers hover over the keys when three little dots pop up at the bottom of the screen. *She's texting me*, and damn if that doesn't make me smile. I stretch out in bed while I wait for her message to come through.

> **KENDRA**
> I think we need to put some distance between us. The women on the show are really great people. I think it's important you find someone to take on a second date. I'm here because of the show. I appreciate your dinner invite tonight, but it's not a good idea to see each other outside of work, even as friends. I don't want to muddy the waters.

I think of the night we had lain in bed at the hotel. "*If things were different ...*" she'd said. But I never asked if the feeling was mutual. I assumed. Have I been assuming this entire time?

> If I wasn't on this show, would we be together?

> **KENDRA**
> If it's meant to be, it'll happen someday. But that time isn't now. Please understand where I'm coming from. Our careers must take priority.

> We aren't done yet.

There's still feelings there. I need her to know that. But her next text has me chucking my phone across the bed.

> **KENDRA**
> We never started, Sully.

Fuck that.

CHAPTER SIXTEEN

KENDRA

Round two, over. Tonight, he went on a date with a lovely woman named Amy. We were staged at a hotel bar. Hotels are great because we can book a suite and film confessionals on-site. I'm in the room checking on equipment with camera operators, Lance and Derrick, and my production assistant, Rachel.

Rachel and Derrick are running out to grab the rest of us food. While we wait, Lance and I go through some of the recent footage on a laptop. "That was a great shot," he says, capturing Amy batting her eyes at him. I swallow, then nod. I am so fucking emotional today, which means my period will show up within the next twenty-four hours.

"We need to have dual-camera coverage. The last date with Candace was a bitch to film, especially when Sully walked off. It's too much to capture with one guy."

"We were limited that night due to permits, but I totally agree. We should have at least two to three going forward."

The shots are great. Captivating, even. So much that I can't tear my eyes away from him smiling and joking with the woman. It's only going to get worse. Both of our careers are riding on this show. It's only hitting me harder today because my hormones are out of whack. I need to pull it together, especially because Sully should be showing up any minute to get his confessional filmed.

"I'll have Rachel double-check our locations going forward," I say. "You handled it really well, though. Nice job."

"He stormed off, had to follow him."

"Shit, I missed that." *Thanks, nausea.* "Do you have any idea what he was mad about?"

"I think … you."

My cheeks feel like they're on fire. "What?"

The knock on the door interrupts us. I suck in a deep breath, and Lance shrugs. He pushes off the edge of the hotel desk he's been leaning on and opens the door. Sully walks in. I don't know if I'll get used to how massive he is walking through doorways. Or the smell of his cologne.

I paste on a smile.

"I gotta grab another mic from the van," Lance announces. "Be right back."

He couldn't have done that earlier?

"Okay!" I say, unaffected and not at all nervous about being left alone in a hotel room with Lee Sullivan. "We'll get you set up here." I adjust the angle of the chair. "We'll go through some more questions, just be honest and share your thoughts, no matter what they are." I flip on the lights and check the lighting and background, wanting a different angle than Amy. "We'll get started as soon as Lance returns."

Then I notice he has a couple water bottles. He hands one to me. "Drink this." It feels like a trap.

"Oh. No, thanks. I'm good. Got my coffee." I nod to the cup of cold coffee on the desk.

"I wasn't asking, Kendra." *Excuse me?* "Drink it. You're

dehydrated."

I grab the laptop and sit on the edge of the bed, trying to look busy.

He steps between my legs and takes the laptop from me. His warm huge hand cups my cheek, and I can't bring myself to pull away. He swipes his thumb across my lips.

"Your lips are dry."

My gaze falls to his mouth, and my tongue betrays me by peeking out and lightly touching the tip of his thumb. He bites his lip, and I swear I hear a slight rumble in his chest.

"Do you want to kiss me?" I ask, then cringe at the impulsive thought that came out of my mouth. I can't even respect my own limits. Though, if he tried, I can say with certainty I wouldn't have the strength to stop him. It seems I can only hold boundaries when there's a screen between us. Because right now, all I can think about is if I was the last person he kissed?

He blows out a breath, staring into my eyes. After too long, he clears his throat and says, "Drink the water, Kendra."

I desperately want to be swallowed up by this hotel carpet. "Shit. I'm so embarrassed." I look away and place my laptop in front of me again, wanting to hide. As if this thin Airbook could somehow provide me any defense against him. "I don't know why I said that." I told him we needed distance, then asked if he wanted to kiss me. *What the fuck was I thinking?* I wasn't! Of course he rejected me. I shouldn't be upset. No. No, actually, this is good. I'm glad he prevented it from going any further.

"Don't be. If I kissed you now, I wouldn't be able to stop."

He unscrews the cap on the water bottle and hands it to me. I take it from him and feel his eyes on me as I swallow every drop.

CHAPTER SEVENTEEN

KENDRA

After leaping from the shower, I drop to my knees at the toilet and heave. There's nothing for my stomach to reject, but that doesn't stop it from trying. I bring my head under the tap and gulp water to give my stomach something. My body shakes as I pull toilet paper from the roll and wipe the spit from my mouth. It's time to see a doctor.

The last few days have been spent throwing up on and off while battling the worst exhaustion I've ever experienced. I feel awful. Is it burnout? Is it stress from the show? It's the first time I've had a role this big. Jeremy is mostly managing the budget, but I'm the producer on-site. Maybe I don't have the stamina for a role this big.

Fuck that, I want this. I can do it. This is simply growing pains.

I stand and rinse my mouth out, then brush my teeth for the second time today.

It's been a month since I interviewed Sully at the hotel, and after he rejected my kiss, it's been easier to maintain a professional distance. A line was crossed when he swept his thumb over my lips, but he's been respectful of my space since.

If only I could find my energy again and start feeling better. Sully has been warning me about this. Eat well, drink water, get sleep. I haven't been good about any of those things unless he's right in front of me with a plate of food or bottle of water, which has become a routine we've fallen into. He doesn't say a word, simply hands me a plate of food or my water bottle, and we go about the day. I admit, my work-life balance isn't healthy, but throwing myself into my job feels much safer than sitting alone with my thoughts. So sometimes I forget to eat, and lately, even when I do remember, I'm often too nauseous to have an appetite.

Once the shakes subside, I return to my shower to finish combing through the conditioner in my hair. After rinsing, I promptly turn off the water. My legs are tired, and it feels like somebody turned up the gravity. I'm exhausted, and my limbs are heavy.

My phone beeps with a notification. I glance at the screen as I dry myself off. *You've forgotten to log your period.*

I roll my eyes. Wait. When was my last period? I unlock the phone and open the app. Scrolling through the calendar for too long. I forgot to log the last one too. I haven't missed two periods, have I? Can't be. The stress of this show has me so distracted I don't even remember. These days I'm so lethargic I'm running on empty all the time. I'm constantly in a daze, just trying to get through the day, but how the fuck would this get by me? Why can't I remember?

I blot my hair and stare in the mirror at my reflection. I can't be pregnant; I had my tubes tied when I was nineteen. What if this is something more serious ... like cancer or some uterine cyst. I shake my head. I'm getting ahead of myself.

With a towel still wrapped around me, I shuffle into the

kitchen for a sleeve of crackers to bring back to bed. I've come to learn the nausea comes on strongest when I haven't eaten. Between being sick and everything else in my life, I need to see a doctor so I can get this under control, whatever it is, because it's starting to worry me. God, this is such a pain in the ass. I pull out my phone and call the doctor's office. They put me on hold. I drop the towel and crawl naked under the covers. I just need a couple minutes more of sleep before I get dressed.

Finally, someone answers and I'm able to make an appointment for this afternoon. I email Rachel and Pierce to let them know I won't be in today. Maybe I can get some work done from home. Thankfully, Sully is traveling with the team to some training facility this week and due to the nature of their training and clients, we weren't able to secure a film permit. Which means my mornings are a little slower until the Rogues come home. My boobs are sore, which means I will probably get my period any day now. Probably late because of whatever flu I'm fighting.

I shove another cracker into my mouth. I'm not pregnant.

That's impossible.

———

The nurse takes my vitals and asks for a urine sample before the doctor sees me. Why is peeing into a cup so difficult? I had to pee before I walked into this bathroom, but all of a sudden, my bladder forgot I had to piss so bad? I close my eyes and visualize waterfalls and dripping water. That finally works.

I set the cup in the pass-through door between the restroom and lab. After finishing and washing my hands, I return to the clinic room with butter-yellow walls and wait for the doctor. I lie on the table, taking advantage of my opportunity to rest. Not that I've been doing any strenuous activities, but the fluorescent lights above are too bright and my eyes feel heavy. It feels good to close them. This is nice …

I wake up to the doctor knocking.

"Yup!" I call, my voice sleepy. I sit up and pretend like I wasn't napping two seconds ago. That's gotta be a record for time it takes to fall asleep. How long was I asleep for?

She looks serious as she takes a seat. Fuck, it's cancer, isn't it? She doesn't turn on the computer, just sits in the chair directly across from me and waits.

"Hi Kendra. It's good to see you. I hear you've been experiencing some fatigue and nausea?"

"*Experiencing* is one way to put it." It's been very hands-on. An up-close-and-personal interaction.

Her expression is blank, and I can't get a read on her. It's causing my anxiety to spiral. "We ran your labs. Kendra, you're pregnant."

I laugh. "That's impossible. I had my tubes tied. It's in my chart. Just a few years ago."

She nods. "I know."

My face sobers. "So, test it again."

"We tested it twice."

I shake my head. No, no, no, no. "I have my tubes tied." I sound like a broken record, but I can't get pregnant. Why do they keep saying I'm pregnant?

"Tubal ligation is ninety-eight percent effective. It's a rare occurrence, but it happens. In general, it's an effective form of permanent birth control, however, the younger you are at the time of the surgery, the higher the likelihood of it being unsuccessful."

This isn't real. She's lying. I can't be pregnant. I made

sure I could never get pregnant. I paid a lot of money to make sure I could never get pregnant.

"How come nobody told me there was a chance this could fail? This can't be happening!" I'm mad. She nods, letting me get my frustration out. My breaths come harder and faster.

"Take a slow breath, Kendra."

I nod, forming an O with my mouth, and try to take a deep breath. My hands wrinkle the paper underneath me.

"Can you estimate what the conception date was?"

Then everything comes full circle, and it slams into me. Tears spring from my eyes. I'm not just pregnant ... *I'm pregnant with Sully's baby.*

Oh my God.

The doctor must see it on my face, so she quickly grabs a blue plastic emesis bag, and I heave up all the crackers and water from earlier. She calls a nurse outside the door to have them bring me a glass of water.

"I'm sorry," I say.

"No need to apologize. I understand this was not part of your plan ... There are still options if you want to consider termination. Can you estimate—"

"Late June. The conception. Or maybe July. Shit, that means I'm, like, *pregnant*-pregnant."

The doctor nods, and a nurse arrives with a cup of water.

"Would you like some pamphlets on your options?"

I swish some of the water in my mouth and spit it into the emesis bag. My doctor hands me a tissue, and I wipe my mouth. She gives me a moment to pull my thoughts together.

"Um ... yes, please. But I don't know yet. What do I do if I keep it?"

"We'll need to get an ultrasound appointment set up so we can get an idea of how far along you are and make sure the baby is growing safely. As far as the nausea and exhaustion, that's very common during the first trimester and can go into the second trimester."

Second trimester. *Second trimester, good God.*

"How is your diet?"

"I'm nauseous all the time."

She nods. "I can give you a prescription to help with the nausea. Unfortunately, the exhaustion is probably hanging around but should be improving based on where you are in the trimester."

There's that word again.

"Ginger also helps with nausea."

The only ginger thing I like are those little spice cakes from Sugar and Ice. Surprisingly, the idea of eating them isn't revolting.

She hands me a folder, and we go through too much information for my brain to take in. My head is swimming with a million thoughts. There's a baby … in my uterus. By the end of my visit, I've already got a to-do list a mile long. First thing is finding an OBGYN I like.

I'm focused on stopping by Sugar and Ice on the way home. Everything else is much too frightening to think about. Am I in shock? Whatever, all I want are those stupid spice cakes. I'm overwrought with my … *condition.*

———

I'm pleased to see a friendly face when I open the front door at Sugar and Ice. Micky's standing behind one of the bakery cases and sliding in some fresh petit fours. She glances up and smiles. This is my go-to place for out-of-the-office work meetings. I spent many mornings and afternoons here while developing my original dating show idea. Over time, I got to know the owner, Micky.

"Hey Kendra! I didn't know you were gonna visit me today!"

I smile. "Yeah, how many of those ginger spice cakes do you have?"

"A bunch, how many do you want?" she says, smiling. She doesn't understand.

I fan my palms on the counter. "How many do you have?"

"I think three or four dozen?"

"Great. I will take three or four dozen."

"Wow, you must be feeding a lot of people."

I scoff. "Just two!" I say, laughing much too hard. My grip on reality is slipping. A tear rolls down my cheek, and I brush it away.

Micky reaches across the counter and takes my hands. "Hey. You okay?"

"Nope. I'm pregnant." More tears, and I try to laugh through them. "Sorry, I just found out. There's a lot going on."

"So ... not congratulations, then?"

I shake my head. "I wasn't trying. One-night stand with a lifetime souvenir."

"Shit. I'm sorry, Kendra."

I shrug. "I feel like I'm still a kid myself, you know?"

She comes around the counter and wraps me up in a hug, and I let her. I needed one. "So, I've got a friend who was in a similar situation. Raleigh? You've met a couple times, briefly."

I remember her.

"She had a child when she was your age, one-night stand. Do you want her number?"

Is that weird? I could use some advice, though. "Do you think she would mind?"

"No! Not at all. I'll check with her, but I'm sure she'd

love to talk to you. She felt a lot like you do. She's a sweetheart, you'll like her."

I nod. That's actually a relief. The pamphlets and brochures I received at the office are adorned with beaming women with protruding stomachs. They look like those advertisements of women laughing into their salads. As if their organic arugula gave them back-to-back orgasms.

I am most certainly not laughing into my salad today.

"Thanks, Micky."

That afternoon, while stuffing my face with ginger cakes in bed, and coming to terms with a baby taking up residence in my uterus, my phone vibrates with a text message.

It's Raleigh.

I don't share much, but we plan to meet for brunch this weekend. I'm really looking forward to talking to her. It'll be refreshing to know there's someone who's been through this and survived.

CHAPTER EIGHTEEN

SULLY

"The second drill is a two-on-one backcheck support drill. This will emphasize some defensive work, backchecking, and transitioning to offense and supporting the puck to attack the net."

Cori, Joey, and Delta get into position. The first try is a little sloppy, but by the fourth round, it's smooth and seamless. "That's fucking perfect. Now swap with Skarbakka."

I hand off pucks to the players, sending them flying in random directions. They have to be prepared for the biscuit to take a different trajectory. After ten minutes, they get a water break, then come back to practice taking shots on Timber and Manon, our goaltenders. Snapping pucks to them as they go, I skate backward, collecting the ones that were blocked and passing them to the players. I enjoy coaching, it allows me to get in ice time, work on drills, but I have so much more control than I did as a captain. And I like control.

Kendra is sitting in the stands with her head down. She's either looking at her phone or the floor, as if she's avoiding making eye contact with me. Actually, she has made no contact with me since before we left for the Hockey Developmental Center in San Diego.

I furrow my brow at her and turn back to my players. "Okay, this next one revolves around competitive play. I'm going to dump pucks in the corner, you are to battle one-on-one, and then make a pass to the coach.

"If you make your pass, you get an ice cream sandwich out of Whit's personal stash." Whit's head snaps up from the corner, then he shakes it. I found out this week that he's a fiend for ice cream sandwiches. Everybody's got a vice. His is ice cream. Mine is Kendra.

Once we finish and I know I've given out enough ice cream to clear out his cache, I send in Jeanine to work with the players on individual skating drills, and head back to my office to go over some scheduling details. Sitting back in my chair, I type in the password and wait for the screen to load.

"Hey, gotta minute?" Rachel, Vault's production assistant, knocks on my open office door.

"Sure." I smile. "What's up?"

"So, the network wants to do a live interview talking about the show, coaching, and your love life. Only twenty minutes or so, enough for a teaser of what's to come, but I need to go over some things with you because live TV is a little different and has a lot more rules."

"Rachel, I've been doing press boxes and playing on live television since I was younger than you."

I don't even get an eyeroll out of her. "Humor me. We're not talking about games, we're talking about your love life, it's going to feel a lot more personal."

"Okay, let's hear your spiel."

She sits down in the orange padded chair across from me.

"Rule number one, no swearing. The network, and you, will be fined by the FCC before you even finish your sentence. There will be a twenty-second delay in case we need to censor anything, but it would make it a lot easier on everyone if you avoid it altogether."

I recline and thread my fingers together behind my head. "Got it." She places papers down in front of me. I pluck them off the desk and flip through them.

"Those are the questions she'll be asking you. You need to come up with your responses so we can clear them before it airs. Memorize what you're going to say, but you know, don't make them sound rehearsed. Add some extra pauses and use inflection so it sounds natural," she explains. "Kendra's included some suggested safety sentences to give you an idea of what they're looking for."

"I thought this was all about unscripted television?"

"*Scoring with Sully* is unscripted, the interview isn't. And you're representing the network during this promo. It will be at the news station, they're going to splice it in between the Lakes intermission."

I see. "Anything else?"

"Day of, go easy on the coffee. Wear something comfortable but professional. Avoid wearing anything with a brand name, with the exception of Rogues gear, but keep it simple like a fleece three-quarter zip or something with a collar. Nothing bigger than pocket branding. That sort of thing."

I nod. "Who's doing the interview?"

Her phone dings, and she pulls it from her back pocket to tap out a response to a text message. "They want someone you're comfortable with, so Kendra will be the one asking questions. You do well when it's one-on-one with her, so just pretend there's nobody else around. You've already got your answers, so you don't need to worry about coming up with stuff on the spot like in the confessionals."

When it's one-on-one with Kendra, it *feels* like there's nobody around.

I nod and she pauses, looking at me knowingly. "A little flirtation is confident, too much and you'll look like a womanizer. Rein it in."

I smirk. Wonder if anyone else has picked up on that. "I'll do my best. Anything else?"

"There's a copy of the questions in your inbox. Kendra needs your answers by Friday so she can critique them before the game."

"Will do." I oscillate in my rolling desk chair, and she stands to leave. "How is Kendra doing, by the way?"

"She's all right, you know, all things considered."

I furrow my brow. "All things considered?"

Rachel hoists the strap of her bag on her shoulder and cocks her head to the side with pursed lips, as if it's obvious. Then she quickly replies, "She just has a lot on her plate right now, she's working a lot. That's nothing new, though."

"Yeah, I've gathered as much."

The last thing I want to do is talk on live TV—with Kendra—about my dating life. Or lack thereof, because so far, every date has been a bust. The only thing worse than going on the dates themselves is talking about them. Sitting one-on-one and discussing other women to the one woman I'm interested in is torture.

I don't want to date all these other women. It's obvious they aren't going to work out, at least it is to me. If people saw what Kendra and I were *really* like when no one's around, they'd see how great we fit together as a couple. I lean back in my chair, close my eyes, and scrub a hand down my face.

How am I going to get through the rest of this damn show?

CHAPTER NINETEEN

KENDRA

Raleigh and I chose to meet for brunch, which I appreciate. I'm hopeful the discussion of my unplanned pregnancy will be less daunting if it's done over expensive avocado toast. I anticipated our introduction being awkward, but Raleigh has a welcoming nature that makes me feel like I belong. Maybe it's her positive vibes or the slight southern accent. Regardless, she's one of those people you trust almost instantly.

"What are you getting to drink?" she asks. "I'd kick a door off its hinges to get to their orange juice."

"Orange juice? Really?"

"Girl, just get it. You'll thank me later."

I'm searching the menu for something that won't make my stomach queasy. Just reading *eggs benedict* makes me want to run for the door. They have lemon-blueberry muffins. Close enough. The ginger cakes from Sugar and Ice are the only thing keeping me alive these days.

"That's it?" she asks. "You're not hungry for anything else?"

"Everything else makes me nauseous."

"Got it. I'll get a muffin too." She sets her menu at the edge of the table.

"The last thing you probably want is the smell of eggs on the table."

The thought alone nearly makes me retch. Luckily, our booth is tucked into a little alcove and the smells of other people's food aren't as pungent as they were the other day during filming.

I drop my chin to my chest. "Oh my God, thank you so much for understanding. It's been a nightmare."

"When I was pregnant with Darby, the smell of raw chicken destroyed me. It's the worst."

I set my menu on top of hers and make small talk about the cute decor in the restaurant. The server comes around, and we order two glasses of orange juice and two lemon-blueberry muffins. The woman smiles and leaves with our menus.

"So," Raleigh says, "should we get into it?"

Here we go.

Once I start talking, it's like I can't stop. I tell her about everything: the failed tubal ligation, about not wanting to tell my job, about the hellish symptoms I've been going through in my first trimester—a word I've gotten used to over the last few days. Well, *almost* everything. I feel a little guilty omitting the minor detail that it's Sully's child, but I can't risk him finding out. Not until I know what I want to do and have a plan of action. All Raleigh knows is that the dad was a one-night stand. Technically, it was two nights, but that's not important anymore.

Once I finish my tell-all, our food arrives and she shares her experience with her first child, Arthur. She was twenty-two when she became pregnant with him. She tried to reach out to Barrett, the father, but due to some miscommunication, they didn't connect again until Arthur was almost five. It's heartbreaking to hear about the struggles she went through, but it has a happy ending. It's especially touching that throughout those five years, Barrett never gave up looking for Raleigh.

Then she goes into the ugly stuff. She doesn't sugarcoat the postpartum depression and anxiety. The expenses and daycare costs. I appreciate her transparency. Thankfully, I'm paid well by Vault Productions, and I've been good about saving money from my mother and grandmother when they both passed, which is how I was able to afford my house—and tubal ligation, which I feel I'm entitled to a refund for.

I take a sip of the orange juice. *Goddamn, that's good.* "What is this?"

"They fresh squeeze it and blend it until it's light and fluffy."

"It tastes like a cloud." I didn't know orange juice could taste like this. "Why do we even bother drinking it any other way?" Best of all, it doesn't make me nauseous. Another safety food!

"Ugh, I know." She takes a sip of hers. "So fucking good."

I peel at the wrapper on my muffin. Nervous to take a bite and have it want to come right back up again.

"I'm going to ask the big question: do you want to keep the baby?" She pauses. "Saying no is just as valid as saying yes."

"That's the weird thing. I do ... but I don't know why. There's no reason for me to keep this baby. I never expected to be able to have children. I always figured I would adopt someday down the road if I wanted to be a mother. The genes I'm passing down to my baby ... it scares the hell out of me, but selfishly, I *still* want it. Does that make me a bad person?"

"Of course not."

I drop my face into my palms. "I *wish* I didn't want it. But I do. It's so fucked up, Raleigh." I pull my hands down, and her sympathetic eyes are brimming.

"It's not fucked up. Feelings are weird. Motherhood is weird. It's not the first time you'll feel conflicted like that. Just know it's okay to experience those feelings fully. Don't guilt yourself over emotions."

I nod, returning to my muffin and tearing off a morsel to eat.

Silence falls between us, and I stare at a woman from another table who's out with her girlfriends. She's rocking a baby carrier at her feet with one foot while she chats with the rest of the table.

"Is it worth it?" I ask, glancing at the sleeping baby inside the carrier.

"For me it was. But that's something every parent has to answer for themselves. Considering you're already worried about your baby shows you want to protect it. That says a lot. You've got a great job, you're strong, and from what I can tell, you're an awesome human, so I think you'll make an awesome mom too. There are great things about motherhood. There are also shitty things, but you'll become stronger than you ever knew you could be. It's okay to do it on your own." She clears her throat. "But …"

"But?"

"But I think you need to tell the father. Try to reach him. He deserves to know either way."

I nod and nibble on another piece of muffin. The last bite stayed down. "I know—and I will. I just need time to figure out how."

"Good. Now … are there any questions you have?"

I laugh and open up the Notes app on my phone. I've got a million questions, and thankfully, Raleigh's an open book. I ask every question I could think of regarding pregnancy and newborns and parenting. Motherhood sounds really fucking hard, especially since I won't have support from family. It's just me. I'm only twenty-three. I don't know if I'm strong enough to do it, but I want to try. I'll find the strength to persevere. Like I've always done.

We say our goodbyes after breakfast is over and part ways, promising to stay in touch. I take the long way home and stop at Lake Harriet. Wrapping my scarf around my neck, I get out of the car and walk the vacant path that circles the lake. In the summer, this place is filled with people jogging, rollerblading, or biking. However, the blustery November weather has all but turned this walkway into a ghost town.

The water on the lake appears thick and sluggish, a telltale sign it will freeze over any day now. Most of the leaves have fallen and blown away, but every so often, a crispy brown remainder scrapes across the path like a lost tumbleweed.

This is stick season. Where life hides underground or nests indoors, waiting for the harsh winter to pass. Maybe that's where I'm at in my life. I'm in my stick season, a period of transition. It will get colder. The days will feel neverending, filled with darkness and air so bitter it bites at my skin. I'll forget the sensation of sunshine on my face. I'll question why I live in such awful conditions.

But ... spring always comes. When the ground thaws and vibrant green life sprouts from the brown sticks and dirt, it will be so beautiful and such a welcome sight that the dark days will have been worth it.

It's worth it.

I lie in bed that night with a spice cake and a frothy orange juice—compliments of myself after buying ten pounds of oranges and a new juicer. After firing up my laptop, I login into Pinterest. This is what the moms do, right? I type *pregnancy* into the search bar, and my screen is flooded with pastel colors and links to every list you could think of. *Ten affirmations for your first trimester. Ten foods you should stop eating. Ten pregnancy essentials. Top ten safest car seats.*

I start with affirmations.

#10. My morning sickness is the overwhelming emotions of happiness my baby has because I'm their mother.

I stare at the words for a while, then read it again and stare some more.

My morning sickness is the overwhelming emotions of happiness my baby has because I'm their mother ...

That's the dumbest thing I've ever read. "Seriously, who writes this stuff? Is there a top ten list of total bullshit?" I shake my head and take another sip of my orange juice, muttering, "Get fucked so hard."

Losing all credibility for the remaining affirmations on that list, I exit the post and hide it so I never have to see it again.

Top ten baby names.

"I suppose it's time we upgrade your name. You can't be Cletus the Fetus forever. Or Cletith ... if you're a girl. I mean, not that you have to choose between just two genders. You've got a lot of options these days, so you do you, boo."

My mind is blank trying to think of names I like. The only names that come to mind are those of my coworkers. That'd be weird.

"My mom's name was Bonnie. Maybe you could be Bo, for now at least." I look down at my stomach. That name brings a whole new level of comfort to me, like mom is with me in some way. This baby really is mine, which means it's also part of her. The notion warms my heart, enough for me to touch my belly, something I've been afraid to do until now. Pressing in, I feel the firm swollen bump. I do it again and smile.

"I promise I'll have my shit together by the time you arrive. Or at least as together as it can be. Everything will be okay … We're going to do this together. You and me, Bo."

CHAPTER TWENTY

SULLY

"How are you feeling?" Rachel asks. "Nervous?"

"No, I'm good," I say. We're using the local network's studio to record the interview today. It's a mix between the people I'm used to being around when we do the show and the network since they are running the control room.

"It'll be just like the confessionals, except, you know, you already have your answers. Kendra said your responses were great, by the way."

I'll bet she did. They were basically the same as the "safety sentences" she gave me.

They usher me under the LEDs inside a room with a raised floor that begins halfway in. On the stage are two upholstered chairs and a step-and-repeat backdrop that includes the network's logo, Rogues's logo, and *Scoring with Sully*. Seeing my name on it is surreal.

Before long, Kendra walks in from hair and makeup and looks stunning. As usual. She takes the chair across from me.

Rachel gives Kendra a questioning look. "You good?" she asks.

Kendra smiles confidently. "I'm good."

"Need any TUMS?"

Her nervous gaze meets mine for a split second. I tilt my head and narrow my eyes. What's she hiding?

"Nope," Kendra answers. "All set."

We get a two-minute warning from somebody on the camera crew.

"Just like you rehearsed," she says.

Wow, not even a *hi*.

"It's nice to talk to you again. Been a while."

She ignores the comment. Jesus, she won't even speak to me outside of this stupid promo. Even now, every question and answer has been scripted and rehearsed. She's taking this professionalism to a whole new level.

My eyes land on the backdrop again. *Rogues.* The word on the step and repeat plants a seed in my brain. I could take the show into my own hands. Fuck it, maybe if I look like a big enough dick they'll decide somebody else should do this show. Like Whit. He's single.

Vault Productions maintains a firm no-fraternization rule, but I feel like she's slipping away every time I'm filmed with another woman. She needs a reminder of how good we are. When I see something I want, I do whatever it takes to get it. I'm stubborn ... or perhaps I just don't know when to quit.

"Thirty seconds!" one of the studio staff announces.

"You look nice today," I say to her. She's preoccupied with the question cards in her lap. I pretend she gave me a compliment back. "Thanks! Yeah, I did something different with my hair today."

She looks up at me, lifting one eyebrow, and I flash her a smile.

"Countdown. Standby, camera one," someone says off to the side.

They countdown and we're live. She looks more nervous than I am, which is unusual for her. Kendra introduces us and summarizes what the new show will be about. Despite the tension coming from her, she has a big smile on her face. God, she's good at faking it.

"So, what has been the most fun about filming *Scoring with Sully*?" she asks.

My answer was supposed to be: *The dates. Definitely. I've met so many fantastic women, I have no doubt I'll find somebody to spend the rest of my life with.*

Does she really expect me to say that?

"Honestly, working with you has been really great. You're a terrific producer and this show is something that's normally out of my comfort zone. You've made every day we film much more enjoyable."

Her smile is frozen. "Wow, thank you so much! I wasn't expecting a compliment like that!"

"You said it's normally out of your comfort zone, have you noticed that the women on the show seem different from the type of women you usually date?"

That's an easy answer: they're not, but it's a rude thing to say, so I go in a different direction—which is also out of my comfort zone—but if it'll shake her up, it's worth it. I want her to see me again. I could understand if there was anger, because it would mean she still was affected by me. Apathy is so much worse. I need a reaction.

"Having my life filmed has taken some getting used to, that's out of my comfort zone. Have you ever experienced that?"

"I can't say I have. Is it—"

"Why don't you experience it for yourself. How about I interview you instead? What do you like most about working on television?"

Her nervous laughter is cute. "I think viewers are more interested in you and *Scoring with Sully*. Let's talk about—"

"Let's talk about you." I narrow my gaze on her.

"That's not really what we're doing here, Mr. Sullivan," she utters.

"Mr. Sullivan ... that's new. I like it more when you call me Sully. How about for every one question I ask you, you can ask me one? Is that fair?"

She laughs again, trying to act casual, but she's staying calm, which can't be easy, considering I'm going off script. Not once does she look toward Jeremy or Pierce for help. She's determined to get me under control.

"I mean, if you'd like to talk after the interview, I'd be happy to answer any of your questions. Right now, we need to hear your update on coaching and—"

"Should I take my mic off and walk out, then?"

There's a gasp from somewhere behind me.

She clears her throat. "I don't know if the network is going to like that," she teases. "You might get fined."

"I'll take that fine." I rest my elbows on my knees. "What are you going to do with your remaining time on air?"

We're at a stalemate. The fire behind her eyes is only rivaled by hell itself.

"Alright, you win. Looks like we'll be interviewing each other today." She claps. "By the way, that last one counts as your question, so it looks like it's my turn. What challenges do you feel the Minnesota Rogues will face this season?"

I smile wide and sit back in my chair. "Lots of challenges from an organization standpoint. The PWHL is a new league, and there are always a few kinks to work out. But overall, it's been very positive so far. We have an incredible team. They're talented, but more importantly, they are good people and I'm very grateful to be their coach." Even though that was one of my scripted answers, I mean every word. Now it's my turn to ask a question. "What song is stuck in your head right now?"

"What song—"

"Be honest."

"The Liberty Mutual jingle."

"Wait, seriously?" I bark out a laugh. "The one with lyrics that consist of saying liberty four times?" I speak-sing it. The corner of her mouth tips up with genuine amusement at my impression, it's not the fake smile she's been sporting for the cameras.

"That's the one, perhaps they should contact you for their next commercial ... What has been your favorite date so far?"

"Easy. One time I shared a hotel room with a woman, we sat around eating calamari pizza and—"

"Sorry, let me clarify: what has been your favorite date you've had while filming *Scoring with Sully*?"

"Technically, I still gave an answer, so it's my turn now. Next time, be more specific. What is your death row meal?"

"Like if I could only eat one more thing? Paella." Good answer. "Are you feeling a connection with anyone on the show so far?" she asks.

"Yes, one woman. What is your favorite part of filming this show?" I want her to say it's me.

She rattles her answer off quickly. "Personally, I've really enjoyed interacting with the women of the Minnesota Rogues hockey team. In addition to being tremendously talented, you can really see their dedication to the game when they're on the ice."

Damn, you'd think she memorized her own answers. The girl knows how to think on her feet, that's for sure. "You said there's a person you connected with on the show. Without naming any names, what do you like about that person?"

"She's intelligent, funny, beautiful ... I think we could have a lifetime of insane se—"

"Insane seats for hockey games? I hope that's what you were going to say."

It wasn't.

"Something like that." I smile.

"Yeah. That's one perk. And moving to the topic of hockey, how—"

"Ope, it's my turn to ask a question ... You sought me out to be on a dating show you were working on. What made you think I would be a good candidate?"

"You know, I'm starting to ask myself that same question." It's a sarcastic answer, but I grin and accept it. She's doing well keeping up with this.

"Good answer. My turn again!" I smile. "When was the last time *you* went out on a date?"

"Couple months ago." Assuming she's being honest, that means I was her last date. She continues. "How has it been transitioning from player to retirement to head coach of a PWHL team?"

"It's been awesome. I love coaching. Obviously, I loved playing for the Lakes. I played alongside some of the greatest players in the league, it was something I always wanted to do, and I feel incredibly lucky that I had that opportunity. Retirement was tricky. I tried playing golf, tried traveling. Most of my friends were still playing or in the workforce. The days could be lonely. But when Whit Moreau called me up and said the words head coach, I knew then and there this was what I was meant to do. I love this team, these players are hardworking and skilled. Practice has been going great. I'm so very honored to be a part of their team." I grin. "What is your ideal sandwich?"

"Scallion cream cheese, roasted red peppers, cucumber,

shredded cabbage, tomato, onion, lettuce, black pepper, sesame oil, and vinegar on stirato," she says.

My eyebrows shoot to my forehead. I really thought I could trip her up on that one. Impressive. "Maybe you can make it for me sometime."

"I'm not making you a sandwich. Unfortunately, we've only got time for one more question. I think I speak for everyone in the studio and, probably, a lot of the viewers, but what exactly were you hoping to achieve by being so ... rebellious, perhaps, in this interview?"

"You wanted real television. This is real. Life is full of unexpected surprises."

The fake smile on her face falls, and she bites her lip, then her eyes become glassy, and I feel like a dick. "Well, that, it certainly is. You never know what you're going to get when you interview Lee Sullivan, people!" She wraps it up with a lighthearted send-off, and as soon as the recording light goes off, she's gone, storming off toward the dressing room.

The studio is silent, making me look like the biggest asshole. One of the assistants ushers me off set and speaks into his headset, but I couldn't make out what he said.

"Think she'll ever forgive me?" I ask him.

"Good luck," he answers.

CHAPTER TWENTY-ONE

KENDRA

I've never felt so out of control! The tears were ready to leak out of my eyes as soon as he hit me with those parting words. *This is real. Life is full of unexpected surprises.* He has no fucking idea. I grab another wad of toilet paper and wipe my cheeks.

"Asshole," I mumble.

I've never had a cast member put me in a position like that. I'm still shaken up. Live television and he made me look like an idiot. My boss is going to kill me, but not before I kill Sully for that stupid stunt. I'm mad—*big mad*—and I will make sure he knows it. I hurl the ball of toilet paper blotted with mascara in the trash and throw the door open. *Where the fuck is he?*

At six-foot-five, he's easy to spot in one of the prep rooms, unhooking his mic. I stride over to him and grab his arm, yanking him into the attached hallway, out of sight.

"Don't you ever do that again!" I whisper-yell. "Your behavior reflects poorly on me. I could lose my job for that, Sully. Do you get that?"

He has the nerve to roll his eyes, as if I'm being overly

dramatic. "They wouldn't fire you." The jerk turns his back to me and reaches back to unclip the battery pack. "You're a fantastic producer," he mutters. I grab his arm and wrench him back, getting a little rough.

"They should fire me! I couldn't control the character on my own fucking set!"

I glare up at him towering over me. He doesn't look very happy with me, but I gulp down any fear I have. He glances at the empty hallway, then steps forward, and I step back. He encroaches until my back is to the wall. *Shit.*

"What are you doing?" I ask, my chest rising and falling.

He braces a palm on each side of my head and lowers himself until he's eye level with me. It's intimidating as hell, but I stand my ground.

His right hand brushes behind my ear, and I shiver. So much for looking unaffected.

"You command every part of my life. I can't focus. I can't talk to other women without thinking about you. I want *you*." His thumb grazes up and down my neck, making me shiver for a second time. I hate the goose bumps spreading from that area. "How does it feel? Not being in control?"

I narrow my eyes at him, and he covers my neck with his giant palm. I swallow and raise my chin defiantly. "Sully—" I warn him to back off, but my voice comes out a lot more breathy than it was supposed to.

"Not very fun, is it?" He tsks. "All that desire floods your senses and makes it impossible to function. Impossible to think. Everything is within reach, so close you can touch it with your fingertips ... but no matter how badly you want it, you can never seem to grasp it." He presses his thumb to my bottom lip and pulls it down. His eyes are on my mouth. I'm full-on panting.

Footsteps are coming from around the corner, so I dart my

eyes away, and he shoves off the wall, walking away without saying another word.

CHAPTER TWENTY-TWO

SULLY

Some days, I regret having it written into my contract that Kendra is my main point of contact. My attraction to her has doubled since working side by side. Maybe it's a forbidden fruit thing that makes me want her so much. It's borderline obsession. She's constantly on my mind; doesn't matter if I'm on the ice with my team or staring into another woman's eyes.

It's what made me flip on her in the interview today. On the drive home, I call my best friend, Barrett. My car seems to be one of the only places I have privacy these days. I hate being in the spotlight, but I must be a masochist because I love being near her.

"Dude. What the fuck?" He laughs, answering. He must have seen the interview. "So, what's it like being the most-wanted bachelor in America?" he says.

I chuckle. "It fucking sucks."

He laughs. "Why?"

Too many reasons to explain. For now, I need to figure out what to do about it. My patience is running out. I answer his question with one of my own. "How did you know Raleigh was the one?" I ask.

"I just knew. It's hard to explain. She was fun, and I knew that if I had to spend everyday with her for the rest of my life —"

"It wouldn't be enough?" I finish.

"Exactly. Falling for one of the women already? That didn't take long. Who is it?"

"I think it's Kendra."

There's a pause. "Kendra? Which one—wait, *your producer*?! That woman who interviewed you?"

I suck my teeth. "Yeah."

"Oh, shit."

"Yeah."

"Does she know?"

"I've hinted at it."

"Yeah … after that interview, it kinda makes sense. You were about as subtle as a brick to the face. Do you think she feels the same way?"

"I don't know. She pushes me away. I can't tell if she's scared or if she really is not interested. Even if she did. We're both in a tough spot."

"Wait, I'm confused. Why do you say 'we're' in a tough spot."

Shit.

"We, ah, kind of hooked up. Before this whole show thing. I really like her."

"Holy shit … Okay. So, drop the show."

"I can't. I'd fuck up my contract, and her career depends on it too. And this girl is driven. I mean, *really* driven. She wants this. More than she wants me, apparently … but I can't blame her. Remember how we used to be when we were drafted? The league was everything."

"So what are you going to do?"

"I don't know, man." I rub the back of my neck. "But I can't even think about these other women. It's like she's some parasite that's burrowed into my brain."

"Ew, what are you guys talking about?" Raleigh interrupts.

"Am I on speaker phone?" I ask. Rude of him not to tell me.

"Yeah, sorry. Folding laundry. Babies have too many fucking clothes—*Sully's having girl problems*—Just be persistent, man. Annoyingly so."

"Of course you'd tell him that. See what you want and steamroll everything else to get to it." I can hear the eyeroll in her voice.

I've never been jealous of Barrett Conway until now. I've never had anyone I've ever wanted in this way, so his fixation on Raleigh never bothered me—unless it interfered with our games.

"No shame in my game. That shit worked."

"Who's the lucky girl?" Raleigh asks.

"Kendra," I answer.

Raleigh coughs.

"You okay, babe?" Barrett asks her.

"Yeah. Yeah. Just drank water too quickly—Kendra? Like, the producer of your show? The one from Micky's party? Kendra Ames?"

"That's the one."

"Holy shit," she says.

"Yeah … I know."

Barrett's voice comes through again. "You're kind of fucked—"

Raleigh interrupts her husband. "Sully, Barrett will call you back."

Then the call disconnects.

"*Gee thanks, Ral.*" I roll my eyes and pull into my driveway.

In the garage, I just sit there. Camera guys are supposed to show up soon. They want shots of me at home. I'd rather hide for the rest of the day. After today, she knows where I stand. It's her move.

CHAPTER TWENTY-THREE

KENDRA

To be fair, I tried to make it to work today, but after throwing up twice on the drive in, I said fuck it and surrendered to the nausea. I need a break, anyway. Especially after yesterday's interview. I can't face him again. Rachel can cover most of my stuff, and Jeremy is on-site for everything else. I'm lying in bed, just rotting.

My phone rings, and I grab it off the nightstand expecting to see Rachel's name on the screen, but it's Raleigh's.

"Hey," I answer, taking a sip of the orange juice that's helping settle my stomach.

Her voice is frantic. "Is Sully the dad?"

"What?" *Oh shit.*

"Don't fuck with me, Kendra. Is he the father of your baby?"

I can't lie. I squeeze my eyes shut. "Yes ... How did you know?"

"Sully was talking to Barrett, I heard him talking about you. He likes you Kendra, a lot. You have to tell him."

"I can't! He could lose his contract with the Rogues."

"No. You need to tell him. You guys can figure it out. When I found out I was pregnant, I tried to tell Barrett. I'd do anything to get those years back with him. He missed out on the birth of his son, you can't knowingly do that to Sully. He doesn't deserve that."

"I know! I know! I'll tell him, just give me time."

"I'm going to give you a month, Kendra. One month. Or I'll tell him myself." She sighs. "I like you a lot, but it's obvious neither of you are over each other. You need to communicate. The longer you stay quiet, the worse this thing is going to get and the harder it will be to tell him. Sully is like my brother, I will tell him if I have to. Don't make me tell him."

I sniffle, the tears coming down my cheeks in full force. He doesn't deserve it. Fuck, this is a disaster. I have no idea how to get out of this mess with both of us intact.

"I will. I'll tell him."

Raleigh takes a deep breath. "Okay … Now, tell me about you. How's the nausea been?"

I sniffle again. "I'm home sick today."

"Okay, I'm going to stop by later with some of those spice cakes from Sugar and Ice. You said they helped, right?"

"You don't have to do that." I don't want to see her. It will only make me feel worse. I'm ashamed of not telling her it was Sully, and even more ashamed that she found out before Sully.

"I'll be there around three. Get some sleep, babe."

I roll my lips together to keep from crying. "Mm-hm."

I disconnect the call and scream into my pillow.

My dumpster fire of a life is no longer contained. It's spreading to everything I touch. Sully. My career. My friends. How can I be a parent if I can't even take care of my own problems?

COACH SULLY

I'm afraid there's only one way out of this. I have to tell him.

CHAPTER TWENTY-FOUR

SULLY

Kendra is gone for the second day in a row. It's got me worried. It's not like her to miss work. I'm supposed to be focusing on my newest date, Becca, but all I can do is speculate on where my producer is. I know I pissed her off with that interview, but she rarely ever misses a day. Today's shoot feels different without her buzzing around, delegating and juggling a million tasks.

I push some of the broccolini around on my plate, wondering if she's home sick or if something happened. What if she was in a car accident yesterday? No, somebody would have said something. Shit, what if that interview shit got her fired? She said something about it, but I didn't take her seriously. Fuck … Rachel doesn't seem concerned, and she would say something, right? People would be talking about it.

"Do you like to travel? Is there anywhere you want to visit you haven't been yet?" Becca asks, taking a sip of wine. I've been avoiding my glass. I'm not in the mood.

"Yeah, I love traveling. Somewhere I haven't been?" I do my best to give her my focus. "I'd really like to visit Vietnam someday. What about you?"

"What?" She looks at me funny. Maybe she didn't hear what I said.

"Vietnam."

"Oh, I thought we were talking about traveling."

Am I having a stroke?

"We are? Vietnam is where I'd like to visit. What about you?"

She tilts her head to the side and furrows her brow. "Vietnam was a war, it's not a country."

I almost choke on my bite of salmon. "Pardon?"

"It was a war. It's not a place you can go. Unless you plan on time traveling, but even then, why would you want to visit a war zone?"

Wait. She doesn't think ... No way. She's got me speechless. My eyes find the film crew. Several are staring at the interaction wide-eyed. One of the audio assistants has his back turned, his ears are red and shoulders shaking like he can't keep it together. I can't believe Kendra is missing this. How do I respond to her without making her look like an enormous idiot in front of everyone? I ignore her comment and continue the conversation.

"Where do you want to travel?" I ask.

"Somewhere tropical. I love the Caribbean, but I'd like to go to Hawaii or Alaska."

One of the crew coughs to cover their laugh.

"You mean somewhere tropical like Hawaii ... *or* Alaska, which is not tropical, right?"

I don't mean to offend her, but after the Vietnam thing, I have to check.

"Huh?" She drops her fork on her plate. "No. Both are tropical ... they're right next to each other on the map.

"No." I quickly shake my head. "Alaska is not an island.

It's along the Canadian border. It's not tropical. A quarter of it is in the Arctic Circle."

"Nooo … They're both islands." She actually laughs at *me*! "They're right next to each other on the map."

"That's not—" I glance around the restaurant. This is a prank, right? This is all an elaborate joke at my expense to see how I react.

She turns her head, following my gaze. "What are you looking for?"

"Ashton Kutcher …" I murmur.

"Oh my God, I love him!"

I snap my eyes back to her. I can't do this. "Okay"—I look over at Jeremy—"Hey, can we take a break?" I toss down my cloth napkin and head to the restroom to get a little privacy.

Pulling out my phone, I send a text off to Kendra. I'm annoyed.

> You told me there wouldn't be scripted conversations.

> Was Becca some kind of test? Next time, be less obvious.

CHAPTER TWENTY-FIVE

KENDRA

Could I have scheduled the doctor's appointment earlier this morning? Yes, they had several openings, but Sully has a dinner date at six with a new woman named Becca, and I don't want to be there to watch it. I made sure I was gone before he showed up.

I recline in the dimly lit small room while the ultrasound tech taps away on the keyboard. My first ultrasound. I keep my eyes fixed on the screen even though it's black.

"Ready to see the baby?"

No. "Yes." There's nothing that could make me ready for something so monumental. She smiles and squirts some warmed-up clear jelly on my stomach.

"Great! Let's see how far along you are."

She places the transducer wand, pressing into my flesh and moving it around, and my eyes are dry as I stare at the screen. I'm afraid to blink and miss it. It's all black and white. I don't know what I'm supposed to even look for. I've never seen an ultrasound performed.

"There," she says, I hear the smile in her voice. "This is

the top of its head, you can see the arms on the side ... Let's see if we can get a better view."

She adjusts the wand and suddenly, I see my baby. "Oh my God," I whisper. My jaw is nearly on the floor. It's a baby.

"There we go. Perfect profile ... You can see the little nose and mouth. Arms and legs."

That's Bo. This is real. I stare in amazement at the life growing inside me. Wow.

"See that little flicker? That's the heartbeat. Would you like to hear it?"

"Yes, please"

The sound of static fills the room before it clears to make room for a speedy thumping. That's the heartbeat? I tense, it's racing too fast.

My eyes snap to the technician. "Is it supposed to be like that? That fast?"

She chuckles and nods. "Yes. It's measuring around 150 beats per minute, that's perfectly healthy."

I swing my head back to the screen and blow out a breath, relaxing my shoulders. Thank God it's normal.

"I'm going to take some measurements so we can confirm how far along you are."

She draws little lines on the screen, getting different angles and drawing new lines.

"This is the spine ..." I can see it. It has a strong backbone. Of course it does, it's my baby. "Right here is a little hand ... And here's the other one ... And the legs and feet." As she takes her measurements, I watch my baby, its arms and legs jerking around. It's ... cute. Really cute. My baby is alive in my belly, with the tiniest nose and mouth. I'm growing a human.

"Looks like you're about seventeen weeks. Baby looks very healthy."

"Will I get one of those little black-and-white photos?" It's the first picture of my baby, and I want to be able to look at it whenever I desire.

"Absolutely. I'll print you a few different pictures today."

I smile. "Thank you." I wish Mom was here to see this.

Afterward, I have a follow-up with my obstetrician. After giving a urine sample and getting vitals checked, I wait in the clinic room for my doctor to arrive. There's a lot of waiting involved with pregnancy. It's pretty much all waiting. Waiting for appointments. Waiting for doctors. Waiting to stop vomiting. Waiting for the next trimester. Waiting to show. Waiting to feel the baby kick. Waiting to tell people. So far, the only people I've told are Rachel, Pierce, Micky, and Raleigh. That's four too many people than I'd like.

There's a knock at the door before my doctor enters. "It's great to see you again, Kendra!"

"I've decided to keep my baby." I shrug. "Suppose that's obvious, huh? Considering I'm here." I wave the ultrasound photo I haven't been able to let go of.

"I saw the ultrasound pictures, they're adorable. It looks like you've got a due date of March fourteenth. That's exciting! How are you feeling? Has the nausea gotten any better?"

Anxious as hell. "A little? It's hard to tell. I throw up multiple times a day. I'm pretty miserable if I'm being honest."

She winces. "I'm so sorry. The good news is you're measuring about seventeen weeks, many women find the nausea improves in their second trimester. Since I saw you last, you've lost a couple pounds. I know it's not easy to eat, but I'd like to see you gaining more weight."

"Even when I do, it just comes back up again."

"Try eating smaller meals but keep them closer together. Don't wait a long time between meals. Nibble all day if you have to. Bland foods. Did you try the ginger like we discussed?"

"The only thing that stays down are these little ginger spice cakes from one of the local bakeries."

"So eat them. We'll get you eating healthy, but for now, I just want you to focus on getting calories in. Do whatever it takes. I don't want to have to put you in bed with an IV."

That could happen? I can't sit around with an IV!

"Okay. Okay, I'll gain the weight back. I'll find a way to do it." The thought of not being able to work scares me enough to try harder than I have been. I need to make it more of a priority.

"Good. Now let's talk about vitamins and nutrition—for when we get you eating healthier."

———

I wander around the grocery store. The meat department was an instant no-go. I had to hustle out of there. The produce section has proven much safer.

I downloaded one of the apps my doctor suggested to help me track my pregnancy. It says my baby is as big as a fig. I've never seen a fig in real life.

As I walk by one of the employees restocking apples, I pause. "Excuse me, do you have figs?"

"No, sorry. You might want to try Garrison's. We have some fig cookies in aisle twelve. Would you like me to show you them?"

I shake my head. "No, but thank you."

Well, I guess I'll wait until next week to see how big my baby is in fruit form. I place a container of strawberries in my cart. Then a container of raspberries. Peanut butter kind of sounds good. I turn toward the shelves in the center of the store and stand in front of thirty kinds of peanut butter. Should I be eating organic now? I didn't think to ask the doctor. I Google my question and get too many answers, so I decide to simply find the peanut butter with the least amount of filler ingredients. By the time I pick a jar, it doesn't even sound good anymore. Oh well, I'm still getting it. Along with some fluffy white bread to eat.

As I wander around the store, I find a display of nail polish and select a pretty sky-blue color. It probably won't be too long until I'm unable to reach my toes anymore. I plan to spoil myself with an at-home pedicure tonight. Peanut butter sandwiches and pedicures. What a party animal, really tearing it up this Friday night.

I'll invite Raleigh, and we can make it a girl's night.

As I stand in the checkout lane, I dig my phone out of my purse. I wonder how Sully's date went, or maybe it went so well that it's still going. I didn't want to watch, not when I have to muster up the courage to tell him I'm going to have his baby. There's a couple text messages from him about scripted conversations? I have no idea what he's talking about.

I'll figure it out tomorrow. Besides, who knows, maybe I'll be out of a job within the week. If anyone finds out the baby is Sully's, I'll never get a job in television again. The other networks will get a hold of the scandal and use it against me. I'll be vilified beyond repair. My only hope is that he'll care enough about his new coaching job to keep his mouth shut.

I need this job to support my baby. It's probably time I formulate a backup plan. One thing's for sure, I can't jeopardize either of our careers. If we can get through the remaining months of the contract, then maybe we can do this whole thing quietly ... Unless Sully ends up in a relationship with someone from the show when it's over. I wouldn't blame the woman he chooses for hating me, but will she hate me enough to do an exposé?

"Find everything okay?"

My daydreaming eyes lift to the cashier, and I grin. "Yup. All good." I glance at some flowers on the endcap. They're pretty, and I'm tempted to grab some. It might brighten up my house. It's been a long time since I've bought fresh flowers.

"This is a cute color." She picks up the nail polish and looks at the name on the bottom. She chuckles and then reads: "Shoulda Blue Him."

Well, then.

"Ain't that the truth," I comment, glancing down to my barely showing stomach.

I'm sure she thinks I'm being sarcastic. Wish I was.

My life is so messy, even my nail polish thinks I'm fucked. I need to tell him. Whatever happens, happens. We'll take it from there. Because if I don't, Raleigh will. That's not the way I want him to find out. Besides, he will learn soon enough, anyway. It won't be long before my clothes don't fit, and there's only so long I can get away with wearing a baggy fit every single day.

Sully's a good guy. He'll be understanding. I hope.

After I pay for my items, I call Raleigh on the way to my car.

"Hey!"

"Hey. What are you doing tonight?"

CHAPTER TWENTY-SIX

SULLY

Rachel helps me get rid of my mic after a short confessional from the insane date last night. I returned after hiding in the bathroom for a minute to get my head right. I don't know how my life became like this. Some stupid reality show, going on dates with women who either don't know basic geography or who fake stupidity really well.

"You did a great job keeping a straight face."

"That's because it was sad." I huff. "Hey … Kendra's been gone two days now. She didn't get fired because of that live interview did she?" I got a slap on the wrist from the network about the interview thing, but after it went viral on YouTube, they didn't seem to care. Publicity is publicity. As long as views are up, nobody gives a shit.

"No, of course not."

"So where is she?"

Rachel looks away. "Oh, um, I don't know." She shrugs too casually.

"Where is she, Rachel?" She knows, the girl is a shit liar.

"She'll be back Monday." She claps me on the back and

walks toward one of the back rooms. "Have a good weekend, Sully."

Whatever. I fish out my phone to see if she's replied. Nothing. I text her again.

> Missed you on set.
>
> You missed one hell of a shoot yesterday.
>
> Everything okay?

I tuck my phone in my pocket, and a couple seconds later, it vibrates. I pull it out and check the screen.

BARRETT
Have you spoken with Kendra lately?

> No, she hasn't been at work. It's weird.

BARRETT
You should go to her house, check on her.

I raise my brow. Didn't expect him to say that, but I was already considering it.

> I'll swing by her place after I leave the arena.

While I'm swapping clothes in the wardrobe room, I overhear Rachel and Pierce speaking in a hushed tone, and it means little to me until I hear Kendra's name.

"She's going to have to announce it soon if she's going to miss more days. Jeremy cornered me about it before we started shooting today. Even Sully asked where she's been. It's not normal for her to take off work like this. Jeremy is going to get suspicious."

"Kendra is allowed to take a sick day. Besides, she was on set this morning before he got here to make sure everything was set up," Pierce says. "It's none of Jeremy's business where she is. If he knew how bad her morning sickness was, he'd be impressed she's only missed a handful of days."

Morning sickness? Did I hear that correctly?

My heart hammers. Fuck stopping at the arena. We're going to talk. Now.

The entire way into the parking lot, my mind is racing. *Kendra's pregnant?* Was she pregnant before we slept together? *After?*

I'm pissed. As soon as I get in my truck, I call her. No answer. I call again. This time, she picks up. I'm so used to her not speaking to me that I'm temporarily speechless.

"Sully?"

I say the first thing that comes to mind. "Where are you?"

"Did something happen with the date? I'm sorry I couldn't be there. I can talk to Jeremy about—"

"Fuck the dates, Ken! I need to see you. Now. You've been gone two days, you never miss work, and you're not taking my calls, you're ignoring my texts. You're my producer. You're supposed to be my liaison. What the hell is going on?"

"Look, I said I was sorry. I've got a friend over right now. But how about we meet for lunch tomorrow?"

"Fine." I scrub my hand down my face and take a deep breath. "Lunch tomorrow."

We end the call, and I grip the steering wheel harder. Jealousy isn't in my nature, but this *friend* she has over has my thoughts spiraling. Is it the dad? Did she get a boyfriend while I've been biding my time and blowing through dates, waiting for us to finish the show?

Is this why she said the chances of us getting together after the show were slim? She wasn't wearing a wedding ring, but I never asked if she had a boyfriend.

My thumb taps the wheel. I'm waiting at a red light to merge onto the highway. Her house is in the opposite direction. I could just go down her street ... The light turns green, and I turn but hit the brakes and do a U-turn at the last second, causing the car behind me to lay on their horn. I'm not waiting until tomorrow. There's no way I'll sleep.

I stomp on the gas and drive as fast as I can until I hit her street. When I pull up to her house, there's a car in the driveway.

Wait. I know that car ...

That's Raleigh's vehicle. *What the fuck?*

Now I'm even more confused. They met at the event at Sugar and Ice, but I had no idea they were hanging out. I'm partially relieved to see it's my best friend's wife at her place, but something about it feels even more unsettling. Like I'm the last one to find out. Did my best friend know and not tell me? *Is that why he said to go see her?*

I climb out of my truck and slam the door.

As I walk to her front steps, Raleigh steps out the front door.

"What the hell are you doing here?" I demand.

She holds up her palms, as if that's supposed to calm me down. "I'm sorry, Sully. She doesn't want to see you. Not right now."

That's all I needed to hear to confirm this has something to do with me.

"Fuck that." I laugh. She's crazy if she thinks I'm leaving. "It's time for you to go, Raleigh. I love you like a sister, but I'll call Barrett and have him drag your ass out of that house if I have to. I belong here, not you. Whatever Kendra needs, I'll do it. I've got it from here." I've never spoken so gruff to Raleigh, but I'm feeling possessive as hell right now.

The corner of her mouth turns up. "About fucking time

one of you gets it together." Then she gets up in my face. "But if I find out you used this tone with her, I'll be the one to have Barrett drag *your* ass out. And he won't be happy about it. Got it?"

My shoulders relax. "Thank you … Is she—"

"Just go in and talk to her, Sull."

I nod and jog past her.

CHAPTER TWENTY-SEVEN

KENDRA

Waiting for Raleigh to return, I can't believe he showed up here, but thankfully, I've got a friend with me to turn him away. We're in the middle of a girl's night, and I still have to get my thoughts together. I said we'd meet tomorrow for lunch, and I have no game plan on how to break the news to him.

Sully turns the corner into my bedroom, and I freeze. *What is he doing here?*

"Goddamn it," I mutter. "Raleigh!" Why the hell did she let him in? I'm not ready for this.

"I sent her home." He raises his eyebrows, letting his blue eyes bore into mine. His voice is deep and commanding. "We need to talk."

CHAPTER TWENTY-EIGHT

SULLY

"Are you pregnant?"

Her chin quivers and her eyes fill with tears. Without answering, she drops her head into her hands and weeps. Shit. I sit next to her on the bed. I should be upset with her—I *am* upset with her, but all I can think is *please be mine.*

I wrap an arm around her shaking shoulders. She's crying too much for telling me she's pregnant, and it hits me that maybe something happened. "Are you and the baby okay?"

She nods, still bawling into her palms. I release the breath I was holding.

"Is it mine?"

When she looks up, she sobs harder. My eyes swell with tears to see her hurt this way.

"I'm the worst person. I'm so sorry, Sully. I'm so fucking sorry. I thought I couldn't get pregnant. I wasn't supposed to be able to have kids. And then I didn't know how to tell you. Everything was so complicated and-and …" She sputters, trying to catch her breath.

"Is it mine?" I repeat. If it's not, I have a decision to make, but I'm prepared to fight for her.

"Of course it is!"

She's pregnant with my baby. It's mine.

She wipes her face on her two-sizes-too-big gray sweatshirt sleeve and takes a deep breath. "I should have told you earlier. I just didn't know how to do it without jeopardizing our careers, and you have this new coaching thing, and I know how important hockey—" Her chest is heaving.

"Okay."

"...and coaching is for you. But if I was going to keep this baby, I needed my job. I couldn't do it without my job. I was going to tell you, I swear I was, I just wanted to wait until—" She's practically hyperventilating.

Cupping her face, I swipe the tears away. "Breathe, Kendra."

She sucks in two deep breaths back-to-back, like she can't get in enough air.

"Slower," I say in a calm voice.

I inhale slowly to show her, then exhale, counting to four. She matches her breaths to mine, and it's not long before her chest softens and she's no longer winded.

"We'll talk about it later. Right now, just breathe. I'm going to get you some water."

"I have water." She tips her head toward her nightstand where a tall metal water bottle sits. I reach for it and place it in her hands, and she drinks without me having to force it.

"Have you eaten?"

She nods. "I had some strawberries and some of those spice cakes Micky makes. Raleigh brought me soup."

I kick off my shoes, put my feet up, and lie next to her. When she's done drinking the water, I place it back on the nightstand and pull her into my arms. Her tense muscles relax, and she rests her head on my shoulder, delivering a final shuddered sigh. Like I knew it would, her body fits perfectly next to mine. I stare at the ceiling.

Holy shit. I'm going to be a father.

My immediate reaction is to panic, but the smell of her shampoo invades my senses and brings me peace. I'm going to be a father ... and she will be a *mother*. She's so young; I can't imagine the stress she's been under.

I curl my arm around her body and haul her closer, then skate my fingers up and down her back. It feels so good to touch her the way I want. She wraps around my middle, nuzzling into my chest. Christ, I missed this.

The show is over. Not sure how I'll break the news that I'm out, but there's no way I'm going back now. I'll get my lawyer involved, and we'll figure it out. It was one thing to do it for the coaching position, but there's zero chance of me continuing to date other women while the mother of my child stands behind the camera and watches. It's not like *Scoring with Sully* was something on my bucket list. This simply makes the decision to leave much easier. I'm done fucking around. It doesn't take an idiot to know Kendra will fight me on it. We can talk about that part later. I'm not about to send her spiraling into a panic all over again.

"Why are you so weird about making sure I drink water and eat and rest all the time?"

I sigh. "Just want to take care of you, Kendra." She's so busy all the time and takes care of herself last. "And now that I know you're carrying our baby ... it's going to be double." I pinch her side, and she retreats. Not willing to let her put an inch between us, I pull her into me again.

"*Our* baby," she murmurs, repeating my words barely above a whisper. "Why aren't you yelling? You should hate me right now."

How could I ever hate her? I'm disappointed she kept something like this from me. I'm scared for the future and what this change will bring. How we'll navigate parenthood together. I worry about the level of involvement she'll let me have. But another part of me feels ready. A part of me that fucking loves our predicament. Our child ties her to me forever; she can't walk away easily. We're good together, and now I get a chance—and a reason—to prove it.

"I wish you would have told me. Have you been going to doctor appointments by yourself?"

"Raleigh was going to go with me to the next one."

"From now on, I'm taking you. Raleigh can stay in the waiting room. I go to the appointments. I listen to the heartbeat. I see the ultrasounds." I tilt up her chin to look at me. "If something happens to you or the baby, you call *me*. From now on, that's how it's going to be, Kendra. Is that clear?"

She nods.

I will be patient with her for as long as she needs me to be, but she can't push me away when it comes to the health of her or our child.

"Are you mad at me?"

I shake my head. "No …I'm not mad." I loosen my grip on her chin and brush my thumb over her full bottom lip. "I'm just disappointed."

She laughs over a sob. "You picked that up quickly."

The corner of my mouth curls into a half smile. "Better start practicing."

After seeing how empty her fridge is, I ordered groceries and a few miscellaneous things. There's a large Sugar and Ice bakery box on the counter, the box is big enough to hold a hundred of those spice cakes, and I'm not sure how many she started off with, but there's half a dozen left. I steal one from the box and find it's stale so text Micky and find out that Kendra's been picking up weekly orders of them. Apparently, it's one of the only things she can keep down. I offer to pay triple if she'll deliver a fresh batch within the hour.

Next, I contact a florist and purchase two large bouquets with rush delivery. When I was here last, she mentioned how much she enjoyed having fresh flowers around. The ones she had aren't there anymore, so I want to get them replaced.

When the flowers arrive, the vibrant pink peonies with golden stamens are exactly what I pictured when I described what I wanted to the florist. The woman included a mix of green spider chrysanthemums, pink and orange roses, and a few colorful ranunculi. It's a cacophony of colors that remind me of her. I place one of the arrangements in the living room and the other in the bedroom for her to see when she wakes from her nap.

Micky's delivery driver arrives with the spice cakes shortly after. I check the time, five o'clock. When I enter her bedroom, she's still in a deep sleep. This woman is exhausted. I'm not sure how long she's been running on fumes, but she has a serious sleep debt to pay off. She barely stirs when I crawl into bed and curve my body behind hers while resisting the urge to touch her stomach. I'll wait for her to invite me. Which I hope is soon, even if there's nothing to feel. I want to be a part of this, but she's got to invite me in.

Her peaceful breaths are soothing as I rack my brain for ways to keep her and my coaching position.

At some point, I fell asleep, then I wake to her stretching next to me.

"Oh my God!"

The sky is dark. I open one eye to check my watch, almost eight. "Hm?" I ask, my eyes closed. I didn't need the nap like she did, but it's easy to fall asleep with her in my arms, and now I'm struggling to move.

"Where did these peonies come from?"

I smile, pressing my lips to the back of her neck. "You were out of fresh flowers. I remember you saying you liked having them around."

She spins and wraps her arm over my side. "You didn't have to do that."

I grab under her thigh and bring it over mine. "It makes me look good."

She lets out a small laugh. "I wanted flowers today … Really. I almost bought them earlier. But then I bought nail polish instead." She yawns. "Raleigh and I were going to give each other pedicures."

That makes me happy to hear. "I'll make sure you always have flowers, baby girl … What would you like for dinner?" She groans. "What?"

"I have a lot of morning sickness—all day sickness, really. The doctor told me to eat little meals often. But I think I waited too long. My stomach feels queasy."

"Does anything sound good? How about one of those spice cakes?" When Raleigh was pregnant with Darby, she would throw up every time she smelled raw chicken.

"Yeah … yeah, I can try that. How did you know I liked those?" She sits up and scoots to the edge of the bed and halts her movement. "Just give me a minute," she says, breathing in slowly through her nose.

"Saw them on your counter … Feeling sick?"

She nods. Poor thing. I get up and walk around the bed, standing in front of her and extending my hand. After a moment, she takes it, and I pull her to her feet.

She keeps our fingers linked all the way to the living room, where I carry a spare table to the couch. I walk into the kitchen to grab her food. "These flowers are gorgeous." She laughs. "How many of these did you buy?"

"Just two," I call from the kitchen while grabbing a plate with a few of those cake things and bring them to her along with a glass of water. She nibbles at the food, taking the smallest bites I've ever seen. "Do you want to watch something?"

"Sure."

I lean back on the couch next to her and point the remote at the television, opening Netflix and scrolling through the options.

She pulls her plate into her lap and settles in next to me, allowing me to put my arm around her. We have a lot to talk about, but it's so nice to act like a normal couple, even if it's temporary. She seems to appreciate the casualness too. We know there's a shitshow on our hands, but for now, I've been waiting months for this. To just *be*.

"Damn it," I say, disheartened.

"What?"

"The oldest thing I can find is *Bridge on The River Kwai* from 1957. You'd think they'd have a bigger collection of talkies for you! Who's running this thing, Gen Alpha?"

"You're such a bitch." She laughs and shakes her head. "There is nothing wrong with enjoying the classics."

I chuckle. "Yeah, I think that's pretty obvious, based on your Netflix algorithm." There's hardly anything made after 2005. "What are you in the mood for?"

"I'd kill for a good squid documentary," she mutters. I

smile, thinking about that night. That was the night I knew we weren't done. "Find us a throwback," she says, chewing a bite. She's finished one of the cakes and is starting on the second. *Atta girl.*

"How big of a throwback are we talking?" There's no way of knowing when it comes to this woman. "*Casablanca* or The *Devil Wears Prada*?"

"Um … somewhere in the middle."

I find the romances and name off titles older than her.

"*Dirty Dancing*."

"No."

"*Ghost*."

"No."

"*Eyes Wide Shut*."

She turns her head to look at me.

"What?"

She smiles. "No … Oooh!" She points at the screen. "*Love and Basketball*. I haven't seen it in forever. I used to watch it all the time, it's a comfort movie."

"That's your *comfort* movie? He cheats on her!" I argue. I saw it in the theaters when I was younger, and that scene stung.

"It breaks your heart and then puts it back together. Makes you feel something!"

"*Eyes Wide Shut* makes me feel something."

"I bet it does. *Love and Basketball*."

"Okay, baby. You hungry for anything else yet?" I ask, starting the movie.

She shakes her head, picking up another mini spice cake. "Are you? I don't have a ton of groceries, but you're welcome to make yourself whatever. Or we can order a pizza or something." The groceries she bought earlier consisted of peanut butter, bread, strawberries, raspberries, and a bottle of nail polish. I don't tell her I filled her fridge, for fear she'll feel smothered. Besides, I ate earlier.

Her pretty eyes glance up at me. "Will you stay the night?" The question warms me to my bones. I want to kiss her so bad. The most I'll let myself do is hold her ... for now. She needs comfort, anything more than that will lead to other things, so I have to keep myself in check.

"Yeah, baby girl. I'll stay." I pause. "But I'm going to sleep on the sofa."

She furrows her brow. "You don't have to."

Yes I do. There's no way I'll keep my hands to myself. It was hard enough sleeping next to her at the hotel. I'm sticking to my vow: I won't sleep with her until she's ready to give us a shot. If I give in tonight, the false hope will be crushing when she fights me on it tomorrow. Something I know she will do—but I'm not going to think about that I'm letting myself have this moment.

"It's not a good idea ... At least not until we talk about everything. Let's just watch the movie."

We have a lot to discuss.

CHAPTER TWENTY-NINE

KENDRA

I haven't felt this at peace since ... well, since our last night together, but he won't share a bed with me, and it takes getting lost in this movie to not obsess over it. He probably hates it as much as me, but he's respecting my boundaries and my career with the production company. We're still attracted to each other, and I treasure that little nugget as I lean into him.

When we're the only two people in the room, we might as well be the only two people in the world. I turn into a puddle of vulnerability around him. Sully is my ultimate weakness.

My phone dings, and I glance down to see a text from Raleigh.

> RALEIGH
> Hope you're not mad I let him in, you both needed each other tonight. How is it going?

> It's going well. You were right. Thank you. Text tomorrow?

> RALEIGH
> You better.

What is he going to say tomorrow? He kissed my neck earlier. That's more than just friends, right? He bought me flowers—he remembered I like fresh flowers. What am I even doing right now with him? Playing pretend? Shit, I can't do a movie now. His touch is conflicting with his words, and I can't think about anything but us.

I grab the remote and pause the film.

"I want to go ahead and have that discussion now."

"We can talk tomorrow, Kendra. Let's enjoy tonight."

I shake my head. "No, it needs to happen now." If he's doing all this only for us to have it ripped away later, then I don't want him to spend the night. It's toying with my feelings.

He withdraws his arm from around me and angles his body toward mine. "Okay," he says, sighing. We stare at each other. I'm not sure where to start. Sully pushes up the sleeves of his white Henley. What we're about to discuss is the kind of mess you have to roll your sleeves up for. His corded forearms are tense. It's not a fair fight ... He looks as nervous as me.

"I'm sorry I didn't tell you. I never planned to keep it a secret forever, but I had no idea how to tell you."

He nods. "I forgive you. I'm sorry I wasn't here for you. You seemed distant. I should have pressed you to find out what was going on."

"Every time I thought about telling you, I thought about the impact it would have on our careers—"

"This is more important than a career."

I take a deep breath. "It's easy to say that when you've had a career. You're a retired hockey player. I didn't know how you were going to react. If it went badly, my career was the only thing that was going to get me through, the only thing that would allow me to keep this baby. I need this job to take care of a baby."

He crosses his arms. "What did you think I was going to say? Fuck you, you're on your own?"

"I had no idea what you would say! Our first night together you told me I was the only one you wanted to call you daddy. We're shooting a show with you dating other women, a show that is critical to your head coach contract. This baby could take all of that away. We already chose our careers over the possibility of a relationship. I was going to tell you."

"And what if I met someone on the show? You thought it was a good idea for me to fall in love before dropping the bomb that you're having my child? Then what?" *Is that what's happening?* Is he becoming serious with someone? "I call bullshit." He shakes his head. "I'm sure those things helped justify your decision to keep it to yourself. But it's not enough."

"I was scared!" I shout, rising to my feet.

"Why, Kendra?" His voice is calm. I feel like I'm being interrogated. It's not like this has been an easy secret to keep.

I throw my arms out to the side. "What do you mean why?!" Pretty sure it's obvious.

His eyes narrow in my direction. "Did you seriously think I would reject you?"

"No, I was afraid that you wouldn't! You're too selfless to leave me to do this alone. If I had told you, you would have quit. I didn't want you to be the reason you quit your dream. I didn't want you to resent me for robbing you of something you wanted so much. I thought I could wait, because at least then I wouldn't be taking away anything from you!" I take a deep breath and continue. "Your anger would fade over time. Eventually, you would forgive me. But if you regret your decision, eventually, that will turn into resentment—and that resentment would turn into hate. I couldn't live with myself if you hated me."

He hunches forward, resting his elbows on his knees. "It hurts that you think I could ever hate you ... but you're right about one thing, I'm quitting the show."

"What? Sully, no! Did you not just hear a word I said?" I won't be able to forgive myself for this. "If you won't think about your career, then think about mine. If you quit, I'll be fired."

"I'll stay quiet about the pregnancy."

"It's more than that, if you quit, they'll tell me to get you back. And if I don't, they'll find a producer who can." I've seen it happen a hundred times. They will find a way to get him back. There has to be a way we can fix this.

He rubs the back of his neck as he stares at the floor. He knows I'm right. I can see him trying to find a solution, but there's nothing we can do.

"Just for now," I reassure him. "Please, Sully. Tell me you won't quit."

It's almost as if I see a lightbulb go off in his head. He sits up and raises a single eyebrow at me. We stare at each other, the devious glint in his eye is suspicious. Then he crosses his arms and leans back. "What's it worth to you?"

"What?" Blood rushes to my cheeks. Is he serious?

"What's your job worth?"

"You're going to *blackmail* me?" I don't recognize this version of him.

He shrugs. "I'll make you a deal."

Fuck him. "What?!" How dare he use my fear as a bargaining chip.

"I won't tell anyone, and I won't quit ... but in exchange, you're going to give me a chance."

I exhale relief and throw my arms up and drop into one of the upholstered chairs. "Fine. Once we're done shooting and the contracts have expired, we can see each other."

"No. Now." He shakes his head. "Starting tonight."

"Sully. We'll get caught."

"Then don't tell anyone." He continues. "When we're at work, I'll keep my distance. But in private, you're mine."

The possessive way he says "you're mine" catches me off guard. Heat floods to my core. Holy hell. I shouldn't want to be anyone's dirty little secret. But for Sully? The idea kind of turns me on.

"What about the women on the show?"

"What about them?" he questions, exasperated. "You have nothing to worry about, Kendra. I know you see me staring at you on set." He crosses his arms behind his head, stretching his shirt over his chest, which only makes him look even more tempting. I see his stares, but I never let myself indulge in them.

"You want to sneak around together." It's not a question.

"No. *I* don't want to. However, I suspect *you* will frown upon me proudly announcing to everyone I'm your baby daddy—but even if I'm not telling anyone, I want involvement in your pregnancy and life. I want to be present at the doctor appointments. I'll take care of the yardwork, or groceries, or whatever the hell else you need. We're going to pick up where we left off."

"I'm not sure that's possible," I say with a chuckle. "I didn't know I was pregnant when we *left off*."

Smirking, he gets off the couch and stands in front of the upholstered chair, then crouches down on one knee. "Then I guess we have some catching up to do, don't we?" His hands cover mine, and he threads our fingers together.

I bite the corner of my mouth, imagining all the ways he

plans to do that. Are we really going through with this? It's dangerous ... and a little exciting.

"Are you here out of desire or obligation?"

He pulls me out of the chair, I straddle his knee, and his palms travel up my back until he's cupping my neck. "I'm not being forced. I'm here because I choose to be. I'm here because there is nothing in this world I want more. So don't ask silly questions you already know the answer to," he whispers against my mouth. "Do we have a deal?"

I smile against his lips and repeat his words back to him. "Don't ask silly questions you already know the answer to."

If he's willing to take the risk, so will I. Are we crazy? Probably. But we won't have to sneak around forever. I'm unsure how this will work out, but we'll figure it out. I just want to be back in his arms and hear him say I'm his.

His daring and mischievous smirk is sexy as hell. He covers my mouth with his and kisses me with everything he has. It releases all the tension we've been holding in for months. All the stolen glances and intense eye contact. I've been reliving all of our old kisses for months, and finally, I can stop living in the past. He's mine again. And I'm his.

"Do you still want to watch this movie?" he asks.

"I'm not married to it."

I slide off him and kneel on the floor. "Good," he says, unbuttoning my jeans and shoving them down. Next, he grabs my shirt and lifts it over my head. His eyes drop to my lower stomach. Does he notice the change? I assumed it blended in with my curves. I shield a hand in front of me, and he sweeps it away just as fast.

"Damn ..." he mutters, his eyes locked onto me. *He sees it.* "Can I ..."

"It's fine," I say with a laugh. "Pregnant women have sex all the time. It won't affect the baby."

He shakes his head, staring at my stomach.

"Did you want to feel …"

His palm hovers over me, and his pleading gaze meets mine.

Oh. *Oh*. "Go ahead." I nod with a smile. Maybe it's my hormones being out of control, but him wanting to touch my barely swollen stomach, that he made, nearly brings me to tears. I watch his face carefully as he presses his fingers to my belly. He swallows, moving his hand over the firm swell.

"Wow."

I'm struggling to understand his awed expression. "Is it weird?"

"No," he blurts, emphatically shaking his head. "Not at all … I love it, Kendra."

I raise my eyebrows. "Really?"

He lifts his eyes to mine. "Is it weird that it turns me on?"

"Stop it." I laugh and nudge his shoulder.

"I'm serious," he says, bringing a second hand to my belly. "You've always been sexy. But, like this? Fuck … I like you pregnant … A lot."

It's gotta be some caveman thing.

"This baby is mine."

Definitely a caveman thing.

He hooks his thumbs in my underwear and drags them down my thighs, peeling them from my slick pussy. "And *you* are mine."

His words take my breath right out of my lungs, and they rush to my head, making me dizzy. It must show on my face because the corner of his mouth tips up in a cocky smile. "You like when I call you mine?"

All I can do is bite my lip and nod. A lump forms in my throat as he tugs my underwear and pants the rest of the way off. He sits on the floor with his back to the chair. Then he pulls me until I'm on my knees hovering over his lap.

His thick fingers glide between my folds, grazing my clit. "You'll always be mine, baby girl." He yanks me forward and licks up my neck. "Say it back to me." My legs tremble as he rubs back and forth. I clutch his shoulders, never wanting to let go.

"I'll always be yours," I say with a shaky voice.

"That's right." He pushes two digits inside me and groans as he stretches them. It feels so good, it's been too long since he's touched me like this. I revel in the control he takes. He moves his palm under my thigh, holding it up and to the side, giving him more room. The obscene noises in the room grow louder as he works his fingers into me faster and faster. "So wet …"

"Oh my god." I drop my forehead to his shoulder and moan. My hips rock forward, needing more.

"Look at me, Kendra."

I raise my gaze, my brows knitted together. He looks at me with reverence.

"Good girl. Come for me, yeah?" His eyes are devious.

My nod isn't enough for him.

"Say *yes, daddy*."

Goddamn. I stare into his eyes. His gaze is so needy, he's desperate for it. I recognize that desire and want him to fill me with it. He's manipulating my body in a million ways, but those blue eyes are begging for my submission. His chest heaves. He exhales through his nose, becoming impatient. I memorize his face; I want to remember him looking at me like this forever.

My lips curl into a smile. "Yes, Daddy."

The growl in his chest is possessive and untamed. I have the power to turn his world upside-down with two simple words—we each have the power to dominate the other. "Don't tease me like that, baby girl." He releases and focuses his thumb on my clit as he continues pumping in and out. I love that he's not being extra careful with me after finding out I'm pregnant. He's fingering me with the same fervor he used to. This is the Sully I need. I've spent months craving his roughness.

With shaking knees, I dig my nails into his back as warmth floods my entire body. Fuck, I can't hold it any longer. Just as I'm about to come, I'm tossed back into the upholstered chair behind me. I squeeze my eyes shut, waiting for his mouth, on the verge of exploding. I grip his hair and then … nothing. When I open my eyes, he's watching me with intense hunger.

"Why did you stop?" I try to shift his mouth between my thighs, but he sits back farther on his heels. *What the fuck?*

He shakes his head. "I don't think you've earned the right to come."

Excuse me? No. I know how to get to him. "Please, Daddy?" I whimper.

His pupils dilate, turning his blue eyes to a stormy gray. He nips at my thigh, and I startle at the sharp sting before he licks it away. A dark soft smile graces his mouth, and I'm eager for whatever he will give me. "Bedroom."

CHAPTER THIRTY

SULLY

I was nice while we talked things out, but now she needs a correction. Kendra royally fucked up by keeping this pregnancy to herself. When I enter the bedroom, she's stretched out on the four-poster bed, naked. I stand at the foot and admire her luscious body sprawled out. *Damn.* I can't take my eyes off her. There are so many ways I want to take her.

I run my hand over the barely there swell of her stomach. The one I put there. I've always been indifferent to pregnant women, but when it's *my* child she's pregnant with? Holy hell. My cock could punch a hole through sheet metal. I plan on fucking her into next week, but first …

"What are you thinking about?"

"How I want to punish you."

She cocks her head to the side, a lopsided smile. "Punish me?"

"You didn't think you would skip out on telling me you were pregnant without getting a punishment, did you?" The surprise on her face tells me she did. "You wanted a daddy … Daddies discipline."

I open her closet, hoping for a belt but only find a slew of scarves. I'll make it work. I touch each of them, selecting the ones that will best suit my needs.

"Your safe word is—"

"Harder, Daddy?"

"No." I cut my eyes to her before returning my attention to the scarves. "That smart mouth isn't doing you any favors."

"Seems a bit wordy, don't you think?" she snarks. After choosing the last scarf, I establish myself at the corner of the bed.

"Your safeword is Mr. Sullivan. Crawl to the end of the bed," I say, wrapping one of the scarves around the corner post. She gets to her knees. "Crawl." I remind her, and she does. "Lay down."

With her head now at the foot of the bed, she relaxes on her back.

"Hand." Her eyes bounce between me and the scarf. "Hand," I say a second time.

She nervously holds her wrist out for me to secure. Afterward, I make my way around the bed, restraining each of her limbs until she's starfished before me. Then I carefully pluck a handful of long-stemmed roses from the vase and drop them beside her on the bed. I pull my shirt over my head and remove my pants but not before wrenching my belt out first. Her eyes widen. I've been straining against my boxers for far too long, it's a relief to push them down.

"Shit," she whispers.

With the belt still in my fist, I climb onto the bed and straddle her waist. Folding the belt tightly in half, I plant a hand beside her head and use the belt to lift her chin. Her eyes are wild, the anticipation mixing with a hint of fear. I love it. I pluck one of the long-stemmed roses from the small pile, careful to keep my fingers between the thorns, and draw the petals between her breasts, then outline her nipples.

"There is no rose without thorns, baby girl. In order to enjoy something that is beautiful and pleasurable, you must also endure something that is difficult or painful."

With that, I take the belt and slap the side of her breast. She jolts, but after the surprise wears off, a slow smile grows and she licks her lips.

"Dirty girl, already hungry for my cum, aren't you?"

Her eager nod is adorable.

"That's too bad." The hope in her eyes fades as I stroke my shaft, using the bead of precum to lubricate myself. My cock is yearning for her. This is as much a punishment for me as it is for her, but it's necessary.

"I'm sorry for not telling you earlier." She's desperate now. "Let me make it up to you?"

"You are going to make it up to me."

Her gaze drops to my dick glossy with precum. I almost forgot how much of a cum princess she is. I move off her, stand at the edge of the bed near her head, place a knee next to her shoulder, and cup a hand behind her neck. From here, I have a perfect view of her body, which I will enjoy watching as she takes me down her throat.

"Make it up to me, Kendra."

She angles her head toward me and opens her mouth for my cock, allowing me to feed it in. *Shit.* The second her wicked tongue drags over me, I know I'm in trouble. This will take serious concentration to not finish early. She's expecting me to come in her mouth, but that would be giving her what she wants. It wouldn't be a correction. I take a deep inhale through my nose. "That's my good girl," I growl.

Bracing myself on a knee, I lean forward and work the belt underneath her. Next, I gather the ends in my fist, lift, and pull her back off the bed. I grab all but one of the roses from the small pile beside her and position them underneath before slowly lowering her and releasing the belt. As soon as the thorns prick her soft skin, she arches her back off the bed. Her mouth protests.

"You've been a thorn in my side for weeks … Now it's your turn."

She moans, and I pick up the last rose, using it to caress her skin while she takes me down her throat. Her tits are pushed toward me, and I focus on circling her nipples again. Fuck, she's gorgeous.

"It's hard arching your back with each of your limbs stretched out, isn't it?"

She mumbles a "Yes" around my cock, and I trail the flower between her breasts and to her stomach, where she's using all her core strength. I slowly spell out my name using the tip of the flower. Her arms begin to shake.

"Are you getting tired?"

She nods again and groans, but there's anger behind it. Can't say I blame her. First, I deny her an orgasm, and now I've got her literally bending over backward for me.

"Eventually, your muscles will fatigue and you'll be unable to support yourself, but you know this already … because your shoulders are starting to shake."

I lean forward on one arm to bring the petaled tip between her thighs. Her pleasure vibrates around my cock. I draw the rose up the center, and over her clit.

"Can you make me come before you collapse?" She definitely can. The question is, can I hold out until the last second? I cluck my tongue. "I don't think you're going to make it."

Her thighs shake as the muscles in her core tire. She hollows her cheeks, sucking harder, and flits her tongue over my crown, and I growl. *Fuck*. I slip out of her mouth and guide her lips back to me. Then I trace her pussy with the rose in retaliation, and she groans around me. The sound is a combination of sex and weariness.

I continue the feather touches as I observe my work. Her breasts jiggle as every muscle in her body shakes. Her brown nipples are so hard I can't resist flicking one. The only thing that would make this better is if I put bells on her ankles so I could hear the sweet jingle of her torture. She focuses her attention on the head of my dick, and I almost lose it. My breathing increases as my attempts to remain calm are tested. I remove one of the rose stems from underneath her.

I push into her throat until she gags. Taking it a step further, I crook her neck slightly, allowing me to burrow deeper. In this position, I can slide another rose out from under her, letting the sharp thorns graze her skin. When it's gone, she rests her upper back more easily and sighs. This time she blinks up at me with appreciation and something akin to devotion. The only stem left is below the small of her back.

Moving my hand between her thighs, I sweep my thumb over her labia. Not giving her the relief she needs, she thrashes her legs, causing her to accidentally press against a thorn. She flinches and arches her back harder, her ankles still held tightly in place by restraints. God, she must be fucking exhausted.

I lean over and notice a damp spot on the comforter beneath her. She's dripping. Reaching over, I part her lips, and she pauses, waiting for the flower to kiss her where she's most sensitive, but instead, I strike her clit. She quakes, teetering on the edge of losing control. Shit, I can't hold out any longer.

"You going to swallow my cum, baby girl?"

Kendra nods enthusiastically around my length.

She's really going to hate this. In one fluid movement, I toss the last rose out from under her back and tear away from her lips, then stand on the floor beside her. She whines, "No!" when she realizes she's not getting anything. "Sully!"

Once I gather my composure, I make my way toward the head of the bed and untie one of her ankles, then climb on and lean over to untie her other ankle. She draws up both knees, and I situate myself between her legs and run my hands from her ankles up her trembling calves and thighs until I can tease my thumbs over her hip bones. Is she shaking because her muscles are strained or because she hasn't gotten to come?

She glares at me. "What the fuck?!"

It's impossible not to chuckle as she wiggles, trying to get out of her wrist restraints.

I almost feel bad. *Almost*.

"This was a punishment, remember?"

"Are you at least going to let me come?" she asks, realization crossing over her features.

I shake my head. "No, baby."

"What?! I'm sorry, Sully! I'm sorry!"

I force her legs open wide and smile at how slick she is. Her pussy is begging much harder than she is.

"Sully." Her big eyes well up. "That's not fair."

"It's more than fair."

"Please? Please?"

I chuck her chin. "Cheer up. I'll let you come next time."

"No! I want to come now! I'm aching!" she begs. "If you don't, I'll just make myself come."

I sigh. "Looks like you're going to be in those restraints a lot longer ... Don't threaten me, sweetheart."

For that, she can watch me finish myself off. I blow a soft

stream of air on her clit and fist my cock. The scent of her arousal is intoxicating. I want to taste her. It's been too long. She cries out. When my eyes find hers, she looks distraught. Tears run down her cheeks. Shit, now I do feel bad about it. I'm powerless against her sounds.

"Please, Daddy," she whispers. It's pathetic. Her voice is so sad and weak.

Goddamn it.

A rumble escapes my chest. Despite myself, I stuff two fingers inside her, and she screams, "Oh my god! Yes!"

I shake my head, disappointed in myself as I pump my fingers into her juicy pussy. She's a sloppy fucking mess. I feel myself rising again. "Tell Daddy how sorry you are," I growl. If she's going to manipulate me this way, she will pay for it.

More tears skate down her face as she apologizes profusely. I pull my hand away and spit between her legs.

"You're not going to keep secrets from me, are you?"

She shakes her head.

"Answer me, Kendra."

"No more secrets! I promise, never again!" she says, with more tears. Shit, she's got me wrapped around her finger.

"That's right, baby girl." Cupping her calves, I lift them, and she plants her feet on my shoulders. I spit again, and my saliva drips between her cheeks.

I bore my gaze into hers, hoping to convey my annoyance that she's exploited my weakness.

"I'm wet enough, please, I need to feel you fill up my pussy."

My lips tip up in a smirk. "Oh, sweetheart," I say, chuckling. "I'm not taking your pussy."

I spit on my cock this time and hold the tip to her ass.

Her eyes turn into saucers. "Safeword, remember?" I remind her.

I proceed forward, fitting my crown past the tight knot. Her lips part in shock, but she blinks and nods to continue. After propelling forward, her ass sucks me in, and I exhale the air that was tight in my lungs.

Goddamn.

I'm kind enough to give her a moment to adjust, then I pull out slightly and drive forward. The way her ass is suffocating my cock has me on the brink. She's so tight I can hardly breathe.

"Oh my god," she whispers. Her eyes blink back tears.

"Have you done this before?"

She shakes her head.

Shit. This is one hell of an intro for her. "You use that safeword at any point, understand?"

"I don't want to use it." Her face relaxes when I thrust, and the anxiety in her eyes is replaced with bliss. I hammer in and out, and the moan that leaves her lips has my grip tightening around her thighs. This woman is everything. I'm not supposed to be giving her pleasure but seeing it on her face almost makes me forget why I was mad at her in the first place.

"Thank you," she mutters over and over again with her eyes locked on mine. "Thank you, Daddy." The submissive nature is so sincere and repentant. My thumb rubs circles into her clit, and her legs begin shaking.

Damn, I wasn't going to do this. That's not how this works, that's not how any of this works. But seeing the ecstasy on her face while I fuck her ass and grind my thumb against her sopping clit, no way in hell am I going back.

Fuck it.

I cast the roses off the bed and lean forward, sinking

deeper into her ass while I untie her wrists. Her hands clutch my arms tight, and she speaks freely.

"Oh my god," she sobs, the relief in her voice gives me chills. "I've missed your cock. I've missed the way you hold me, the way you fuck me. I've missed *you*—I've missed you so fucking much, Sully." I swallow her words. They're everything I want to hear. I need to know she's been longing for this as much as I have. Her body limps with exhaustion, yet she still strains to be an active player. I sit on my heels and dig my fingers into her hips as I pick her up and fuck her ass on me. Her lips part, allowing me to further admire her tear-stained cheeks while I drown her in pleasure.

"That's it, baby girl, just relax." She encircles my wrists at her sides, and the devotion in her gaze has me clenching my jaw. I'll do anything to keep her looking at me like that. I want to see it every day for the rest of my life. "You are so beautiful."

Her whimpers are passionate and frenzied.

Fuck me.

Her voice wraps around my heart and fills my chest with pride. With my thighs wedged under her ass, I release one side of her waist and press my thumb to her clit, rubbing circles and watching her eyes light up. Her muscles contract and shiver. "There she is …" I grin, god, I forgot how pretty she is when she comes.

"I think I have to pee."

I smile. "No, you don't, push through it."

Fuck yes, she's about to squirt for the first time. I'm taking two of her firsts tonight, and I could not be more happy.

I drop my chin and spit on my dick so I can pound into her harder, and her chest rises and falls as she takes all of me.

"Your cum is as much mine as you are, Kendra. Give it to me."

Her hands find the gold chain at my neck, and she wraps her fist around it.

"Sully …" is all she says before her pussy gushes. She screams and writhes like nothing I've ever seen, and I'm forced to pin her down while she orgasms. As much as I love hearing daddy, nothing beats my name on her lips as she comes. She moans, and her ass puckers around me.

"That's it, baby girl, let me have it."

Her pussy twitches, and I resist shoving my fingers inside. When I finally feel the way her pussy throbs again, it will be around my cock. Watching her shatter sends me over, and I cover her mouth with mine, swiping my tongue over her plush lips as my hot cum pulses inside her. Kendra has destroyed me. I'm hers.

CHAPTER THIRTY-ONE

KENDRA

17 weeks pregnant

I'm a mess, but not as much as my bed. It doesn't matter. I don't have a care in the world right now. Who would ever want to come down from this euphoric high? He starts the shower, then turns me away from him, and his hands roam over my back like he's searching for something.

I laugh and turn my head, trying to see him. "What are you doing?"

"Making sure those thorns didn't nick you."

They didn't. I felt his palms on me the entire time I was sucking him off. Every now and then, he would skim his fingers along my sides, feeling for the stems and making sure they were in place. The threat of being punctured was what was so fun. Deep down, he's a teddy bear, no matter how mad he is with me. Although, I don't doubt for a second he would have denied me that orgasm if I hadn't begged as much as I did. Sully is like no other. When I realized he didn't intend to let me come, I sobered up instantly. I'm not sure what made him change his mind, but I'm happy he did. Very happy. I had no idea my body could do that.

"I'm okay," I assure him. "I just need to get some of that stuff out of my hair." I think it happened during our kiss, but I love when he drives his fingers into my hair to kiss me.

He checks the water temp, then his eyes find mine. "I'll get you cleaned up," he says, guiding me toward the shower.

Chuckling, I take his hand and step into the shower's steam. He removes the detachable showerhead from the wall and sweeps my hair to the side as water cascades over my shoulders, ass, and legs. It feels like heaven.

"I'm still going to wash your back, to be safe." After two rounds of soap and a thorough rinse, he deems my back safe from any infection the thorns could bring. Then he plucks my bottle of shampoo off the shelf and actually does a pretty good job washing it. I'm impressed.

"Thank you," I tell him. "I can take it from here." To a man like Sully, I'm sure it's intimidating seeing all these hair products. He's not going to know how to wash textured hair. To my surprise, he selects the leave-in conditioner I would have chosen and starts working it into my ends. Huh. While it sits, he washes himself, then leans down to press his lips to mine. His cock thickens against my stomach, and I lean into his kiss as he deepens it. It's sensual and packed with emotion as his hands glide over my body. My whimper is muffled when his tongue darts across mine. I'm about to wrap a leg around him when he reluctantly pulls away, leaving me in a lust-filled fog.

"Damn," he mutters. "You're such a distraction, baby girl."

He smiles and turns me away from him, picking the comb off the shower shelf and detangling my hair with it. *What the hell?* "How did you know to do that?" I immediately regret my words, assuming he's already had practice washing another Black girl's hair. I don't want to think about him with other women.

"I watched a video," he says.

I spin around to face him. "When?"

"A couple weeks ago. I know how important your hair is to you, so I wanted to be able to do it. Besides … it's my mess, I should clean it up."

He watched a video so he could wash my hair.

"Oh." I slowly turn back and let him to continue working the comb through my curls.

I'm thankful to be facing away from him because I'm quickly overcome with emotion. That might be the most caring thing any man has ever done for me. Nobody asked him to learn this. Weeks ago, when I was sure he was falling for other women, he was spending his free time watching videos on how to wash *my* hair. I wipe away the tears as he brushes away my tangles.

After we're done in the shower, he wraps me up in a towel, then takes the oil I have sitting on my counter and dabs a small amount into his palm.

"About this much?" he asks, as if it's no big deal.

I smile. "A little more than that."

He adds more and shows me.

"Perfect."

I look down as he massages it into my hair.

I'm falling for Sully. Hard.

My fridge is full of food. There are fresh flowers on my kitchen table and nightstand. My hair is expertly tended to. And he's holding my back to his front as we snuggle naked in bed. I feel so protected with his strong arms around me, and the skin-to-skin contact has me melted into a puddle. Strong, warm palms skate over my body, leaving goose bumps in their wake. He concentrates mostly on my stomach and belly, as if he's going to feel the baby kick at any moment.

He enjoys spoiling me. I was suspicious at first. To be honest, it's kind of a lot, but now I see it's just the way he is. It's in his character to be caring and nurturing and protective. He's a daddy by nature. He enjoys being a provider—of food, flowers, and multiple orgasms. Probably what makes him such a great captain and coach ... and partner.

"Can I ask you something personal?"

I laugh. We're well beyond that. "Yes."

"Why did you have your tubes tied? Did you never want children?"

My heart sinks at the reminder, and I clear my throat. It reminds me of my greatest fear.

"I always wanted children, just not ones that *I* made. I told you how my mom died when I was young ..."

He nods against my neck and plants a kiss to my bare shoulder.

"She died of late-stage cystic fibrosis, and I'm a carrier of the gene. Watching her slowly deteriorate, struggling to breathe, and transforming into someone who was not my mom, was awful. My mom was my world, she was my best friend, and I watched her die. I was alone. I could see in her eyes that she didn't want to leave me, it hurt her as much as it hurt me."

Sully's arms wrap around me, cradling me to him.

"The memory of Mom's funeral was mostly a blur, but I'll never forget watching my grandma that day. The pain she went through burying her own daughter stayed with me. I didn't understand the magnitude of it at the time, but as I grew older, I saw how it changed my grandma. It aged her. She was a fabulous caregiver, I loved her very much, but she was never the same."

"I'm so sorry, Kendra," he whispers against my skin, and pulls me tighter to his chest.

"When I was eighteen, I received the money my mom left me. I used some of it for college and the rest of it I used to make sure I could never have children. I didn't want to take any chances to bury my own child."

"And then you got pregnant."

I nod and wait a moment before adding. "The gene is more common in men of Northern European descent."

His hand stills on my stomach. I roll over to face him.

"I'll get an appointment for genetic testing on Monday."

I hate how somber his voice sounds, but it was something I needed to bring up either way.

My fingers trace the edge of his jaw. "Really?"

"Of course. We'll find out if I'm a carrier, and we'll go from there."

CHAPTER THIRTY-TWO

SULLY

First thing I do on Monday is make an appointment with my primary care physician to put in orders for a genetic test and to meet with a genetic counselor. I did some of my own Googling and it's a concern, but I don't have it in family history that I know of, and I'm using that to keep the glass half full. After all, I have Kendra, and we're in this together.

The fact she's agreed to see me, even in secret, has me practically whistling into work. It's the best I've felt in weeks. I finally have my cake and can eat it too … I have to eat it in the closet, but only temporarily.

In my office, I spend about an hour going through my inbox and responding to emails. Most items get forwarded to the public relations coordinator. At five minutes to ten, my calendar flashes a notification reminding me that I'm meeting with Whit to go over lineups.

I grab my laptop and head toward his office, then knock on the open door.

"Ready?"

"Yup."

He closes a couple windows on the shared screen and brings up the software we use to monitor our players and their stats. I want to be a coach who's known for running a good bench. It's all about getting the right players in the right situations, not being tripped up by unexpected changes, and making sure our athletes are put in positions that allow for successful plays.

"I noticed that Paulson has a better rapport with Walters than she does with Grattle," Whit says.

I sigh. "Unfortunately, Grattle does best with Paulson. She's improving, but it's taking longer than we anticipated."

He nods. "What about Delta Makkonen?"

"She and Cori Kapowski are a powerhouse. I'm very hesitant to split them. They make a killer training drill for the other players. Add in O'Hara and they're a dream team. We have to watch Delta, she tends to push herself a little too hard sometimes. But the trainers have been talking with her about it."

He furrows his brow. "If it becomes a problem, let me know."

I cock my head to the side, looking at him. Why would I let him know? This feels like a line is being crossed. I can't quite place it, but there seems to be a strange tension between Whit and Delta Makkonen that I can't figure out. It caught me off guard when he postponed her pick on draft night. Yet minutes later, he was on board to make her captain. In addition, he's more acutely aware of her than the other players. I don't know if that's because she's the captain or if there's something else going on.

"Will do," I respond.

We continue going over our O line and make a few changes, but overall, things are looking pretty good for a new team. It's not as smooth as what I've experienced in the

NHL, but we're dealing with all new players and a new league.

"Great job," Whit says. "I think we're on the right track."

I shrug. "The real test will be game time, you know as much as I do lines can change minute to minute." The more we learn about our players and the way they operate, the better prepared we'll be when we need to make those adjustments in real time.

Jeanine has been working with the players this morning, so she arrives halfway through the meeting. She and I spoke earlier today to go over the changes I planned to present to Whit, just to make sure she was still on board with everything we discussed after the last practice. She's a great assistant coach and has a good eye for our defense positioning. It's nice having a female coach as part of our team, as she brings a lot of knowledge and insight to our players.

"How much did I miss?" she asks, taking the seat next to me.

"We're just about to start defense. Whit is on board with implementing the changes we discussed previously."

"Excellent," Jeanine states. "I want to talk about Joey Breck."

After the meeting, I make a quick stop in the gift shop and notice there's way more Lakes gear than there is Rogues merchandise. The Lakes have a larger fan base, but still. It shouldn't be this obvious. I was hoping to pick up a Rogues onesie to surprise Kendra with. However, the smallest Rogues apparel is youth sizes. I should talk to somebody about that.

Our kid will require both Lakes and Rogues gear, so I head to the other team's baby section. The pickings are slim.

Lots of branded items, but I frown when I stare at the onesies on display. There are two. One in Lakes team colors that reads: *Future Hockey Star*. The other is pink with sparkly white letters spelling out *Cutie*, with a small Lakes logo underneath. *Jesus, really?*

I pull out my phone and dig through my email contacts until I find the director of merchandising. I snap a photo of the two onesies side by side and attach it to the email with the caption: *WTF?* I make sure to CC the public relations manager to remedy this situation before it gets picked up on social media. I'm not sure what the sex of our baby is, but it makes me mad as a goddamn hornet that these are the options young future hockey fans are given. I add a PS to the bottom of the screen with a request for more Rogues gear in our gift shops. Everything Lakes players have, Rogues should also have. Hell, our team needs the funding more than the Lakes do.

There's a lot of misogyny in women's hockey—that's already been established, especially when you look at salary caps, sponsorship deals, and physical game play. I would not be surprised if a few fights break out this year. I wouldn't be surprised if some include my players. These women are tough as nails, they play hard, and they have just as much aggression as their male counterparts—if anything, they have more since the option to throw a punch is taken away from them. I certainly anticipate our left defense, Joey Breck, in the penalty box a couple times.

Had I walked past this clothing display before coaching the Rogues or having a baby on the way, would I have even picked up on the inequity between the PWHL and NHL? There are so many things hardwired in my brain since playing in the NHL. Our female players have to put up with way more shit than we ever did. For example, the comments during the player draft about Makkonen's appearance. It makes me respect Whit Moreau more for putting that shit to bed on the spot.

It's late when I finally get out of the arena. I spent a couple hours in the gym training center. The only exercise I did over the weekend was in Kendra's bed, so I was overdue for a workout. By the time I get to my truck, it's almost seven. I use the time on my drive home to return Barrett's call since I ignored it when it came through during my treadmill run. I haven't spoken with him since last Friday before I ambushed Kendra at her house.

"Hey *Dad*," he drawls.

I chuckle. "I take it you heard the news."

He laughs. "Raleigh can't keep secrets from me. When I found out is when I told you to go find her. She would have killed me if I came out and said it, and to be fair, it wasn't my news to tell." That's fair. "From what I hear from my wife, things went well this weekend?"

It's impossible to keep the smile off my face. "Yeah. It went well."

"Does this mean you're quitting the show?"

The smile falls from my face. "Unfortunately, no. But we're going to keep everything under wraps until my contract is up. I'll still have to do the dating shit, but it's going to be performative, and I made sure Kendra knows that. Not ideal, but that's all she's giving me right now, so I'll take it."

"Hope all that passes quickly. Raleigh really likes Kendra, they seem to get along, which is pretty fucking convenient for us." He clucks through the speaker in my truck. "Hey, speaking of, Raleigh wants to go to Florida for Christmas so we can spend some time with my mom while she snowbirds down there. She suggested you and Kendra come along, what do you think?"

"Spend the holidays together?"

"I mean, we'll be doing the Conway thing, which you're welcome to join. I'm thinking I'll rent a boat so we can cruise around. You know how my mom is, she can be a little *much*. Figured we could rent a few houses on the beach, and y'all could get your own place." He singsongs the last part.

My grin spreads ear to ear. I love the sound of that—and love that our girls are becoming close friends. The thought of being out of town with Kendra over Christmas, where we don't have to hide from cameras, sounds like a dream come true. It would also be a good time to have contractors work at the house without raising suspicion. However, spending the holidays together is a big step, then again, so is raising a baby. I'm not sure how she will feel about it. I'm coming on strong, but after not having her for months, I don't want to waste a second. I don't want her to be alone on Christmas—and truthfully, I don't want to be alone on Christmas either. Since my brother married, he has been spending the holidays with his wife's side of the family.

"That sounds great. Let me talk to her about it."

Absentmindedly, I pass by the studio we've been filming at. I do a double-take when I see Kendra's car is still there. Why is she working so late?

"Hey, I gotta go. But I'll get back to you about holiday plans later this week. Tell Ral and the kids I say hi."

"You bet. Take it easy."

I end the call, pull off the boulevard, and park next to her car.

CHAPTER THIRTY-THREE

SULLY

I stand at the opening of her office and observe for a little while. Her eyes are fixed on the screen in front of her as she bites into what appears to be a tough, stale green-apple licorice whip. Damn, she's beautiful when she's disheveled and has her hair piled on top of her head like that. I can picture her in my house, like she is now, working late from home. From our bed. The image is clear as day. I can see our future together as if it's already happened.

The licorice hangs out of the side of her mouth, and I step over the threshold.

"You're here late," I say.

She jumps back and clutches her chest. "Jesus Christ! Don't scare me like that!" She looks up toward the ceiling as she catches her breath. "I could say the same about you. What are you doing here?"

I grin and turn to shut the door, quietly locking it. I'm pleased the blinds are already closed on the windows. "Saw your car and decided to check in on you. What are you working on?"

"Going through footage … I saw your date on Friday."

I raise my eyebrows as I recall the dinner conversation. "Yikes."

"My grandma used to say some people couldn't pour water out of a boot with the instructions on the heel ... She's hot, though, so people will forgive her for it."

"How hot can you be with a room temperature IQ?" I ask.

She tries to hide her smile. "They don't cover geography in contestant interviews. Though, if they did, I'm sure Jeremy would have been feeding you lines to quiz her."

"Damn, that's low."

She shrugs. "That's television ... it's got an ugly side, that's for sure. I don't enjoy exploiting people. I've already emailed the editing department about cutting that segment, though I highly doubt they will ... God ... *Alaska*? Really?"

"I thought for sure it was scripted," I say.

She shakes her head in disbelief.

"So, got any good footage of me? Anything you wanna save for the spank bank?"

She glances over at me with a dull expression, and I smile.

"That good, huh?"

"Wait ..." She stills in her chair. "Oh my God!" She looks down at her stomach.

"What?"

She's beaming at me. "I think I felt the baby kick ... I thought it was just weird gas bubbles or something, but that felt like a kick. This is the fluttering they talk about."

I can't believe I get to have a baby with this woman. I walk over to her chair and kneel in front of her. She lifts her shirt, even though I know damn well it will be a while before I can feel it. I just want to touch her. It makes me feel closer. I press a kiss to her stomach, then it growls.

"Kendra."

She looks away. "Hm?"

"When did you eat last?"

She throws her head back. "Oh my God, Sully. What is this obsession with you and making sure I eat? I'm eating right now!" She swings her licorice in the air like a lasso. I can't help it. I'm incredibly protective over her, especially now that she's pregnant.

"Eat better, and I won't have to hound you about it."

"I'm fine, Bo is fine. We're all fine."

I grin up at her. "Bo?"

"Oh." She worries her lip. "My mom's name was Bonnie, I thought Bo was a good nickname that worked for either sex."

It's perfect. "Bo is a great name. Do I get to use it too?"

"Only if you stop fussing over me so much."

I chuckle at her sass. "You need an outlet for that frustration. Want some help?" I lean forward and bite her thigh through her jeans.

She squeals a laugh and nudges me away but rolls backward in her chair, putting herself farther from her keyboard. "You're an animal."

I grab her legs and haul her back. "You have no idea."

We stare at each other, then she drops her gaze to my mouth. That's all the motivation I need to get up and seal her lips with mine. Her tongue meets mine, and the tart green-apple flavor is bright on my tongue. "You taste like sour candy."

She reaches down and fumbles with my belt. "What do you taste like?"

I peel her shirt off, and I swear to god, her tits are bigger than they were before. They're growing heavier, and the thought turns me to steel. An image of her bouncing on my cock pops in my head, I visualize the milk leaking from her

COACH SULLY

nipples, dribbling over my hand as I massage them. Fuck. *That's new.*

I unhook her bra and suck a nipple into my mouth. Popping off, I relish the jiggle and nip the side of her breast, then find her mouth again. Our kiss is steamy, hot, and urgent. Her chest rises and falls as I lift her, then deposit her ass on the desk. She works my jeans and boxers down.

"Lift," I say.

She braces both hands behind her, raising her ass for me to pull her pants and underwear down her pretty legs. Her left hand is firmly smashed on the center of her keyboard, causing the computer to blast an angry beep, she startles and pushes it over the edge of the desk, letting it clatter to the floor. We laugh against each other's lips and remove our clothes.

I lower her bare back to her desk. I've always wanted to fuck someone on a desk. I glance down and nod at the papers in a pile next to her. "Are these important?"

She looks over. "Why?" A smile forms on her lips "You want to shove them off?"

"So badly."

"I'll organize them later," she says, giggling. I sweep my arm across, and they whoosh off the side, floating to the floor.

A wide grin stretches across my face. "Sort of a bucket list thing," I explain.

"I totally get it. I've always wanted to be fucked on my desk."

"That makes two of us."

I spit on her already wet entrance and bury myself to the hilt. She's so tight I see stars and have to take a second for the fog to clear. My entire lower half is humming.

"Have you been a good girl today?"

"Yes, Daddy."

"Christ, Kendra."

My palms glide up her body to squeeze her full breasts. "This fucking body …" I drift one down to her clit and rub circles over it with the pad of my thumb, and she tightens around my length. I draw out and plunge inside again. "You have the neediest little pussy. Look at you taking every inch of this fat cock." I withdraw almost completely, then drive inside again. She accepts it like a champ. I love the way her mouth drops open when she makes those sexy noises.

Outside the door, two people walk by, talking among themselves. I cover her mouth and lower my voice. "You better quiet those noises, you wouldn't want the entire office knowing what a greedy girl you are for Daddy, would you?"

She shakes her head side to side. One of the passersby knocks on the door and calls out to her "Don't work too hard, Kendra."

I slow my movement, dragging myself in and out of her tight pussy, her muscles tense, and I'm relishing the pained expression as she tries to remain quiet.

"You're working so hard, baby girl …" I grin, then nod toward the door. "Answer him."

I lift my hand from her lips. She struggles to calm her breathing, then forces her eyes shut to focus. "I won't," she calls out.

My wicked smile grows. "Good job, baby girl." I wrap my fingers around the base of her neck and fuck her harder, making the desk rattle. I'm unsure how far away her fellow employees have traveled. I don't really care. I just want to see her come. She gasps and claps a hand over her mouth, groaning against it.

"There's my loud girl." I chuckle and slide the hand on her neck up to her cheek and give a shallow controlled slap.

She moans again. "I love the sounds you make when I'm fucking you. Get up."

She moves to sit up, and I release her, then help her the rest of the way to the floor. I spin her around and press her breasts and the top half of her body against the desk. With my foot, I nudge her foot to the side, spreading her legs wider, and marvel at her dripping, puffy cunt as it twitches with need.

"So beautiful ..."

"Please, Daddy?"

"You are so polite when you want to be filled with my cock." My palm rubs her ass before I deliver the spanking. Then I stuff her with every inch. I am feral for her; there's something about fucking the woman who's carrying my child that's erotic as hell. I want to tear my claws into her.

Ever since the first time she called me daddy, it's all I think about when I jack off. And now she's made it come true. She's made me a literal daddy, and it fuels the fire in me. I never thought this would be something I'm into, but damn, am I ever into it. Pregnant Kendra makes me feral.

Panting, she reaches forward and grabs the edge of the desk, clasping it with strained fingers.

"Is my pretty girl enjoying herself?"

She sobs. "I'm going to come."

"Let me feel you come on this cock. Say my name ... Who gets you off, baby girl?"

I grab her legs, lifting her, and use her like she's my own personal toy.

"Oh fuck," she cries out, neither of us caring who hears. "Always you." I want to feel her shatter.

She clenches around me, and I grip her ass in my hand, digging my fingers deep. She groans into the desk, and I explode. "Oh, good, good girl." I flood her with me, continuously thrusting until it's dripping down her thighs.

Gently, I lower her calves and pull out. Holding her back to my chest, I turn her chin to the side so I can kiss her. "Holy shit," she says, panting on shaky legs. "Have I told you how much I love our sex? It's like nothing I've ever experienced."

It fills me with pride. If I do my job right, she'll never know another man's cock.

I chuckle. "You make me crazy … I've never had anyone like you."

She spins in my arms and rolls her eyes. "I'm sure you've had your share of hot little groupies."

"I have. But none were you. Their sex was never ours. I didn't yearn to keep them the way I want to keep you. You're untouchable, Kendra." Her eyes are big as she ingests my words. "I never gave my heart to them. You are the only woman to get all of me."

I don't want to say more because these feelings are new and I don't know what to do with them. Maybe it isn't love, but it's something similar. Instead, I kiss her with all I have. Letting her know she's the only woman for me. She's the only one I want. No matter how many dates they film me on, no matter how many women I pretend to be with for the next several weeks, she will be the only woman I give myself to.

I help sort the papers I swept onto the floor, then walk Kendra to her car. The thought of her walking to her car alone when it's this dark makes me uneasy. I'll have to talk to security about giving her an escort.

She unlocks the driver-side door and swings it open, and

before she sits down, I grab her hand. "Hey, before you go … I want to ask you something."

Her smile is filled with postsex haze. She's glowing, and I wish I could take her home with me. "Yes?"

I brace an arm on the top of her car. "I know it's coming up soon, but Barrett and Raleigh are going to Florida for the holidays … They've invited us to join them. I don't know what plans you have but—"

"Yes."

I'm a little stunned she said yes so quickly. I raise my eyebrows, and a slow smile grows on my lips. "Yeah?"

"Definitely."

Grabbing her chin, I kiss her, loving her grin against my mouth. I nip at her bottom lip, and she giggles, retreating from me. I forgot we're supposed to be curbing any public affection. Even though it's dark, she doesn't want to take any chances. I respect it, even though I don't like it. She climbs into the driver's seat, smiling back at me. "I'll see you tomorrow at the arena … Daddy."

"Yeah you will." I chuckle and shut her door, making sure she gets the car started. She waves before pulling away.

Fuck, I'm happy.

CHAPTER THIRTY-FOUR

SULLY

Kendra 20 weeks pregnant

After her urinalysis came back with normal hormone levels, we were ushered into a different room for the ultrasound. I thread our fingers together and squeeze, and she gives me a small smile. The technician enters the room and introduces herself before beginning. The screen turns on, and before long, I'm seeing our baby flickering on the screen before me.

I'm awestruck.

I swallow, staring at the image. Each finger. Every toe. We made them.

"You okay?" Kendra whispers, clasping my hand.

My eyes find hers, and emotion swells inside me. "Yeah … I'm good." *So damn good.*

The technician discusses the stats of measurements. So far, our baby is measuring on the bigger side. That's probably me.

"Do you want to know the sex?"

I glance at Kendra and smile. "Do we?"

She shrugs. "I think I want it to be a surprise."

That's more than fine by me. "Then let's keep it a surprise."

Today has been stressful. I want to know, but I'd rather us find out on our own time. Together.

The ultrasound tech nods. "Surprises are fun."

Kendra smiles and nods.

"Is there anything we should be doing to make sure she and the baby stay healthy? Anything we should be watching for? Anything with sex?" I know this isn't her doctor, but I feel like I should ask.

"The placenta has good positioning, everything looks normal and is on track measurement wise. You'll have to ask your OB some of those questions, but as long as you're feeling up to it, sex is fine."

"Good," I confirm.

The tech nods. "Mom is healthy. Baby is healthy." She smirks. "Sounds like Dad is doing pretty good too." The tech taps the keyboard a few times, and a printer below spits out a bunch of ultrasound pictures.

She passes me some tissues, and I wipe the clear gel from Kendra's slightly rounded stomach and resist putting my palm out to feel. I know the baby is moving right underneath my hand, I wish I could feel them.

"Have you been feeling kicks yet?" she asks us.

"I can feel them, but the baby has been a little quiet today. Sully hasn't gotten the chance to feel anything yet."

"Well, baby's still very active, just maybe not giving you those big kicks. I'm sure you'll feel them by tonight, especially if you have some orange juice and rest. I'm guessing Dad will be able to feel them in the next few weeks."

Dad.

CHAPTER THIRTY-FIVE

SULLY

A few players are talking along the boards as I get on the ice. I'm going through Jeanine's notes from the last practice when my thoughts are interrupted by their conversation. Are they talking about what I think they are?

"Most guys have tried it. I mean, why wouldn't they? They'd fuck a fruit pie, I feel like this should be expected," Joey says.

Timber laughs. "No fucking way."

Cori chimes in. "What are you guys talking about?"

Yes. Thank you, Cori. I need some clarification too. I pretend to go through papers while eavesdropping.

"Guys trying to suck their own dicks."

That's what I thought I heard. This I gotta hear.

Cori huffs a laugh. "How would you even know that?"

"Because I ask them."

Now Timber's involved. "Wait, who is *them*? You just walk up to men and ask them if they ever tried to suck their own dicks?"

"Makes for one hell of an icebreaker," Cori mutters.

Joey casually fixes some of the tape on her stick. "No, but if I'm on my knees about to blow a dude, I'll ask him. So far, one hundred percent of men have tried to suck their own dick at some point in their life."

I mean, she's not wrong.

"Shut the fuck up." Timber groans with a smile, clearly not buying it.

"Damn, that's a big population study."

Uh-oh, sounds like gunfire. I glance at them out of the corner of my eye in time to see Joey put up her middle finger.

Delta pushes off the wall nearby. "Okay, I wasn't going to get involved with this, but fuck, now I'm invested. So, could any of them do it?"

Joey nods. "Several could."

Cori leans on her stick. "Did they say what it was like?" She narrows her eyes like she's genuinely curious.

This time, Joey laughs. "Yeah." I already know what she's going to say. "They said it felt like having a dick in their mouth."

The women laugh. Ask any guy who's accomplished this task, it feels way more like sucking dick than getting your dick sucked. Not proud that I know that, but here we are.

Delta narrows her eyes. "Wait, what about jacking off? Wouldn't that just feel like giving someone else a handjob?"

Cori jumps in. "That's why I can only use vibrators!"

Okay, that's way more than I needed to know. Backing out of this.

"No, it's gotta be the same as women fingering themselves," Timber says.

"Maybe you should ask Whit." Joey snarks, talking to Delta.

Hold up. What? Why did she mention Whit?

Delta cuts her a look. "Maybe you should work on your stickwork."

"Didn't you hear? My stickwork is great."

"I'm ambidextrous! I can use anything!" Timber says.

Fucking abort.

"Jesus Christ!" I shout, and cover my ears with one hand and a clipboard. "Fucking stop talking. All of you. Go. Skate. Do ... something! Just stop talking."

I shake off the mental image of my players strumming their clitars, or worse, why Timber said "*anything!*" with so much enthusiasm.

Everyone laughs, except for Joey. Ever the button-pusher, she adds, "Hey, Coach ... can you do it?"

I wouldn't answer that question if there was a gun to my head.

"Wait a minute ... weren't you out with a back injury a few seasons back?" she asks.

"Fucking hell," I mutter, pinching my brow. My head snaps up, and I scowl at her. "Get out there and do some lines!"

"Oooh, no thanks. I'm trying to quit. Gotta get that whole *Trainwreck Breck* thing under control."

I swing my head toward Jeanine. "Is this a nightmare?" We are weeks away from our first game, and her attitude needs a serious adjustment before then.

Jeanine points to the ice. "Breck. Lines. Now."

Joey aims a finger at Jeanine. "There we go! Cracking the whip, Ice Queen Jeanine! I like it!"

"I swear to God ..." I say to my assistant coach, shaking my head.

"Same," she replies.

Joey Breck is a pain in my ass. Usually it's harmless shit-talking, but I received a text from one of our staffers that they saw her partying pretty fucking hard at a club last night. I'm sure those bag lines she's skating right now are making her regret every decision she drank at the bar. She better not puke on my ice.

The PWHL is too new to have one player drawing a lot of negative attention. There's a double standard for women athletes. Nobody thinks twice about an NHL player throwing a fist or leaving a bar drunk with a couple of women on his arm. However, as soon as one of our players is seen drunk and dancing up on people, all of a sudden it's news. Annoying, but it is what it is. Our new organization can't afford a catch-and-kill everytime Joey goes out and throws back a few.

The frustration creases my brow until I notice one of the camera guys coming out of the tunnel. Kendra's here, and I can't help the half smile that graces my face. I'm also thankful the crew didn't get a chance to pick up the players' fellatio discussion earlier. It'll be a while before I can bleach that from my brain.

She carries in her bag of gear and pulls out a tablet, tapping away. I skate to the visitor bench where Lance, the camera operator, is setting up.

"Either of you need anything?" I ask, looking at Kendra. She knows I'm talking to her.

"Nope, we're good," she says with a fake smile and a firm stare.

"I'll have one of the assistants bring over some water and snacks." I wink at her.

Lance is oblivious as he hooks up a contraption that he wears like a vest to hold the video camera to help stabilize the shot or something. He stands and heads over to one of the holes in the plexiglass to set up a secondary tripod for filming. Jeanine is out on the ice running drills with defense. I've learned as soon as pucks start flying, the cameras hide behind barriers. Probably smart.

"Stop, I'm fine." I smile at the way her lips roll together to form the *p* at the end of the word.

"You're going to the sin bin."

"Why?"

I point to the penalty box. "Because you're not wearing a helmet and those pucks are flying through the air around eighty miles per hour. Go." Not to mention, hockey benches are fucking disgusting. Full of spit and who knows what else.

She rolls her eyes and reluctantly enters the penalty box next to the bench. I make a mental note to have a better chair put in there for her. She doesn't want me fussing over her, but there's only so much control I have regarding her comfort. I enjoy taking care of her. Especially now that she's pregnant with my child. The next few months will test my self-restraint like no other.

"Sully."

Whit's voice has me spinning around, the curious flicker in his eyes tells me he's been watching my interaction with Kendra for the last few minutes. The way I smile when I'm around her probably makes it look pretty flirty.

"A word?"

I nod and skate to the home bench where he's standing. He nods toward Kendra. "How's the show going?"

With my most casual shrug, I glance back at her before responding, "Meh. Not my favorite thing, but it's getting easier to deal with."

He nods. "That's good to hear. I'm sure you know there's a lot riding on this production. A lot of money exchanging hands—money this team needs." His stare conveys his message more than his words do. He's telling me not to fuck this up.

I nod. "Got it."

"It's unfair to put it all on your shoulders, but having a corporate sponsor could make or break our success this season. This show is critical."

Somehow, I hold back my eyeroll. I understand what he's telling me, but damn, I look forward to the day this show doesn't matter. When flirting with Kendra in public won't draw attention and my only job is coaching this incredible team and taking us to the finals.

CHAPTER THIRTY-SIX

KENDRA

26 weeks pregnant

He kneels on the floor in front of me, cupping my foot in his hand as I squirm a little on the edge of the bed.

"Hold still," he says, grinning wider. He keeps his eyes trained on my toes as he paints my toenails with a surprising level of precision. The little brush looks absurd in his massive palms. It's not like my belly is so big that I can't paint my own toes, but he wanted to do it, and I thought it would be entertaining to witness. However, now that I've discovered he has a steadier hand than I do, I'm not going to stop him.

My wiggling is unintentional. "I can't help it, I'm ticklish."

"Maybe I should bust out the restraints again," he mutters. He glances up at me a second with one raised brow. *Oh.*

The seductive threat distracts me from the touchy sensations on my feet. Visions of the night he tied me up put a soft smile on my face. My body heat rises as the memories flood my mind. Ugh, that was so hot. The control he exerted was like nothing I've ever experienced. He's the only man who can quiet my busy thoughts so I can escape reality.

"Weather looks like it's going to be great while we're there."

"Huh?"

He cocks his head and narrows his eyes. "Something on your mind, baby girl?"

I glare at him with a smile as I'm brought back to the present and discussing our holiday trip to Florida with the Conways. The reason he's painting my toes a *Shoulda Blue Him* blue. A delicate cerulean that perfectly matches the new sundress I packed. We'll only be there a few days, but after weeks of sneaking around, I'm looking forward to us existing without cameras. A chance to unplug from the show and all the stress that comes with it, mostly for Sully. Being discreet has been hard on him. Pun very much intended.

"You're mean."

He chuckles. "As soon as these nails dry, I'll make it up to you." He winks at me. He's so sexy. I'm such a sucker for his winks, and he only gives them to me, which makes them more special.

"You're going to have to wait until Florida. We've only got three hours till we need to leave." Raleigh and Barrett are the only two people who know we're spending the holidays together. Sully blows on my toes, and I jerk away from his touch. It tickles so much. Then he unscrews the clear polish next to him and adds a topcoat.

"I'll be fast."

I bark out a laugh and shake my head. That's funny. "No, sweetheart. You won't."

I'm positive Sully couldn't perform a quickie if his life

depended on it—that's not a complaint. He's *thorough*. He takes his time, and every minute is pure bliss. The stamina of this man is like nothing I've ever seen. He's a machine.

After speaking with Raleigh, it seems that's not unusual for hockey players. A few days ago, I made it my mission to wear him out. I had to tap out at the two-hour mark. I'm curious what a record length of time would be for him, but I'll never know. I wouldn't survive the results.

He finishes the topcoat on my pinkie toe, closes the bottle of polish, then sets it aside. "There," he says, satisfied as he admires his masterpiece. "Not bad, right?"

He's a natural. "If the coaching thing doesn't work out, I'd say you have a real future as a nail tech."

Picking up my calf, he presses a kiss to my ankle. "I'll be sure to update my resume."

I wiggle my toes. "Thank you for taking care of me ... *Daddy*," I add, smiling sweetly.

Slowly, he rises from the floor and kneels on the bed. *Oops*. Sometimes I forget uttering the d-word is the equivalent of a spy's handler activating its sleeper agent with a trigger word.

I shake my head vehemently. "No, my toes aren't dry!" I say between laughter.

He advances, throwing my ankles to the side, causing me to fall flat on my back. I settle into the mattress like a cloud.

Tucking his head into my neck, he nips at my earlobe. "You should have thought of that before calling me daddy." His teeth sink into my shoulder, and I shriek. His playfulness is such a turn-on.

"How do you want it, Kendra?" he growls. *Fuck*. "Keep your legs open like a good girl ..." My eyes practically roll back in my head just from his words. His hands grip behind my knees, and he wrenches my thighs apart. "I bet if I fuck you just like this I won't mess up those pretty toes of yours."

I know how this ends. I'll end up passed out, exhausted, and absentminded, and I haven't even finished packing. After mustering all the self-control in my possession, I push him off me and shake my head. "I promise, as soon as we check into our rental, I'll let you do whatever you want to me, but every time you fuck me, my brain turns to mush, and I still have to finish packing my bag."

Groaning, he plants one more kiss to my neck before rolling off and dramatically flopping on the bed. He knows it's true. Before he changes his mind, I hop up and walk into the bathroom, piling my makeup into a travel bag and packing the rest of my toiletries. Have I ever traveled for something that wasn't work related? If I have, I don't remember it. Hell, I hardly remember the last time I took Christmas off! To be fair, it's the only day I can work through without being interrupted by phone calls.

Sully has crashed into my life ... and my landscape is forever changed.

SULLY

She looks out the small oval window as the plane cuts through the clouds. She's so beautiful. Everything I want in my life is so close. Her hand rests on her lap, nails painted to match her toes, and I cover mine on top, threading our fingers together. It's the first time we've ever held hands in public. It's a small gesture, but for us, it's a monumental milestone. It's a promise that someday we'll have this all the time.

We kept our distance in the airport and when the plane was boarding, but the first-class seats provide us with extra privacy, and with our friends across the aisle, we can be ourselves. On set, I find little ways to conceal my caresses. When she hooks up my microphone on my collar, I discreetly graze her stomach with the back of my hand. If she's issuing me a new battery pack, our fingers brush. When no one is looking, I squeeze her side. Small gestures to remind her that no matter who they shoot me having dinner with, she's the only one I want. Without fail, she gives me those bedroom eyes with every clandestine touch. She deserves more than secrets, but if that's what she needs right now, I'll follow her lead.

She glances down at our linked fingers, then back up to me and beams as we stare at each other. Her understanding of the importance of our public display of affection hits me in the chest. I swallow. This is big. It's the first time I've felt this strongly about someone. Without letting go, I twist my body in order to cup her neck and lean over, placing my lips on hers. She sucks in a small gasp and grips my palm as she kisses me back, reciprocating every intense feeling I have for her.

We just arrived, but I'm already wishing our vacation was longer. Being ourselves and not having to hide our affection in front of our friends is everything. Barrett and I rented two small bungalows next to each other right on the beach. It's perfect.

A shared firepit sits between the two, and we sit comfortably in adirondack chairs around the flames as the sun dips below the horizon. The wind from the ocean keeps our fire small, but it's enough to keep us warm. Barrett's mom, Sue, is playing in the sand with her two grandkids. She brackets Darby, who will be one year old before we know it, between her legs while she digs in the sand with Arthur, who will be seven next May.

Barrett smiles at me as we watch our women get on like a house on fire. When it comes to friends, I'm a believer of quality over quantity. I'm a quiet guy, Barrett is my closest friend, and it means a lot that he understood how important a vacation like this would be for me. He and Raleigh reconnected in Hawaii, and I suspect he was hoping this would do the same for Kendra and me.

She seamlessly fits in with the people closest to me. I've already pulled Raleigh aside and thanked her for supporting Kendra before she was ready to tell me she was pregnant. I wish it could have been me, but I'm just happy she had somebody to lean on, and I'm grateful that person was Raleigh. I like Raleigh, she has a good heart and went through a similar situation with Barrett when she became pregnant with Arthur. It warms my heart to see the friendship between them grow.

The sky turns to dusk, and Grandma Sue picks up little Darby, heading in our direction with Arthur excitedly running ahead and waving something in his hand. As he gets closer, I see it's a big seashell.

"I found a big shell!" he shouts animatedly.

Grandma Sue passes off Darby to Raleigh, who's holding her arms out for her daughter, then takes one of the open seats and chuckles as Arthur proudly presents his shell, displaying his find for all to admire.

"Wow! Can I see it?" Kendra asks.

Arthur hurries to show her up close. She leans forward in her adirondack chair, and he offers it to her.

"This is a special shell," she tells him. "It's a lightning whelk."

"You guys! It's a lightning whelk!" he announces over his shoulder as if we didn't just hear it for ourselves.

"What makes it special?" he asks.

She turns the shell, showing him the top. "It's a left-handed shell. See this?" She traces her finger over the whorl. "Its spiral goes in a counterclockwise direction, most shells coil in a clockwise direction."

"Cool!" Arthur stares wide-eyed, hanging on her every word.

"Long, long ago, they were used in special ceremonies."

She hands it back to him, and he stares at the shell like it's the rarest treasure on earth. It's amusing as hell. Arthur's a sponge when learning about something. Koalas are his specialty, and how the kid rattles off facts is wild. I have a feeling Kendra earned major points with him after sharing her lightning whelk knowledge.

Not sure why it's such a turn-on when she busts out knowledge about niche subjects, but it is. I like seeing her geek out about something she finds interesting. Brings me back to the night we watched that squid documentary. That night was bittersweet. The more we got to know each other, the more I fell for her. There was no awkwardness, and our conversation would have lasted till morning if she hadn't checked her phone to see what time it was.

I've been with other women, most of those connections were purely physical, but when we talk, the hours melt away like seconds.

The inconvenience of losing my hotel reservation turned into the best night of my life, but by the end of that night, I couldn't have her the way I wanted. The way I craved her kiss was painful, but instead, I pulled her into my side and held her as tightly as I could. As if I was holding onto the memory of us, not wanting to let go. It was difficult knowing I would have to set her free in the morning. I barely slept that night, breathing in her scent, feeling her skin against mine, and memorizing the curves of her body. If it was the last night I had with her, then I was going to take everything she was willing to give.

I swallow down the bitter reminder that I'll have to give her up again when we return. For the next week, she's all mine, so I don't need to dwell on it now.

Reaching over, I cover her hand with mine and squeeze. She nods.

"Well, I think we're going to call it a night," I say. Kendra sets the blanket on the side of the chair and stands, adding a yawn for extra measure. We've had a big day of travel. She's probably exhausted. If not, she will be by the time I'm done with her.

CHAPTER THIRTY-SEVEN

SULLY

Back in our bungalow, Kendra sits on the edge of the bathtub in the en suite bathroom.

"Are you hungry at all?" I ask.

She shakes her head. "I'm still full from dinner. Feels so good to be able to eat more again." Those words are such a comfort. Now that we're in the second trimester, her appetite has been returning and the nausea is staving off. I was worried we would have to take extra measures to make sure she was getting the nutrients she needed.

"Ooh! Baby kicked!" she says, glancing up at me. I grin, loving her excitement. Soon I'll be able to feel those kicks too. Reaching into the shower, I turn the water on and let it warm up so we can wash the sand off our feet and bodies.

"Are you washing your hair tonight?"

"No, I'm leaving it."

I nod and turn a knob to redirect the water to the detachable shower head. I strip down and make a gruff noise as I take a seat in the shower on the tiled bench. My joints are killing me. The older I get, the more I feel the toll playing professional hockey has had on my body. After a day of travel and running around the beach, my knees are giving me a big *fuck you*. I shower the steamy water over my joints and sigh loudly. That's nice.

"You okay in there, old man?"

I chuckle at her dig. "Take your clothes off and get in here."

"Yes, Daddy."

Fuck yes. I know what that means. She's been struggling to lie on her back lately now that Bo is growing bigger. That's an easy fix.

Cocking my head to the side, I watch her strip through the glass shower door. So perfect. I'm growing harder with each article of clothing that falls at her feet. I groan when she unclasps her bra. Her eyes sparkle with mirth as she observes my reaction to her, then she tortures me with her slow striptease. When she opens the shower door and steps inside, I grab her hand and lead her in front of me. She leans down to kiss me, and I rest my palms on her sides, my thumbs rubbing circles on her hip bones, then land a strike on her ass. Her breath hitches and she pulls back, laughing, and I rub the sting away.

"What did I do to deserve a spanking?"

"Teasing me … but mostly because I wanted to." I want to smack her ass whether she deserves it or not; it's so pretty with my palm prints. She rolls her eyes, and I seal my mouth around one of her nipples, their color deeper than before. Her quiet hum sends more blood to my dick. She cradles my head to her, but I pop off and press a kiss between her breasts before moving to the other one. They're heavy, and those thoughts creep into my head again. Images of milk dripping from her tits to my cock. I learned this fetish I've developed is called a lactation kink.

I suck harder and she moans.

"Oh my god," she whispers. I glance up and love the dazed look in her eyes as she watches me. "Jesus, Sully ... if you suck any harder you're going to end up with a mouthful of milk," she jokes. The thought turns me on even more, and I realize it's time to tell her about this lactation kink I've developed—I did some online research after my last fantasy about it. It was a relief to see I'm not the only dude out there getting off to their woman's breastmilk.

I release her nipple. "Would that be bad?"

She chuckles. "Huh?"

"Would you let me?"

Her eyes grow wider, and I can practically see the wheels turning in her head as she considers what I'm saying. She smirks, then takes my hands and brings them to her breasts, and I begin kneading them. "Does this turn you on, Sully?"

I swallow, feeling lightheaded that she's not disgusted by the thoughts I've been having. "Yeah."

"What do you think I'll taste like?"

I groan. "Like fucking candy, baby girl."

Her eyes glance down in time to see my dick flinch. She grins. "Yeah, you can taste me."

I freeze and stare at her. Is she serious? "Really?"

"It's—it's kinda hot ..." She gives a nervous laugh. "Is that weird?"

Holy fuck, this woman. "Goddamn it, Kendra." I flatten my tongue and lick her nipple, relishing the gasp that escapes her. "No ... You're incredible, you know that?"

I love that she's so open-minded about this need I have but can't believe she's willing to indulge and let me be a part of this when the time comes. There's nothing sexual about her breastfeeding our child, it's simply beautiful that she can provide life that way, but imagining breastmilk dripping down her body and me licking it up is a crazy turn-on.

Spinning her around, I pull her into my lap. I bite the sweet spot between her neck and shoulder, and she hooks her palm behind my neck for support. Cupping under her knees, I massage the flesh. Her breathing increases the higher I go. Hooking her legs over each of mine, she's fully exposed. I could play with her for hours.

Withdrawing my hands from under her, I rest my palms on her hips, then slide them down to her calves and back up again, teasing her with my touch.

"You're such a sweet little thing," I growl in her ear. "Aren't you?"

She reaches down, grabs my quads, and holds on. The soft, desperate mewl is so fucking hot. Traveling between her legs again, I let my fingers explore and drag them up to the crease on each side of her inner thighs. I cup her there, and she twitches in my hands, all her muscles tensing.

I stop at the apex before kneading again. My fingertips become slick from her wetness, and her whimper is pathetic as her grip tightens on me.

My right hand parts her lips to brush her engorged clit. She's so coated in her arousal that I have to blink twice. I want it all over me, but this is about her.

God, she's adorable when she's like this. I'm pretty sure if I wanted her to come now, I could stuff her with two fingers, blow on her clit, and she'd explode. I pick up the showerhead and adjust the settings to misting.

"No, no, no," she whines. "I want to come."

"Aw, but it's so fun for me to watch you turn into my needy little girl." I slap her clit without warning, and her body writhes on my lap when she cries out the moniker I love.

"Good girl ... Let Daddy have his fun."

I position the misting showerhead away from her clit, the tiny droplets giving her the tiniest bit of sensation. Her hips undulate as she seeks more. She exhales a shudder. The frustration building inside her. I bring it slightly closer, giving her a little more, and nudge her forward so she's sitting closer to my knees. Then I wrap my left arm around her and lay her back, exposing even more of her. I adjust the showerhead to a pulse and align it with her ass.

"Oh fuck," she sobs. Her legs part as she becomes more relaxed. Then I switch back to the mist, raining a light spray across her clit. I do a couple more rounds of this until she's grunting and wiggling all over my lap. She hoists herself to line her pussy up with my hard-as-hell cock.

After picking her up, I slowly lower her onto me, and she moans the entire way down until I'm settled inside her. Her calves are really shaking now.

"Better?"

"So fucking good ..." She leans against me, and her petite hand snakes down to grip my balls, tugging on them. *Damn.* "You never said I couldn't play." The smile in her voice is so playful. Kendra is my kryptonite. Switching the showerhead back to pulsing, I bring it to the side of her thigh, less than an inch from her clit. "Oh my god," she whines, squeezing me so hard my eyebrows shoot up.

"Goddamn, you've got my dick in a vise."

She hums, trying not to rock back and forth.

Her shaking hands are so sexy, and the way she aches to be touched is beautiful. I set the showerhead to a powerful spray, running it up and down her legs. She mumbles something incoherent. Her sticky arousal pools at the base of my cock. So pretty.

"Mm-hm," I groan in agreement. Leaning back, I reach

down and part her soaked lips, then bring the showerhead right where she craves it, sending the spray up and down her clit.

She tries to jackknife forward, but I throw an arm around her chest and haul her against me, keeping a palm at the base of her neck. "Hold still, baby. We're not done yet."

Her head rests on my shoulder as she looks at the ceiling and pants.

I cup her chin, angling myself and tilting her head to face me.

"There's my girl." My hand retreats slightly to increase the water pressure against her clit. Her brows push together as her pussy tightens. Her whole body shakes on my lap, and I grin wider as her face contorts into sweet relief. Still gripping her chin, I stroke her cheek with my thumb and force her to look me in the eye while she comes. She tries to get words out, but it's all jumbled. I nod, understanding that she's lost in pleasure. The way her pussy flutters is killing me. "Shhh, just like that. Damn it, Kendra, look at you … Absolutely stunning." I don't stop with the showerhead, and the overstimulation has her trying to bat my hands away.

"Almost, baby. Give your daddy one more …"

She twitches like mad until I feel the slow constriction of her pussy on me again. Here it comes … I press my lips to hers briefly before another orgasm barrels through her.

"That's it! Fuck, baby girl!" I praise, growling through gritted teeth as I try not to come with her. I pull the showerhead away and let her rest. Her chest heaves like she ran a marathon. "No question, you were made for me."

She nods, then climbs off my lap, leaving my cock covered in her. Damn, that looks good. Her legs wobble, and when her knees buckle, I reach out to steady her. "Whoa, easy. Just take a beat."

She shakes her head and drops down, spreading my legs wide, then taking me into her mouth. My mouth drops open.

Jesus Christ, this woman.

"Fucking hell," I groan. "Kendra."

The grasp she has around my cock is shaky, but her mouth is solid as she takes every inch. Those big gray eyes look up at me, and I shake my head in disbelief. "Unreal," I mumble, awed by the woman before me.

Her hand twists at the base as she hollows her cheeks and focuses all the suction on the tip. I roar as I all but lose it. She moans around me, and my palm finds the back of her neck where I set the pace for me to finish. I wrap my fingers over the fist she's made around my length and squeeze it three times.

"Look at me," I say.

Her gorgeous eyes find mine, and my breath gets lodged in my chest. The vision in front of me is ecstasy. This unbelievable woman who makes me feel things I never thought I could. With her belly round with my child and her mouth wrapped around my cock? She's everything I've been missing. Everything I've been waiting for but thought I'd never find.

"You're mine. Always," I tell her. "I promise."

Her eyes swell with tears, and I cradle her chin. The need to lock my lips on hers is strong, but I'm afraid what will happen if I don't come right now. I've been edging myself for way too long.

"Ready?" I ask her. She nods, and I cup her face and make eye contact. "Good girl." I drive inside her mouth, and my jaw drops as I surrender to the orgasm, shooting my cum down her throat. She swallows, and I bite my lip, groaning as I get the very last drop out.

Thank god I'm sitting, or I'd probably collapse. I find the

strength to pull her into my lap and sink my fingers into her hair as I kiss her with everything I have.

"Forever, Kendra." I want her to know it wasn't an in-the-moment thing. There's no post-nut clarity bullshit. She's my everything ... and I fucking love her.

She releases a small whimper. "Forever," she says, and I groan against her lips.

CHAPTER THIRTY-EIGHT

SULLY

When my girl put on that dress this Christmas morning, she chose violence. It's the best present. What I got her for Christmas is back home. Goddamn. I haven't seen her wear anything that hugs her bump before today, and my fingers itch to explore every inch of her. Again. After last night, I'd been satiated enough to get through the day—I thought—but as soon as she walked out in that sundress, all I wanted to do was throw her over my shoulder like a caveman and hide in the bedroom all day. She's too excited about today's excursion for me to deprive her of that, though.

Barrett rented a boat to explore the coast and soak up some sunshine to celebrate Christmas without a ton of gifts. His mother, Sue, is joining us on the cabin cruiser, along with Raleigh and the kids. Memories over material things. When we went to pick it up from the rental, one of the guys at the counter couldn't take his eyes off Kendra. I pulled her back to my front and placed a protective hand on her belly, then glared at him. I've never felt so possessive over someone. I'm usually pretty levelheaded, there's not much, outside of a bad referee call, that gets me worked up. Until her.

Ocean water sprays over the side of the boat as we cruise the area. I'm with Barrett in the cockpit while everyone sits in the deck seating at the bow.

"So ..." He begins, handing me a beer.

I twist off the top and stow the bottlecap in my pocket. "So," I respond.

"And how was your night last night?" he asks with a smirk.

Shit. Did he hear us? We're in separate bungalows, but I suppose we had a few windows open ...

"Good." *Phenomenal.* "Why do you ask?"

He shrugs. "I had to go out to the truck to get Arthur's stuffed koala ..." He cuts me a look, and I feign ignorance.

"Twas the night before Christmas, when all through your house, the neighbors heard you screwing and making her shout—"

"Yeah, yeah, okay." I smirk.

"I can keep going ..."

"We'll keep it down next time."

He chuckles and steers the boat down the shoreline. After a moment, he clears his throat. "I like her. Raleigh *really* likes her. Just want to say I'm happy for you, man. I know it wasn't the most conventional way—"

I scoff. Yeah, you could say that.

"But neither was the way I met Raleigh. I'm just glad you found somebody you click with."

I nod, looking down at my beer. "We definitely click ... I really appreciate you extending the invitation for us to tag along on your holiday. It's been really nice not having to fake it. Not to turn into a total sap, but it's the best gift you could have given me. So, thanks."

He nods. "You love her?"

"Yeah."

"Okay, so now do you fucking understand why I was such a mess that season?!"

I laugh. "I'm sorry, I get it."

Barrett raises his eyebrows and holds his bottle out for me to clink. "Have you told her?"

"Nah." I shake my head. "I don't want to freak her out, but I know she's as serious as I am … we just have to get through the next couple months. It sucks, but I'll wait as long as I have to. I'm sure you understand that better than anyone." He waited five years for Raleigh, a few months should be nothing. I want her to move in with me. If I have to wait until we're outside of work to see her, I don't want to waste a second of our time off the clock.

Barrett nods. "Yeah, but damn, life is good now. We might try for a third."

I shake my head and laugh. "Hey … personal question for you. When Raleigh was breastfeeding … did you ever …"

He grins wide. "Fuck yeah."

I laugh. "Wait, seriously?"

"Absolutely." He lifts his shoulders. "I dunno why it's so hot, but it is."

He and I have far too much in common. "I knew we were best friends for a reason."

He nods out the window, toward the bow of the boat. "Ready for that?"

Following his line of sight, Kendra cradles Darby in her arms, and it sucks the air out of my lungs as I'm filled with visions of our future together. Family barbecues, our kids playing side by side, family vacations, celebrating birthdays and milestones. Hell, maybe they'll go to school together.

Darby's tiny feet are braced on Kendra's thighs, where she uses them as a springboard to bounce.

"Yeah. I'm ready." I don't know everything there is to know about being a dad, but I'm definitely ready to find out. "Do you mind if I …?"

"Go for it … Hey, send Ral in here, would ya?"

"Gonna try for baby number three?"

He bounces his eyebrows at me and smiles before he takes a sip from the bottleneck. "Maybe."

That's what I thought. I grin and shake my head. "Fuckin' perv."

When I get to the bow of the boat, I squeeze next to Kendra and slide my hand up her back to massage her neck. It's chilly out here, everyone has a weighted blanket they're wrapped up in. Darby must have tired herself out, because she's resting peacefully against Kendra's chest. Well, as much as she can while wearing the smallest life jacket I've ever seen. She hasn't fallen asleep, but it won't be long, based on the lazy blinks she's doing.

Arthur is updating his grandma on the latest and greatest drama from the elementary school playground. Some kid gave another kid stickers but didn't give them to a different kid … or something equally heinous. Raleigh and Kendra are discussing smart sleepers, which I've learned are basically robotic cribs. Parenting has changed a lot from the days when I used to babysit cousins. When their conversation dies down, I lean over to face Raleigh.

"Barrett mentioned he wanted to talk to you about something." I gesture behind us to the boat's cabin.

She rolls her eyes with a smile. "I can take her back if you're getting tired?" she asks Kendra. "That girl doesn't skip leg day."

"Nah, she's doing great. I think she's about to fall asleep."

"Perfect! I'm not going to get in the middle of that." Raleigh hands me her blanket and hops up to make her way over to the bridge.

Kendra turns to me. "Hey, could you fix the blanket to cover her back?" She leans forward to give me access, and I tuck it over Darby's shoulders.

"There we go," she says to the baby, then turns to me. "Thank you. I think the temp has dropped a little."

I adjust us so she's leaning her back on my chest rather than the seat and rub my index finger over the tiny hand that's clutching my girl's dress strap. Pressing a kiss to Kendra's temple, I wrap an arm around her and the little bundle she's cuddling. My chin rests on her shoulder, the one facing away from Arthur and Sue.

"I was watching you and Darby from inside," I mutter. "Couldn't help but wonder what you were thinking. Does holding a baby make it feel more real?"

She grins. "I thought it was going to be weird, but it doesn't feel awkward."

I nod. "I can tell, you make it look natural. Like you've done it a hundred times before. You're going to be so good at this."

"Yeah?" she says. "I think there's a lot I don't know. I'm going to screw something up."

I chuckle. "We both will. I think that's part of it."

She hums agreement and combs her fingers through Darby's white-blonde curls. "Are you nervous?" she asks.

"Terrified … but I don't think there's any first-time parent who isn't."

"True," she agrees.

"I'm also excited." I don't want her to think that just

because I'm nervous, I'm not thrilled to be starting a family with her. It may not be the way either of us envisioned our journey going, but I regret none of it. Darby moves her mouth as if she's eating in her sleep. I wonder what Bo will look like. Will they look more like her or me or be an equal mix of both of us?

"Damn ... We're having a baby, Kendra." I squeeze my hand under Darby to rest it on Kendra's belly.

"What? Since when?" she whispers, panicked, before smiling.

Turning my head, I nip at her neck. "Smartass," I mutter. "How are you feeling?"

She nods. "Good. Just a little bit of nausea this morning—" I know how her body is feeling, but I want to check in with where her head is at.

"Mentally. How are you doing?"

She sighs. "Scared ... I'm also excited, but I'm young, Sully. You were able to focus your whole life, up until this point, on your career. I thought I could do the same. Grind for a few years and work my way up the ladder. When I chose to keep our baby, I knew I was trading it for rungs on that ladder. I won't be able to climb as high—"

"Kendra—"

"It's true. They can say women can have it all, but you and I both know that's not true. I won't be climbing as high as I would without children. *But* I'm at peace with it. I want this baby. I already love them ... I just need you to understand motherhood isn't enough for me. I need to have a career. I want to be creative, I want to make more than just babies. Okay?"

I hurt for her in that way. She's growing up quickly. Even if she continues working, she's still sacrificing her dreams.

She's right. Society will likely gift opportunities to those without children. I nod. "I'll do everything I can to make sure you have the resources you need to keep creating for as long as you desire."

CHAPTER THIRTY-NINE

SULLY

My phone buzzes with a video call from Whit. I slowly get off the bed, where Kendra is still napping, and creep out toward the living room, gently shutting the door behind me so she doesn't wake up. Whit knows I'm in Florida, but he doesn't know it's with Kendra.

"Hey," I answer. "Ever try taking a day off?"

"Somebody's gotta get shit done around here while you're on vacation."

"Fair. How's everything going?" I take a seat on the sofa and listen to him go over some scheduling details for the upcoming season. We've got our first game in a couple weeks against Boston.

"How's the shit with the TV show?"

I sigh. Before we left town, I had three dates in two weeks, and I swear they're only getting worse.

"Meh. Same old. Just trying to get through the contract." I don't get into it. The longer the conversation lasts, the more nervous I become that Kendra will wake up and walk out here. "Well, if that's all—"

"Do you know where my lotion is?" Suddenly Kendra is right behind me. "I think your Viking baby is already giving me stretch marks—"

I swing my head around at the same time she glances at the phone in my hand. She and Whit are looking at each other.

"Oh my God," she says, frozen in place.

"One sec," I tell Whit, setting my phone face-down on the coffee table. I take Kendra's arm and guide her into the hallway.

"I'm sorry," she whispers on the edge of tears. "I'm sorry. I'm so sorry. I didn't know—I shouldn't have said—"

"No." I wrap my arms around her body and pull her into me. "You did nothing wrong, Kendra. I'll talk to him. Just give me a couple minutes, okay?"

She nods into my shirt, and I release her.

"It's going to be okay," I reassure.

On the way back to my phone, I hear him sighing a curse. I pick the phone up in time to see Whit slam the door to his office. "She's fucking pregnant?!"

It's a rhetorical question. I let him get his anger out as I take a seat on the sofa again. Might as well get comfortable, I will be here for a while. This ass-chewing will not be brief.

"How did—When is she due?"

"March. She got pregnant before the show, this all happened prior to the paperwork being signed. We didn't know. She didn't know she was pregnant when the contract was made."

His eyes look less menacing after I explain. He nods, rubbing his fingers over his mouth, his gaze fixed on the floor. I won't be surprised if there's a scorched hole forming in the commercial berber carpet as we speak. It's clear the wheels in his head are turning, assembling the timeline I've laid out. He's searching for a loophole. There isn't one, trust me. I've looked at this situation from every angle possible. Our situation is still hairy as fuck, but it sounds a lot less scandalous when you lay out all the facts. It was an accident, but one I have zero regrets about.

"We gotta put something together. Talk to PR. Get ahead of it. Why the fuck didn't you tell me when you found out?"

I roll my eyes. "Would you?"

"Yes!" he shouts.

Bullshit. Before I can stop myself, I bark back, "Then why don't you tell me what the fuck is going on between you and Delta Makkonen?" That shuts him up. I level him with a stare. "Are you involved with one of my players?"

He cuts his eyes to me, then looks away. The silence hangs heavy between us. The stillness is loud and clear.

"Then back the fuck off," I say slowly.

He takes a deep breath and relaxes his shoulders.

I do the same and clear my throat. "We just have to wait out the contract. I'm still going on dates with every woman they throw at me. Hell, I've got another one already lined up for when I return. I'm going to flip through as many as I need to until production wraps up. Kendra is keeping things quiet on her end."

"Who else knows?"

"You, Barrett Conway, and his wife, Raleigh."

"Oh, is that all?" His voice is laced with sarcasm.

"The Conways won't say shit," I mutter. After summoning my courage, I say what I'm thinking. "If you think I'm not a good enough coach without the reality show, then you never should have asked me to join this organization."

He stops pacing and scowls at me. "Our team has their coach. You are their coach! Why the fuck do you think I'm sweating bullets right now? I don't give a shit about the reality show, I don't want to lose you or this sponsorship."

I appreciate that. Leaning forward on the edge of the sofa, I glance at the floor, and nod. I am their coach. I feel it in my bones, the Rogues are my team.

"The organization can't find out about this," Whit says. He rubs the back of his neck as our eyes meet. "Look, that production company needs you more than you need it. If the network sues, let them. I'll bring you back myself if I have to. We'll figure it out."

KENDRA

The Conways are at Sue's place to ring in the new year. We opted to celebrate with the two of us in our little bungalow. I can't believe Whit found out about us and the baby, but Sully seems convinced he won't say anything because, apparently, he's got dirt on him too. It's a lot to take in, and it hasn't helped the anxiety regarding our secret. For now, I will enjoy our night. I'm surprised I'm still awake this late. All the fresh air we've had has had me feeling like I'm in the first trimester again. I'm exhausted.

"Eleven fifty-nine," Sully announces, handing me a champagne flute.

Laughing, I take it from him. "Can't believe you got sparkling cider. Such a cornball."

He plops down next to me on the sofa. "First New Year. We gotta celebrate," he says firmly, as if it's a mandate. For being a giant, he's adorable.

"Do you have any new year's resolutions?"

He keeps an eye on his watch as the second hand moves around the clock face. "A couple."

"Oh, yeah?" I didn't peg him for the type of guy to have resolutions, though it makes sense. He's the type to make a plan and do it; when he wants something, he goes for it. His first game is coming up, so I'm sure that's been heavily weighing on him. "Wanna share any of them?"

Looking up from his watch, he smiles. "Happy New Year." His giant hands cup my face, and he tilts his head to kiss me. Endorphins flood my brain, and it's as if I'm floating. As soon as his tongue glides over my lips, I open up to him. A small whimper escapes my throat. Blindly, I set my stemmed glass on the coffee table and pause for a moment to straddle his lap.

"Happy New Year," I say against his lips, returning to our kiss.

His hands drop to my waist, then down to my ass where he hauls me tighter against him.

"Want to know my resolution?"

We're doing this *now*? I take a deep breath and retreat from his lips. "Um. Sure," I say with a small laugh.

"Moving you in with me."

I gaze at him while the words register in my brain. "Moving in? As in, moving in? Like where I move in with you?" That might be the most absurd string of words I've ever stitched together, but he caught me off guard.

He chuckles. "Are you surprised?"

My mouth opens and closes. "Is this because of the baby?" What am I saying, *of course* it's because of the baby!

"It makes that part more convenient ... but it's mostly because I want to move in together." He waits for me to say something. I forget to speak. "Shit, am I reading this wrong?"

"No!" I shout. "I just wanna make sure it's really what you want. Make sure it's not some emotional thing."

He laughs. "Of course it's an emotional thing!"

"You know what I mean, I want to make sure you're not suggesting we do this impulsively. It's a big step."

Sully nods. He tucks me to his chest, and I wrap my arms around his neck while he skims his fingers up and down my back. "I'm ready to take the big steps with you."

"Okay." I smile, rest my elbows on his shoulders, and press my forehead to his. "How do you picture this going?"

"I'd love to have you move in with me. You don't have to get rid of your house if it makes you feel better. Or if you're dead set on staying where you're at, I'll sell my place."

"You just built it."

He shrugs. He fucking shrugs like it's no big deal that he dropped close to a million on a new lot and build. Let's be real, my place is not big enough for a man his size. He'd be contorting himself to rinse the shampoo out of his hair in the shower. There would be weekly chiropractor appointments and concussion checks because he'd hit his head on everything. "No way. You said you'd teach me how to skate. You at least have to wait until you make good on your promise."

He smiles and wraps both arms all the way around my back. "I'll teach both of you to skate."

He squeezes my sides, and I laugh into his chest. "You really want me to move in? You don't think it's too fast?"

"It's probably a little faster than normal, but this baby will be here before we know it. You should be comfortable in the house before Bo arrives. It's going to be a big change, so the more time you can spend there, the smoother that transition will be. You need time to nest."

My heart clenches every time he uses the name Bo. I want us to live together. I want to raise a child with him, under one roof. I want to *be* with him. I want the forever he's offering me. Sully can tell them he's no longer comfortable filming at his home. We barely have any shots of him there anyway since he spends the majority of his time at the arena …

"Fuck. Okay. Let's do it."

CHAPTER FORTY

SULLY

Hunching over the bench, I tighten my laces and tape up a new stick. It feels good to be at the arena again, but going back to pretending Kendra and I are simply colleagues fucking sucks. It was way too easy getting used to being a normal couple. I'm counting down the days for this show to be behind us.

Before the team arrives, I warm up by skating a few laps and hitting pucks into the net. It feels good. When I'm alone out here, it reminds me of the old days when I played with the Lakes. I miss the boys and the camaraderie of being a player, but damn, being a coach is equally great in a different way. I get to watch the players improve and come together as a team. It's more challenging, and there's more pressure to make sure everyone is where they should be. It's so rewarding.

The closer we get to our first game, the higher those stakes seem. I can't fuck this up. Between balancing the show in exchange for keeping our sponsor and making sure the team is performing at the necessary level … it's a lot. Oh, and let's not forget, Kendra and I have a baby on the way. Someday, we will look back on this and laugh. Unfortunately, that day is not today.

"No cameras today, Coach?"

When I look up, Timber Healy is skating out to the ice.

"Thought I saw your car in the lot. Trying to earn extra credit by showing up early?"

She scoffs. "What would I need extra credit for? Certainly not to warm up extra early so you put me on the starting line in Vancouver."

"Want some practice shots?"

"Yes, please. I've already warmed up with reaction balls in the locker room," she explains, doing some stretches on the ice.

"Finish your warm-up and let me know when you're ready."

I practice some of my edgework while collecting pucks around the ice for her, then notice a couple of Kendra's camera guys setting up. I'm supposed to be going on another date tonight. Now that I'll be traveling for games more, they're trying to get a bunch in beforehand. Wish I could tell them what a waste of time this all is.

I slap a few pucks toward the opposite end of the ice.

"Ready?" I shout to Timber.

She drops her mask and bends her knees, lowering herself to take up more space in the net. Affirmative. I rush the net, passing the puck while watching her small movements and preparing to dart in either direction. When I come from the right, she covers that side. I'm coming at her hard. How long will she hold out in this spot? Long enough for me to get the puck by her on the left? Or will she cover the left too early, allowing me to strike on the right? Anticipating moves when someone is barreling down on you is a mental mindfuck. She stays cool and collected. In the end, I get it by her on the right. She pulled a split second too early after I gave her a small deke, and couldn't react fast enough in the crease. Reacting is a goaltender's last line of defense. Positioning and reading a player comes first. Her reflexes are lightning quick, but sometimes it's not enough.

She shakes it off, tapping her stick on the ice. "Let's go again."

The next one she blocks, and I smile. "Nice job. Notice how you were able to cut down on those angles? Your positioning was better."

She nods, and I do close plays with her until the other players filter onto the ice.

Delta skates up and takes over for me while I do a couple drills with Joey—who actually showed up on time today.

"How's the dating life, Coach?" she asks. "Any winners?"

"Nobody yet," I tell her.

She dekes me to the side, and I lose the puck. Damn. "I'm going to tell you my tried-and-true method, ready?"

I scoff. "Pins and needles."

"Okay, here's what you do ... You look them in the eye"—she skates in front of me, looking serious as can be—"and then you say, 'I'm a hockey player.'"

I chuckle and grab a new puck.

"Works every fucking time," she says.

I roll my eyes. Yeah, I may have used that once or twice back in the day.

Timber blocks one of Delta's pucks, who then spins around, grabbing a new one. She's frustrated. Jeanine is on the other end with a few cones, setting up for edgework drills. The rest of the team is on the ice stretching.

"See, it's more of a relationship show," I explain to Joey. "If it was a hookup show, I'd already be done, right?"

"How embarrassing," Timber pops off. It makes me laugh. I kinda walked into that one.

"Hey-o," Joey adds.

"What about Kendra?" Cori asks.

I keep my head down, collecting pucks, making sure I don't react. "What do you mean?"

"I dunno, you did that little live promo thing, seemed like there was some tension there."

Shit. "No, there isn't. She's my boss."

Delta barks out a laugh. "Do you think we're blind, Coach?"

"Nah," Joey says, disagreeing. I'm shocked—but grateful —she doesn't add to the conversation.

"Have you ever thought about her like that?" Timber asks.

Delta waves a hand. "He's not going to answer that."

I shake my head. "I'm not talking about this with my players. Besides, I'm not supposed to be discussing the show at all, I signed an NDA."

"Did you see how Twitter blew up after that live interview?" Cori asks the other women.

"Oh yeah!" Timber adds. "See?! Even the internet was talking about all the chemistry you had with her."

Joey pipes up. "I don't buy it. People love drumming up speculations on things they know nothing about. Lord knows all the shit they say about *me* online." She gives me a subtle wink. Fucking *great*.

"Don't worry, Coach. America just wants to swoon and kick their feet over your love story," Cori says. "I'm sure you'll find someone. Give it time."

I have someone. The whole conversation gets on my nerves. She skates around, and I follow up with "Cori, you're doing too much stickhandling. *Push* the puck. The other team knows you're a killer. You don't have to prove it with all the fancy stickwork."

"Yes, Coach."

There, that ends that. My phone rings in my pocket, and I glance down to the caller's name, it's my doctor's office. My genetic results.

I fish it out and nod to Jeanine. "I gotta take this, can you?"

She nods and rallies the girls. I answer the phone after skating off the ice and tossing my stick to one of the equipment managers.

"Hello?"

"Hi, Lee. We're just calling to let you know your genetic test was negative, we found zero gene mutations."

I pump my fist in the air and jump on my skates in the arena tunnel. "Awesome. That's great to hear. Thank you."

"Happy to give you the good news," she says with a small chuckle. "Did you want to schedule an appointment to discuss anything further?"

"Nope, all set."

"All right, have a good afternoon."

"You too."

A second later, Kendra walks out of a locker room and into the tunnel looking down as she fiddles with one of the walkie-talkies along the band of some of the new maternity pants she bought. I stride over and crowd her against the concrete wall of the dark tunnel, and she gasps when I delve my hands into her hair and kiss her. Our baby is healthy.

"Sully!" she whispers, shoving me away.

"The test was negative," I say, with a small laugh. "No gene mutations."

She stares at me while the words register in her brain, then she grips my sweater and tugs me close. Her small palms frame my face, and she kisses me once more before pulling away. "Oh my God."

"Bo is fine," I reassure her.

She nods over and over, her eyes swelling with tears. I wrap my arms around her. "You okay?"

"Yes!" She laughs through a sob. "Just emotional. Okay, okay. We can't do this here. Um, go back out there. I'll be behind you after a minute."

"Okay. Celebrate later?" I ask.

"I'd love that."

Smiling, I walk backward out the tunnel, watching her pull her emotions together as she faces the wall. This is a huge weight off our shoulders. It's fine. Our baby will be fine. There's a chance they'll be a carrier of the gene like Kendra, but we don't have to worry about our baby developing cystic fibrosis.

As soon as I spin around at the mouth of the tunnel, I all but run into Whit Moreau. He shakes his head, telling me everything I need to know.

We weren't being careful enough.

CHAPTER FORTY-ONE

KENDRA

28 weeks pregnant

He places his hand on my thigh while we drive through the trees. Using my nails, I scratch lightly over the back of his palm, and he squeezes, sending a wave of pleasure up my spine. I love when he's grabby. I agreed I would start moving in, which is how six boxes of my things ended up in the backseat before we decided to head home from our record store excursion.

I packed some clothes, bathroom toiletries, and a bunch of refrigerated food I don't want to spoil. Seeing my fridge empty made it real. It's fast, but it feels right. It's not heavily weighed down by pregnancy or obligation. If we weren't having a baby, I'd still be moving in. The problem is I have no idea where I will put all my things.

He parks and runs around to open my door. "You go in, I'll grab these boxes." Lately, he doesn't let me lift a finger to do anything. He's been very protective. I grab my oversized purse stuffed with a few items and head in. There's no use in fighting him.

"Thank you," I say with a smile, and pull his arm so he leans down and I can kiss him. I miss no opportunity to love on him. We've fallen into casual affection so easily. As soon as I enter the house through the kitchen, I'm surrounded by the smell of new construction. Fresh wood shavings and a slight odor of new paint. It smells like the studio after a new set build. I glance around the kitchen and notice nothing different, but as I walk through the house, I see the change. The entire living room has been redesigned, and along the longest wall are brand-new built-in shelves. My purse falls from my arm and clunks on the floor.

Oh my God. Are these ...

"You needed a place to keep your records."

I spin around to Sully leaning against the wall. He built shelves for my records. He didn't give me a room, or a corner, or tell me there wasn't space. He redesigned the main room of his house to fit my things. *He made room for me.*

"You remodeled your living room?"

"*Our* living room, baby girl. No more his and hers."

My lump forms in my throat at the actions of this thoughtful, considerate, gorgeous man of mine.

Pressing my fingers to my chest, I stare at the shelves. "Oh my God, Sully."

He pushes off the wall and stalks toward me. "Thought we could start moving them over this week, what do you think?"

"Yes," I say, laughing. "This is way more room than I need though."

"I'm sure you'll find a way to fill it up." He grins and walks to the center of the room. "You can pick out a rug to go here ... and I thought this would be a good place to set up a spot for your record player." He points to the striking record stand made of rich walnut. The craftsmanship is stunning. He's recreating the room where I spent so much time with my mom. When we'd lay on the floor and stare at the ceiling listening to music for hours. Dancing or holding hands while on our backs. I get to do that with our child someday. Does he know how much this means to me?

I'm speechless. I meet him in the center of the room and wrap my arms around him. "You're giving me future memories like the ones I had with my mother. Thank you."

Leaning forward, he kisses me, and his lips curl into a smile.

"What?" I ask.

He says nothing, just takes my hand and leads me toward the bedroom. *Our* bedroom? The grin on my face grows, and I bite my bottom lip; I'm about to get some. Then he passes by the bedroom, and I pout.

"Hey, I thought—"

He leads me into one of the guest bedrooms, and as I step over the threshold, I'm hit with the natural light from all the windows on the back wall. A black river flows behind the house, and the dark water meets the dense snow blanketing the world. The landscape looks like something from an Ansel Adams coffee table book, sans the white-capped mountains.

This bedroom had furniture in it before. Now it's empty, except for a rocking chair.

"Thought this could be the nursery. I know it's really blank, but I wanted to give you a blank canvas for you to decorate. Make it colorful. Put some Kendra in it."

The thoughtfulness of this man is unparalleled. He wraps me up from behind and rests his hands on my stomach. The baby kicks at that moment, so I guide his hand over where I feel the little thump. The kicks are getting stronger each day, but every time the baby is active, it seems Sully is at practice or in the office.

"Feel that?"

"No," he whispers, as if staying quiet will help him feel it more.

I probe his fingers deeper, and Bo kicks again. He drops to his knees in front of me and places his palms near that side of my belly again. "Was that—"

I chuckle as he feels around, seeking more. Another kick.

"That's your baby, Sully."

The pride in his eyes is palpable, and my throat thickens with emotion. He will be the best dad.

―――

Wedged between Sully's massive thighs on his sofa, his arms are wrapped around me as we listen to music together ... It's perfection. My right hand curls behind his neck, drawing small circles at the nape. His breaths are relaxed and steady, and I'm almost positive he's sleeping, as every once in a while his leg twitches, and it makes me smile. It's adorable. I resist giggling. I'd hate to wake him when he's this relaxed. He's been so attentive lately, he needs to rest. He's earned it. His palm hasn't left my stomach since feeling Bo kick. I close my eyes and relish the safety I feel at this moment.

Yup. This is it. My happy place.

"I love you," I whisper, knowing he won't respond but needing to tell him anyway.

His breathing stops, and mine follows.

Sully shifts and spins me so I'm straddling him, my round belly between us. His eyes search mine while his fingers skate up my arms and cup my neck. He tucks a lock of my hair behind my ear and brushes the edge of my jaw with his thumbs. The air between us is thick. He heard me. I know he did. But I don't dare take it back. I meant it. I love this man whether he reciprocates my feelings. Still, the empty air feels thick. What is he thinking?

He swallows. "I love you so fucking much, Kendra."

Finally, I exhale the breath that's been burning in my lungs.

He loves me too.

Sully pulls me close and kisses me, and my hand covers his and our fingers link.

This is love. Deep, true, sacrificial, ends-of-the-earth love.

The rest of the night is spent lying in bed together, our bed, feeling for kicks and watching movies. Better rest up, the movers are coming tomorrow.

CHAPTER FORTY-TWO

KENDRA

28 weeks pregnant

"Figure it out, Kendra!" Jeremy yells. He's the executive producer on the show and is giving me shit because Sully has taken none of the women he's dated on a second date. I'm trapped in his office with him while he screams the house down with a red face. He's pissed because this show isn't the cheap-and-easy reality productions he prefers. He gets off on exploiting others in the fastest way possible and wants to fabricate his own drama. All he cares about is putting up numbers. I thought I could learn a lot from this guy, but his style is not mine, and there's nothing beneficial for me to learn here.

My argument is that we can achieve the same results by working the story from a different angle. Sully has depth! The entire story has depth, it's Minnesota's first pro-female team. Why are we relying on only these dates for the storyline? It's lazy.

"How? I can't force him. If he wants to find out what's

behind door number two, we can't intervene. That's the show."

He grimaces at me. "We're halfway through production, and he hasn't had one second date! What show, *Kendra*?! Where's the story arc of him not finding a partner? Nobody cares to watch him speed date a bunch of bimbos! They want to see him fall in love!"

This asshole.

"Your arc is with the Rogues!" I argue. "He's a coach first and foremost! It's a great story, we can play the NHL to PWHL angle, having the hotshot male hockey captain coming face-to-face with athletic misogyny. It's a big issue! We don't need the fake shit. Let's work with what he's given us." Before I even finish speaking, I can tell he will shoot it down. Jeremy doesn't give a damn about ethical filmmaking or the important matters at hand.

"Fuck that—make it happen! Fix it! Talk him into it, trick him, I don't care. I want a second date from him before I get on set."

He throws open the door to his office with enough strength to rattle the door handle in its wake, then stomps out. He's ranting under his breath out in the hall. What a dick. I close my eyes and take a deep breath. I'm growing sick of this production.

Normally, I don't get flustered when a producer starts yelling. Most of the time, they're blowing off steam, throwing fits because shit isn't going the way they want—um, hi? That's the job. It's never fun being the target of someone's anger, but it's never gotten under my skin like it has today. Probably because the person in question is Sully. Being under the weather isn't helping either. I don't want to force him to pick a woman twice—I don't want to watch him date those women in the first place.

I look at my phone and check the time. Shit, I needed to leave ten minutes ago. I feel ill, it's probably the stress from the ass-chewing I just received, or possibly the recent traveling from Florida. It's not exactly nausea, but an overall not-well. I need to rally if I'm going to make it to ten o'clock. I've been here since six. It's going to be a long day.

We've secured a film location at a local brewery for Sully's date tonight. I text Rachel, my favorite production assistant.

> Hey. You on loc already?

RACHEL

Yeah, what's up?

> We need Sully to take this girl on a second date. How's his attitude right now?

RACHEL

He's thrilled lol what do you think?

Super.

> Get him a beer or something, I'm on my way.

> Oh! The owner, Cliff, has the branding he wants in the shot. Everything has been set aside already, he should be on-site to show you where it is.

RACHEL

10-4

> Thank you!

I haul ass to the local craft brewery, Citra, and see that Rachel has taken care of most of the prep. Thank God, because I have to pee.

"Sorry, I'm late!"

"You're not late," Rachel says with a laugh.

"Jeremy here?" I say, heading toward the restroom sign in the corner.

"Not yet—oh, nevermind, there he is." She shifts her eye contact behind me, so I spin to see him walking in from the parking lot with tonight's date.

I scan the room and find Sully signing a couple autographs near the bar. Lance already has a camera on him. I do my best not to stare, but damn, he's handsome. *How many days until this contract is over again?* Then I remember why I have to talk to him.

I'll try to convince Sully, but I know that man, he's not gonna do it. It's hard enough getting him to do the show. He's been adamant about not having any repeats. For now, I need to find a bathroom; I can't think until I pee. Once that's done, I'll have a snack, drink some water, and clear my head. We'll sort this out.

Pushing open the heavy door, I take the first stall. Sweet fucking relief—*there is a God*. Finishing up, I spot blood on my underwear.

Washing my hands, I try to remain calm while my mind races with the possibilities. None of them are positive. I have to get out of here, but I have to tell Sully. I made him a promise there would be no more secrets. And truthfully, he's the only person who can comfort me right now.

When I find him, he's still at the bar, giving his fans all the attention. I hustle over to Jeremy and let him know I've got to leave, keeping him informed of the situation.

"Shit." He snaps at Rachel, "Hey, I need you to drive Kendra to the ER."

Rachel's eyes rove up and down my body. "What's going on, are you okay? What happened?"

COACH SULLY

I nod and briefly explain without sounding too frantic.

"Do what you gotta do, I'll cover it here. We'll talk about the date stuff later," Jeremy says.

Oh good, I was *so* worried about the date stuff. Whatever, at least he's not being a massive dick about it. Now I have to let Sully know.

I head toward the bar, and he's chatting about his new role with the Rogues, enthusiastically promoting the players and team. When I press my fingers to the back of his arm, he spins to face me. His smile grows, and he goes to touch me but stops himself, and the smile slides off his face.

"What's wrong?" he asks.

My eyes find Lance's and look to Sully again. The fans are no longer circling him like vultures, but the camera is on us. Shit.

"I need you to casually turn off your mic for a sec," I say.

He reaches behind and fumbles with the button on the battery pack.

My voice catches in my throat, but I force it out, speaking as level as I can. "I have to go to the doctor. I'm bleeding, and I want to make sure everything is okay."

"You're bleeding—where?"

I look down. "I saw blood in my underwear a moment ago. It's not a lot, but I want to be sure."

"Let's go." He puts an arm around me and is ready to take off for the exit.

I plant my feet on the ground, and he whirls around when he notices I'm not moving. "You stay. Rachel is going to take me. I will call you as soon as I find out—"

His nostrils flare. "Kendra, you are out of your goddamn mind if you think somebody else is taking you to the emergency room. Let's. Go."

Next to me, Rachel's gaze is ping-ponging between us.

He looks at her. "I'm taking Kendra to the ER. Tell them we can reschedule this for another time."

"Ohhhkay?" Of course Rachel is confused. This whole situation is a clusterfuck.

I open my mouth to speak when Jeremy shouts, "Sully, we need you over here." He points to one of the empty chairs. Sully rolls his eyes and shakes his head, so naturally, Jeremy clomps over in our direction. *Fuck. Fuck, fuck, fuck.*

As soon as Jeremy is within earshot, Sully glances down at him. "I'm taking Kendra, we'll reschedule."

He rears his head back with a pinched expression. "Sully, we've got it under control. Rachel is taking her. Please sit so we can begin shooting. The crew is already set up and waiting. Stay out of this."

Sully invades his space, and I hold my breath. *Shit, what is he doing?*

"That's my child. Kendra is leaving with me. We are done." He disconnects his mic and shoves it into Jeremy's chest.

I'm frozen in place. He told them. He revealed everything.

"Now, Kendra."

My blank stare is echoed by Jeremy's. I don't know how to explain. There's nothing to explain. Nothing can be said. It's over.

A big arm braces my back, then I'm being ushered toward the exit. Without saying a word, my feet shuffle all the way to Sully's vehicle. *One thing at a time*, I think, trying to compartmentalize what happened. I can't have a breakdown here. Bo needs my attention right now. Bo is my priority.

CHAPTER FORTY-THREE

SULLY

I return the clipboard to the front desk clerk and ask when we'll be seen. It's the same as before: *shortly*. When I get back to Kendra, she's hunched forward in her chair as we impatiently sit in the emergency room waiting room. This is purgatory. About fifteen other people sit in chairs around the room. I don't understand why she isn't being rushed back.

I crouch in front of her and take her hands in mine. "It's going to be okay."

She sniffles and wraps her arms around my neck. "Don't talk to me right now."

I'm sure there's a better way I could have snuck out of filming, but I panicked. I apologized in the car numerous times, but there was no getting around it. I needed to be here, and whether she admits it or not, she needs me here too. I nod, stay quiet, and hold her.

She clutches my shirt, and I swipe the tear that falls down her cheek.

"Kendra?" a nurse calls from one of the doors.

Fucking finally.

I stand, pulling her to her feet. She walks ahead, not letting go as I follow behind.

"Hi, Kendra, how are you doing today?" the nurse asks.

I roll my eyes. We're at the emergency room, the answer to that seems pretty obvious.

"I've been better," she answers.

We are led to a small room with a sliding glass door. Inside is a bed, two small chairs, the same kind they had in the waiting room, and a small sink. "I'm sorry to hear that. It looks like you're almost twenty-nine weeks?"

"Yes," Kendra mutters, her voice beaten down.

"Tell me what's been going on."

"Um, I haven't been feeling well, and then I noticed a small amount of blood in my underwear while I was at work, and I didn't know what to do." Her voice shakes. "I looked it up and saw that maybe some of my symptoms for being sick might actually be ... I-I don't remember feeling the baby kick at all today. Or last night."

"Have you had any cramping?"

Kendra shakes her head. "I don't know. I've been achy, but it just seemed like normal discomfort from pregnancy. Maybe I didn't know they were cramps?"

"Are you still bleeding?"

She shakes her head. "I don't think so. I don't know."

"And roughly how much blood would you say there was when you found it?"

Kendra makes a shape with her hand, and the nurse nods. The woman passes her a thin polyester gown and closes the curtain that draws across the glass doors. "Let's have you put this on. While you're doing that, I'm going to get a fetal doppler so we can check for a heartbeat."

The nurse exits the room, and Kendra begins undressing. With each layer she removes, I take them from her and fold them into a small pile. She slips the gown on, which has a bunch of snaps and fits like a robe.

She sits on some pad the nurse put on the bed, then we wait. A minute goes by, and she speaks.

"I didn't even want to be a mom until a couple months ago. And then I wanted it. I wanted it so fucking bad." Her voice is hollow, and I wrap my arms around her. Grateful that she's letting me be here to support her. I clench my jaw and swallow. I'll be strong for her right now. "Lay back and relax." I pull a chair close to the bed and sit, holding her hand in mine and rubbing circles on the back of her palm. "We're going to leave this room together, regardless of the results. Is that clear?"

She rolls her lips together and nods.

Before long, there's a knock on the glass.

"Come in," I answer.

The sliding doors part, and the nurse returns with a physician's assistant. They introduce themselves and put on gloves.

Kendra lies on the bed, and they unsnap some of the buttons around her belly.

"Bleeding doesn't always mean miscarriage, though you are past the time we usually see it," they explain. After squirting this clear jelly stuff on her stomach, they push a small microphone-looking thing around on her belly. The sound of static fills the room. We're all silent while we listen. I don't even want to fucking breathe. They continue to move the device. So much static. Waiting, waiting, waiting. What the fuck is happening right now? The blood drains from my face. I have never hated the sound of empty static so much in my life. I squeeze her hand tighter.

Then a galloping thump fills the room.

"There it is!" both the staff give small cheers.

Kendra exhales a sob, and I take my first full breath since we got here.

Leaning forward, with an elbow on my knee, I blow out another shaky breath. I kiss her palm and stand, wrapping my arms around her trembling body, then press my lips to her temple. "It's okay," I whisper, trying to soothe her. She nods but doesn't answer.

They pass me a paper towel, and I wipe the clear gel from her skin. While I'm doing that, the nurse hands her a plastic cup. "We're going to take a urine sample to check hormone levels, and then we're going to put in orders for an ultrasound to cover all our bases. Sometimes these things happen, other times there's a cause for the bleed, so this way we can know if there's anything else going on."

There's a shitstorm waiting for us when we exit those doors. I will make sure everything is secure with our jobs, but all I care about are the health and safety of my family. Because that's what Kendra is, she's my family. She needs to be healthy, and our baby needs to be healthy. Everything else can wait.

CHAPTER FORTY-FOUR

KENDRA

This scare has sent Sully into the deep end. I doubt he'll let me out of his sight until the baby is here. We stopped at my place to pack a bag, and now he's making me stay with him. Which is probably good because who the hell knows if I even have a job anymore.

I feel a lot better knowing our baby is healthy. Other than sending Rachel an update letting her know everything is okay, I've been avoiding every call that comes through my cell phone. Something I've never done in my life. His deep sofa swallows me up, and I'm wrapped up in a blanket and watching the fire crackle ahead of me. Sully hands me a cup of peppermint tea. I take a deep breath, hoping to calm my nerves.

He curls up next to me. "Whatever happens, happens. We'll figure it out. This mess is temporary, baby." I want to believe him, but this only ends badly. "I'm not giving up on us. You're it for me."

"They're going to fire me," I say, looking into the steaming mug. The show is toast. Sully's heart was in the right place, but he might as well have thrown a grenade on our careers. I'm not innocent in this either. I agreed to sneak around with him. For now, I'm thankful the baby is okay. I'm sure I'll wake up tomorrow and mourn the career I lost, but for now, I'm just thankful Bo is healthy and Sully cares enough to possibly destroy his own career or team sponsor for the sake of my safety.

What's done is done, and there's no coming back from it, so we might as well stick together.

"We don't know that."

I do. I know that. "This isn't one of those glass half-full situations, Sully. I'm going to be fired. My only hope is that my reputation isn't destroyed beyond repair. This will follow me for a long time."

"We can prove that you were pregnant before the show began."

I nod. "It doesn't matter. I'm the villain in this story."

"I'm so sorry, Kendra."

"We knew we were playing with fire. I just need to figure out how to do damage control." This was supposed to be my debut as a producer, and instead, I've sabotaged my entire career. I lost it. I'm so fucking tired of having to choose. Choose between a social life or success, career or family, independence or love. *These days, women can have it all ...* No we can't. Not really. One thing will always be forfeit for another to some degree. Sure, we've made progress, but it's not enough. Why do women have to make the sacrifices?

"I'm going to take a nap," I say.

"Kendra—"

"I'm fine, Sully." I smile. "I just need some time alone right now."

His eyes are full of sympathy. I can't sit around feeling sorry for myself; I'd rather rip the bandage off and figure out where I go from here. He takes the untouched tea from me, and I trudge over to his bedroom and shut the door.

I pull out my phone and click Pierce's name. I want to get this over with.

"Kendra," he answers.

"What do I do?"

He sighs on the other end. "Shit, I have no idea. I will help you as much as I can, but you gotta tell me everything."

So I do. I tell him everything.

CHAPTER FORTY-FIVE

SULLY

Our first game is away, in Boston, and it's the absolute worst time to leave Kendra. I feel like I blew up her world, then left her to clean up the mess. My lawyer is pissed. The organization is pissed. My PR team is pissed. Whit doesn't have to say anything for me to know he's disappointed—it blew up right after I told him nothing would get out.

They've buried four news stories. The players knew something was up when a different producer showed up instead of her. We still don't know what is happening with her job. She's basically been put on a suspension until they decide what to do.

With Whit's approval, I privately explained what happened. I figured if I'm pushing these women to bond as a team, maybe this could be a moment for them to bond with me. While initially disappointed, the team seems elated with the news of Kendra and me expecting a child. I've made it clear that it's not to be publicly discussed and any details relating to Kendra are to be kept under wraps. In exchange for their silence, I've agreed to let them throw her a baby shower.

Now that everyone is on the same page, I want them to stay focused. They've got enough to worry about with the season starting.

I have to prove to the Rogues they need me. Bring them a win and keep my career going forward. I'll still fight for this and for Kendra's job too, but tonight is about this team. We've already gone through the first game's fanfare. My team is back in the locker room, and I recognize the nerves in the players. After a deep breath, I focus my mind. I owe it to these women, who have been busting their asses to get here, to be present and on my game. Once we get home, I can start making phone calls, but tonight is for them.

"When you skate tonight, I want you to remember this is bigger than Boston. This is bigger than tonight's win or loss. Just by stepping out there, you are making a difference. And you did not work this hard and sacrifice this much to feel fear, so shake that shit off. Each one of you deserves to be here. This ground we stand on isn't ours, but that ice sure as hell is. Show the world why you fucking matter."

They've fought tooth and nail to play this game. I've never seen so much passion and drive from every single player. I'm so fucking proud of this team and what they've built. Jeanine glances up to me and nods her approval.

Quoting Shania Twain, Delta shouts, "Let's go, girls!"

I've come to learn that this phrase is the equivalent of "Avengers, Assemble!"

These women are ready.

CHAPTER FORTY-SIX

KENDRA

29 weeks pregnant

The words keep replaying in my head: *We've chosen to let you go.*

I was fired.

Sure, they gave me the option to tender my resignation and step down, which I did to salvage my reputation. If I went quietly, so would they. Pierce can tell me all day long that it's only because of this incident, it's not because of my work ethic or performance, but who the fuck cares when the end result is the same?

I pick up my phone to text Sully, then drop it. Shit, *the game*. I'll tell him when he returns from Boston. With a fresh box of desserts from Sugar and Ice, I plop myself on the couch and turn on the television to watch the game. It feels weird staying at his house when he's not here.

All I want to do is crawl into bed and sleep forever, but it's Sully's first game, and I can't miss it. When I turn it on, they show the players I've come to know over the past few months, and I'm not sure if it's the shitstorm of emotions brewing inside, but I bawl. There's a familiarity in them that I recognize in me. They fought like hell to get there, and they've spent their lives trying to prove themselves. To be good enough. And I'm so fucking proud of them.

Then they show Sully in the box yelling and pointing down the ice. It's not anger, though, it's him in his element. It's Sully coaching. I don't know if he was born to play or coach hockey more, but he was made for *this*.

About an hour after their win, my phone rings, and Sully's name pops up on the screen. I put a fake smile on my face, hoping he can hear it through the phone. I don't want him to worry.

"Hi! Oh my goodness, the team did incredible! How are you feeling?!"

His relaxed chuckle on the other end turns my smile less fake. "I'm feeling great. I'm so proud of them. They played like champions."

"They did! That save from Timber in the first period? Oh my God!"

"She's been working really hard and putting in the extra time. Her start tonight was earned … How are you feeling? I'm sorry I can't be with you right now."

I trace over the letters on one of my album covers. "That's okay, I'll see you tomorrow. I'm doing fine. Things are good. Just about to order a pizza and put on some tunes."

"Have you heard anything from Vault yet?"

"They didn't say much." It's not a lie. It was a short conversation.

"That's good, right?"

I shrug, even though he can't see me. "Maybe? Who knows. We can talk more tomorrow."

"Okay, I want you to take it easy until I get back. I know you're bored while we wait this out, but don't try to do any work. Got it?"

That shouldn't be a problem.

"Got it. Why don't you go out and celebrate with the team, enjoy your win."

He laughs. "Nah, I'm going back to my hotel to crash. I hardly slept last night. Besides, I've got a bunch of other stuff to take care of … I miss you. I wish I could be with you tonight."

That wouldn't be fun for him—I'm a mope, but having his arms around me would lessen the sting of today. "I miss you too." I swallow my feelings, then slide the record from the sleeve and place it on the turntable.

"I can't wait to come home. I need to immerse myself in that good Kendra energy for a bit." There's a hint of innuendo, and it gets a sincere chuckle out of me.

"Yeah, I suppose that would be all right."

"Better be …" he says. "I love you."

"Love you too."

After ending the call, I drop the needle onto my Tina Turner album and sprawl out on the rug like I used to do with my mom. Her melodic, raspy voice relaxes me as I think about her. Remembering her and how fun it was to lay on the floor and laugh, I hope I can make the same memories with our baby someday. My mom died too young, and she would have been a fantastic grandmother.

My career might be over, but I still have a responsibility to this baby and Sully. I refuse to lose anything more. They are all I have. Careers can be rebuilt, and our love will weather the storm. Maybe I'll look for a smaller production company this time, one with a focus on documentaries or independent films. Something I actually *want* to do. Besides, I probably won't be allowed in production of any reality projects. I wonder if it's pointless to try and find work before the baby is here. Maybe I should wait until Bo is born.

My phone rings, I glance at the screen and see Sully's name. I'm working through my feelings, and if I answer the phone, he'll hear right through my fake smile. I can't handle another conversation with him tonight, not without spilling my guts and telling him everything. It has to be an in-person conversation. I stare at the screen and watch it ring and ring and ring before it eventually goes to voicemail.

I glance at the ceiling, then close my eyes and take a deep breath. This isn't the end. Good things will come. They have to, because I need more. I need to be more than a mother. More than a girlfriend or wife. It's not enough. I want to grow, develop my skills, and work in filmmaking. I want to create.

My phone dings with a text message. It's Sully.

SULLY

I just got an email from my lawyer. You quit?? What is going on?

Damn. Looks like the cat is out of the bag. Great, now he's really going to go out of his mind. He calls again, I ignore it. I don't have the energy to discuss it.

SULLY

Kendra! Pick up the phone.

No thanks.

Who knows how long he'll keep doing this if I don't reply. Reluctantly, I pick up my phone and hold it above my face while I tap out a reply.

> I'm sorry I didn't tell you. I'm fine, but I don't want to talk about it tonight. Please? Tomorrow we can go over everything. It's going to be okay.

SULLY

> I will fix this.

> I'm okay, Sully. Really.

I'm not.
But I will be.

CHAPTER FORTY-SEVEN

SULLY

Staring out the plane's window, the state I call home comes into view. I'm so happy to be back and can't wait to get my arms around Kendra. After the email I received last night from my lawyer, it seems the network, MNSports, was "displeased" to hear about the show's termination. Which is code for really fucking pissed off. Thankfully, they've chosen to break their sponsorship contract for the inaugural year. In some ways, I'm glad Kendra is out of there. She shouldn't have to deal with the fallout of this.

I don't want her to worry about anything but being healthy and having this baby. This show has brought on way too much stress over these last few months. I have no problem with her working, hell, I encourage it if it makes her happy, but every time I had to look into her eyes while I sat across from another woman ... fuck, it gutted me.

The guilt has been eating me alive. Kendra said she quit, but I know she didn't leave by choice. She wouldn't go unless she was being forced to. This all happened because of me, I caused her to lose her dream job—so I will be the one to fix it. Which is why I'm Facebook stalking her friends list so I can contact Lance. Found him.

> Hey.

LANCE
Hey. I'm guessing you heard the news.

> I did. But there's an idea that's been rolling around in my head and I'd love to run it by you.

LANCE
Let's hear it.

> Any chance you can meet for coffee in fifteen minutes?

LANCE
Yeah. As of yesterday my schedule is wide open …

Well played. By the time we land in Minneapolis, I've got a plan. At least, a Plan *A*. If it doesn't work, I'll move to Plan B. Then Plan C. I'll go through the entire alphabet if I have to. I spoke with Kendra this morning, and hearing her voice was a punch to the gut. I hated that I couldn't be with her, and as soon as I finish meeting with Lance, I'm going straight to our place.

―――

MNSports is the network that Rogues wants for the sponsor, and lucky for me, I used to play with one of the NHL commentators. I've got a Hail Mary meeting with my lawyer, theirs, and the execs in three days, which gives me a short amount of time to meet with Lance and ask him for an enormous favor. I can't do this without him. As much as I want to rush home and see Kendra, I'm afraid to look her in the eye without having something in play.

Warm air and the scent of roasted coffee beans greet me when I enter the coffee shop. It's a welcome reprieve from the dipping outdoor temps, where the roads are being blanketed in big fluffy flakes. I stomp the snow off my shoes on the rug while I scan the room for Lance. He's already sitting at a table in the corner when I arrive. He lifts two fingers in the air, and I head in his direction. I was hoping to get here before him so I could buy his drink, but it took longer than expected to disembark from the plane.

I slide the chair out and sit across from him.

"Hey. Sorry I'm late."

"No worries. What's up?"

I take a deep breath and get into it. "First, thanks for meeting with me. Since we all know what went down the other day and secrets are out, I'm going to get straight to the point. You've been filming me for the last few months, I'm sure you've caught some of the moments with Kendra and I, right?"

"I mean, that's none of my business." He sighs. "We all love Kendra, myself included. You don't have to worry about me going to the press or talking about what happened."

I close my eyes and shake my head. He thinks I'm coming here to make sure he doesn't talk, so the rest of what I'm about to say may come as a shock to him.

"Forget that. How much footage do you have of us?"

"Shit, I don't know. It's a lot. But technically, the network owns the raw footage—"

"Do you think it's enough for a show?"

"Oh ... um ..." He rubs his jaw and raises his eyebrows.

"I'll pay double your rate to have you pull the footage and make me a sizzle reel, or whatever Kendra called it.

Something to pitch to the network, about Kendra and I meeting."

What Joey said the other day hit me, America just wants a love story. They want to root for somebody.

"You want a pitch tape." His eyes light up with recognition when he sees where I'm going with this. Kendra is my love story, so if that's what they want, then I'm ready to give it to them, but only if it's real. "Okay. Yeah … Yeah, I'm loving this idea, actually." He rubs his hand over his mouth and stares at the table, the wheels turning in his head. I'm so thankful he's on board.

"But Vault can't know about it. I don't want the show unless Kendra can do the storyline herself."

"How are you going to do that?"

"Still working on that side of things. But it's gotta stay quiet for now."

He nods. "I'll need to bring in an editor. You'd be pitching the show without a proof of concept, it has to be perfect. That's out of my wheelhouse."

"*Scoring with Sully* didn't have proof of concept, and they picked it up," I argue.

"Yeah, and then it bombed—no offense—so they're going to be extra cautious the second time around. I'm not going to sugarcoat it for you, man. It's going to be a hard win. And how are you planning on getting rights to the footage?"

"You still have access to the files, right?"

Lance sits back in his chair, crossing his arms. "Man …"

I dip my head and nod. I'm asking him to take a risk. "Look, I have a contact at MNSports. I'm meeting with the network in a few days, along with my lawyer to run it by them and see if I can pull some strings. But this can't get back to Pierce or Jeremy."

Lance takes a sip of his coffee. "There's a lot we can do

with editing, but it might take a little bit of time. How much can you give me?"

I wince. "Couple days?"

"Seriously? Okay. Let me go through some of the highlights tonight and see what I can come up with. Luckily, I've got a little extra time since they scrapped it."

I exhale a sigh of relief. "I owe you, man."

He chuckles. "You definitely do. I'll be sending you a bill. So will the other guys."

"Done."

CHAPTER FORTY-EIGHT

SULLY

Lance got the promo reel over to me less than an hour before my meeting with the network. Now I need to pitch it to MNSports and have them agree to it. Walking into that conference room feels like walking into the lion's den. The tension is palpable. It's awkward. They're disappointed in what happened, but deep down, I feel zero shame. I love Kendra. I'm happy I met her. Vault Productions on the other hand? Fuck 'em.

"I understand you want to get Kendra's job back, but it seems your motives are personal. There's a zero-tolerance policy for fraternization. We aren't going to be airing a scandal."

"Why … Because you think that will make people watch *less*?" I respond. One of the network reps clears their throat and passes a glance with another. I didn't major in marketing, but after being in the spotlight for most of my life, I know for damn sure a love child scandal is more exciting than any run-of-the-mill dating show. My lawyer's gaze burns into my temple. He tucks his phone away and places a relaxed palm on the black marble conference table. It's a signal for me to stand down. I take a deep breath, then continue.

"You've already paid for the footage, you can't pull your sponsorship until next season, so why not do something with what you have. It's better than whatever dating thing you're currently working with. The coach that fell for the producer of his own dating show? You want a story, this is a fucking story. Better than anything you're going to get with Vault."

The MNSports creative director waves a hand and shrugs. "Yeah, 'kay. Let's see the demo. Is it ready to play?" They're writing it off before they even see it. Fuck, this will be a hard win.

The room is quiet as the A/V assistant loads the media file that Lance put together. I only saw a snippet of it, so I'm counting on Lance and the editor he brought on to make it something the network will want.

My hands sweat when it begins. I don't know what these things are supposed to look like, but it seems solid. The guys did a good job from what I can tell.

One of the execs whispers to another while it plays. On the screen, there are small clips of me and Kendra. Little snippets of our hidden relationship. Snapshots of our affection that we've had to hide: the discreet touches, making her laugh at my jokes, moments I'm caught staring at her from across the room. It's like watching us fall in love from a distance. I can't wait to show this to her, hopefully soon.

There's a long-distance shot of me with her in the hallway when I've got her pinned against the wall. Shit, I didn't know that was going to be in here. I didn't even know that was captured. Three people at the conference table exchange glances. I don't know what it means. There's a lot of judgment coming down on me. They must have hired a voice actor to narrate the premise, which they nailed. The end of the reel features my mic'd up audio telling Jeremy I'm taking Kendra to the hospital. I never was good at working those mics, and this time, I'm glad for it. They had a lot more material than I thought. I would watch this.

The trailer ends, and the lights turn on again. It's quiet.

One of the ad execs rubs his chin. "This is ... something. Who put this together?"

I've got them. That's all I needed. I school my expression to not give away my excitement.

"A couple of contractors from the show." I'm not snitching.

"They've signed NDAs," my lawyer adds.

"And this is all real?" another woman asks.

I nod. "*Scoring with Sully* was about me finding love. I found it, but it wasn't orchestrated with a dating show."

"Why isn't Kendra here?"

I clear my throat. "She, uh, she doesn't know."

"What the fuck? You can't just offer a show featuring her as a main character and not get permission."

Shaking my head, I respond, "I *will* get permission. I just need to know that you would consider running this instead. It's a little different, but it's real. It's the true story."

The ad exec. from before chuckles. "It's scandalous, but damn, it's kinda wholesome too." The guy is wearing a big smile on his face; he's seeing dollar signs. "I say we run it up the ladder. I think it's got legs."

"It's worth a shot," another one agrees. "Dating show love affair between the producer and hero?"

It may have been hidden, but it wasn't an affair. It's always been Kendra. She's the one who insisted on it being secret, not me. "There's enough footage to make viewers fall in love with her. We're not letting her be the villain to the public. She's adorable. She's funny. Relatable and kind.

People will fall in love with her, but I need to know that Kendra gets the final say on everything. This is still her show. She'll be the one to construct and control the narrative."

One of their lawyers speaks up. "If we take the show, we aren't paying extra. We already paid Vault. We have the footage, we're not footing the bill for a show we already paid for."

"We know you've already cut ties with Vault. We ask that you allocate the editing fees to cover final production," my lawyer cuts in. I'll fund this shit myself if I have to. "And if the show meets or exceeds the profit margins you anticipated for *Scoring with Sully*, you stay on as the Rogues sponsor and honor the contract previously in place."

"That's going to be another discussion," their lawyer responds.

"How long is it?" one of the executives asks.

"I'm told there's enough to fill the season," I answer. My knee bounces under the table. "We can start it like the dating show and transition into what really happened by adding more and more of Kendra."

The creative director smiles at another exec. "Almost like a behind-the-scenes ..."

"We can market it as *real* reality tv, not manufactured like other networks." My lawyer and I watch carefully as they discuss pros and cons in front of us. It's sounding positive, so I keep my lips sealed.

One of the women nods and turns to me. "Get her to agree, and then let's talk more ... Who else knows about this?"

"A couple of cameramen and the editor. I think an assistant was involved too."

"We'll want whoever had part in making this demo."

"I'll get them," I assure. They're contractors. I'll do whatever it takes.

Off to the side, one of the network liaisons mutters to the creative director, "Jeremy is gonna throw a fucking fit."

They scoff and reply with "Any way we can get tickets to that show?"

"So, what are the next steps?" I ask.

"Next steps are getting Kendra on board. We can't do anything until we get her to sign off on it."

CHAPTER FORTY-NINE

KENDRA

30 weeks pregnant

"Where are we going?" I ask, tapping my fingers on my thighs in the passenger seat. This isn't the normal route he takes to the grocery store.

"You're running errands with me," he says, flashing a grin.

We must be stopping somewhere else first. I relax in my seat and trace his features with my gaze. Damn, he's handsome. My staring is interrupted when he parks in front of a record store. My *favorite* record store.

"Sully." I look at him. "You don't have to keep doing this stuff. I'm doing okay, really." I believe it. The more I've sat and thought about it, the more I see this as a way to challenge myself to take the next step. Like when a wildfire ravages a forest. It's devastating but necessary for new growth. That's what this is. Devastating but necessary.

"I know I don't. I want to."

I shake my head with a smile. "Well, since we're here ..." I pop the handle on the passenger door.

"That's my girl."

Sully runs around the front of the car to help me out. I accept the help because even though I'm not waddling yet, I'll take any excuse for him to touch me. He holds the door to the shop open for me. "This reminds me of Florida," I say.

He looks behind us, to the cold city street with small snow piles along the edge.

"What?" His brow furrows and I laugh.

"Not the weather, just ... this. Being together without it being some big secret, ya know? It's nice." It's the silver lining to all this. I get Sully to myself. I don't have to share him with other unsuspecting women. He's mine in record shops and grocery stores, not just private residence rendezvous. I walk toward the rows of brown cardboard boxes housing the used albums, with his hand in mine.

"Wow. Yeah. Guess that means I get to do things like this, then, huh?" He retracts his arm, tucks me into his chest, and kisses me as if he just came home from war. His palm cradles my neck as he licks the seam of my lips, and I automatically open up for him. I can't breathe or think. It's pure manipulation when he nips at my lower lip. Finally, I remember we're in public and laugh, concealing my blushing cheeks against his chest. This man's mouth makes me dizzy.

"No, you can't kiss me like that in public." I laugh nervously. "It's indecent!"

He presses his lips to the top of my head and mutters, "Most of my thoughts about you are."

I shake my head at his boldness, then grab his hand and drag him along. "Come on, buy me some new music."

We flip through the selection. I'm looking to add more rock to my collection.

"Shit, I forgot to ask you, do you think you can get me seats behind the bench for Thursday's game?" I love watching him coach.

"You don't want to sit in the box? It's comfy up there."

I roll my eyes. "Hell no, I want to be by all the action." Seeing him all focused and yelling like that turns me on like no other. I shiver just thinking about it. My man is a Norwegian god, seeing him all authoritative and commanding in a fitted suit—at six-foot-five—is the hottest foreplay. Good lord.

He chuckles. "Yeah, I think I can hook you up … it's going to cost you though."

Resting a hand on my hip, I raise one eyebrow at him.

"You heard me," he says, doubling down. "Payment due up front."

My teeth dig into my lower lip as I resist squeezing my thighs together. What a hardship that will be … I love the way his eyes roam over my body. Having my body change shape hasn't deterred him, if anything he's become more attracted to me. He's insatiable. If this playful happiness is what I get in exchange for losing my job, then I'll get fired a hundred more times. He's worth it.

I return to perusing the albums until I come across a winner. "Oooh! Lou Reed! Can I get this one?"

"Whatever you want, baby girl."

———

Sully has been spoiling me rotten since he got home from Boston. Most of that afternoon was spent talking and ended with his face between my thighs. Besides that part, nothing has made me forget I no longer have a job, but the distraction of all his other methods of treating me definitely helps.

Today, he picked me up from my lovely prenatal massage, and I left feeling so relaxed and cozy I practically collapsed onto the sofa when we got back home. He's nestled in beside me. One thing I love about Sully is that he always naps with me when I'm tired. We've perfected our spot on the couch together. I never sleep as soundly as I do when I'm in his arms. The fireplace crackles across the room as the speakers croon out John Coltrane.

Sully's chest evenly rises and falls, telling me we're both on the edge of sleep, then my phone rings. We jerk in surprise. I feel terrible that it interrupted the nap he desperately needs after all the games, practices, and traveling he's been doing.

"Shit, I'm sorry!" I grab it quickly, hoping to silence it when I see Pierce's name on the screen. "Oh …"

I swipe my finger across the screen to answer. It's probably some offboarding paperwork that needs signing or something.

"Hello?" My brow furrows.

"Hey! How are you doing?"

I swallow. "I'm all right."

"I've got some good news. I've been talking with the team, they are willing to bring you back on."

"They want to give me my job back?" I sit up and glance at Sully who furrows his brow.

Pierces continues. "So, that's the thing, you couldn't be a producer, but we could make that a probationary thing. You could work your way up again, maybe in a year or hell, maybe even a few months, you could take part in another show."

"Oh …" My heart sinks. "So I'd be, what, a PA?"

"Hang up the phone, Kendra," Sully says softly. I crane my neck to look at him. He shakes his head beside me. "No."

"Yeah, executive PA." Pierce continues. "You would still keep some of your same tasks as before though. We could give you more responsibilities."

"For less pay, I assume."

He sighs on the other end. "Unfortunately, yes. But it's something, for now. The studio knows you're an asset."

I nod. Sully pinches my thigh to get my attention, and I'm torn on what to do. I had come to terms with them letting me go. I accepted it, but if they're willing to give me another shot, it would be nice to have something locked in before the baby is born. That means no break on my resumé, and if they hired me back, I could someday use them as a reference again. Maybe after a couple years?

"Can I think about it?" I ask.

"Of course, but don't take too long. I would hate for somebody to change their mind and have the window of opportunity close on us."

"Okay … okay. I'll get back to you soon. Thanks, Pierce. I appreciate it."

"You bet. It would be great to have you back. Take care, okay?"

"You too."

I end the call and turn to Sully. "They want to hire me back," I say with a smile—one he doesn't return. "What's wrong?"

"Don't take it."

"Sully, this could be really great for me. It would get me in with a studio. I don't know if I'll be able to find a new production house that will take me before the baby is born."

He sits up and takes my hands in his. "I was going to wait until dinner to bring it up, but …"

What does he have to say? I'm getting nervous. "But what?" I ask, my voice is high pitched with anxiety.

"I've been talking with MNSports."

"What? Why?" Did he get in trouble? This is news to me.

"They own the rights to the raw footage that Vault shot."

I know this already. "Get to the point, Sully."

"I think you should start your own production company?"

"Huh?" In a flash, I'm on my feet. "But what about the network, finish telling me what's going on. Why have you been meeting with them?"

He smiles, and it gives me an inkling of relief, but I'm still confused. "Don't be mad … but I met with Lance after I landed earlier this week to find out how much they had of us. I want them to do the show, but it needs to be real, to be our story. I had him put together a promo reel thing—with footage of us. He had one of the editing guys help him, and it was beautiful, Kendra. I met with MNSports a few days later and they took the bait. I think they're all in. You just have to sign off on it. They want to meet with you."

Holy shit.

"But here's the best part, you would get to produce it. Fuck Vault and their bullshit offer, start your own production company. You can pick your own team of people. We can start hiring contractors. I'm sure a bunch of your colleagues would jump at the opportunity to work with you again. People love you, it's why they want you back so bad … But they don't deserve you—they fucked up and they know it. Please, Kendra, don't take a step backward when you're capable of doing so much more. You were born to do this, you're a creator. You can knock this project out of the park."

"And they would continue to sponsor the Rogues?" I ask. I want to make sure this would save the team's sponsorship.

He nods. "But even if they didn't, it wouldn't change anything. This is a great opportunity for you to spread your wings. We can even take more footage, all decisions are up to you. We pitched it to show some of the dating show in the beginning, but as the show progresses, you can see all of our little moments and you can see something develop between us. It's a love story among chaos. But it's your footage. You can do whatever you want with it."

By the time he finishes, I've got tears streaming down my face. This is unbelievable. "You did all this? What if they would have said no?"

"I would have figured out something else ... This is my apology to you. Not once did you give up on me after Vault let you go. You didn't blame me when you had every right to."

I could never put that on his shoulders, it would have crushed him, and I love Sully far too much to ever hurt him. No matter how upset I was. Deep down, I knew how that story would end. I knew the consequences, but my need for him was too great to say no. "Sully, we were both playing a dangerous game, baby. That responsibility doesn't fall on you."

He takes a long look at the ceiling, shakes his head, then kisses me. "You are the most incredible woman ... and you're great at what you do. There is no one else I would want in charge of documenting the Rogues, my career, and us."

I nod. This is our love story. It's messy but it's ours.

"And after this project is done, you can get started on the list of projects you told me about at the hotel."

Time stands still, a weightless sensation comes over me. Am I dreaming?

"So ... what do you think?" he asks.

This is huge. I can't believe he did this for me. This is my dream. I'm unable to speak because I'm holding back a sob, so I nod profusely against him. "Oh, and yes," I say with choked laughter. "Let's do it."

"Hell yeah …" He kisses my temple and rubs a hand up and down my back. "You are going to nail it."

I inhale and let it out slowly before swallowing the lump of emotion clogging my throat. "I can't believe this," I say, my shoulders shaking.

"Deep breaths." He chuckles. "I'll take care of MNSports and let them know you're in, and we can get a meeting set up. Now all you need to do is figure out what demeanor you want to use when you tell Vault to pound sand."

I laugh, and another wave of happiness rolls over me. "Oh my God!" I squeal with a huge smile. "Sully, I have my own project!"

This is the best day of my life.

I kneel on the sofa in front of him so we're eye level. "I'm so happy."

"Me too." His smile is so gorgeous. It reminds me of the first night we met.

"I love you."

I've never smiled so big in my life. "I love you too."

He cups my face in his massive palms and kisses me, and I know he's telling me the truth because I feel his love in it, and I accept it, giving him all of me in return.

"Do you have the reel? Can I see it?"

He nods and digs out his phone, tapping the screen. We settle into the sofa again, with me between his legs resting my back against his chest. My heart is soaring. He holds the screen in front of me and taps the button, starting a video.

I stare in awe as it plays through. Oh my God, I'm watching us fall in love. It's the best footage ever. It's real and honest and raw. The feelings shared between us on camera are subtle yet, under the context, so loud. You can see everything in our eyes and the way we look at each other.

Sully drops his mouth to my ear. "I love you so much, baby."

I bring my hand behind his neck again and smile. "This is so beautiful … It's us." I can't believe how much of us was caught on film. It's almost as if Lance and the guys knew I'd want this someday.

"You'll still be the producer and work with editing to go through footage. You control the narrative. Regardless of what this trailer shows, it's still your show, Kendra."

Once it plays through, he shows me some bonus footage that Lance sent over just in case they needed extra persuasion. Some of it shows me behind the scenes. I've never watched myself do my job before. My brain is already reeling with ideas. It's an amazing project.

It's perfect, and I can't wait to get started.

CHAPTER FIFTY

SULLY

Kendra has hit the thirty-four weeks and is more gorgeous than ever as we walk toward Joey's place. When I agreed to let the team throw a baby shower for Kendra, it was under the condition I could supervise. After that dick-sucking conversation, I'm not going to abandon her with these feral women. And if the twenty-four inch vagina piñata is any indication, I'd say I made the right call. *What in the actual fuck?*

The entire team is here, along with some of the Lakes wives and girlfriends. It's cramped in Joey's apartment; I can't believe the team let her host. This looks more like a bachelorette party than a baby shower.

"If you feel uncomfortable and want to leave—at any time—just blink twice."

She chuckles, placing her hand on my forearm. "I'm fine, Sully. Why don't you go find a beer and take a seat on the couch? I'm going to see if there's anything I can help with."

Kendra heads into the crowd, and I stand awkwardly off to the side. Then Raleigh walks in. She freezes, and her eyebrows practically hit her hairline as she takes in the room.

Yeah, my sentiments exactly. She fixes her gaze on the wall, and I follow the line of sight to a giant art print of some gory crimson blob. It looks like it belongs in some cheap house of horror production. *Okay, seriously, where is Joey?*

Being the tallest in the room aids me in spotting the host in the kitchen. I call out to her from across the room. "Joey!" I raise my arm and point to the big red thing. "*What the fuck is that?*" I mouth.

"Huh?" She cocks her head to the side, then sees what I'm referencing. "Oh!" She holds up a bag of Ping-Pong balls. "Pin the ovum on the uterine lining!"

You've got to be shitting me. Kendra laughs.

"Do you mind setting them up over there?" Joey shakes the bag at me. I make my way over to her and snatch the bag from her hand. Raleigh has followed me into the kitchen, and she stands in front of Micky, who's pouring ... shots?

"Seriously?" Raleigh asks. "She's pregnant."

"Don't worry, we made a nonalcoholic version," Joey says, transferring a bag of chips to a decorative bowl.

"Yeah, I don't care about that part, why do they *look* like *that*?" Raleigh says with a grimace.

"They're placenta shots!"

I audibly gag. "Unreal."

Micky's eyes light up. "I know, right!? Joey did a phenomenal job. No notes."

"Aww! Thank you!" Joey accepts the compliment and smiles with satisfaction.

Raleigh and I share a look filled with equal confusion and concern. Of course Micky would say that. She's probably mentoring Joey. It's sweet the girls wanted to throw Kendra a shower, this is just very ... unexpected.

I take the bag of balls and head toward the wall of gore. Raleigh follows behind me, still holding a big pastel gift bag in her arms. We don't exchange words, just look on at the chaos unfolding in front of us. After a moment, she says, "I think it's a fair assessment to say Joey Breck has never attended a baby shower."

"What gave it away?"

"The chocolate cupcakes were lactating."

"Christ." *If Joey ruins my new kink, I will be pissed.* "It was the crowning cheese ball for me."

After watching the women play the most demented baby shower games I've ever seen, it's time for her to open gifts. It's a welcome reprieve. I almost had to leave when they were sucking on ice cubes that contained little plastic babies. The discussion over who had the best oral skills was disturbing—worse than the fellatio conversation at the arena. I've heard things a head coach should never have to hear. Kendra doesn't seem affected by the unhinged baby shower. She's taking it all in stride, like everything she does. She's full of beauty and grace as she accepts each gift. I've never seen a woman glow the way she does. Pregnancy looks phenomenal on her. I'm hoping to see her like this again the future.

"Where did you find a vagina piñata?" Micky asks Joey while the rest of the party oohs and ahhs over one of the new Rogues onesies that reads "Future Rogues Player."

"I think the better question is *why*?" I ask.

Joey smiles, watching Kendra open another gift, then through her tight smile, whispers, "Because Kendra's vagina is about to be wrecked, just like this piñata when we bust it open."

"Joey …" I respond calmly without looking at her. "You are going to skate so many laps at Tuesday's practice they'll have to pay the Zamboni driver overtime just to clear your tracks."

She has the audacity to look surprised. "What!"

"Don't."

"Yes, Coach." She takes a drink from her beer bottle, muttering, "Buzzkill."

God, I can't believe we drafted someone who thinks pacifier beer pong is a good idea for a baby shower. Even more disturbing was the strawberry-flavored nipple butter she apparently thought was for breastfeeding. I'm not saying it won't get used, but ... damn.

I sit back and enjoy the rest of the show. If Kendra is happy, that's all that matters, but if there's one thing I've learned today, the Rogues know how to go rogue.

CHAPTER FIFTY-ONE

KENDRA

36 weeks pregnant

Sully has been throwing slapshots into the basement hockey net while I finish ordering the last of the items we need. As soon as I submit the last order of diapers, his phone rings, and he spins in a circle on his skates while pulling his phone from his pocket.

"Hey Nick."

That's his lawyer. We've been waiting for a call back.

I slowly close the laptop and sit on the edge of my chair as I listen. The inflection of Sully's voice gives nothing away. I wait patiently, but I'm dying to know what Nick is saying.

He chuckles. *That's a good sign, right?* Then his face sobers. "Yeah, I understand." *Shit, maybe not?*

"Okay, yeah, send it over and I'll take a look." I swallow and stand up. "Yup ... Thanks, Nick."

He ends the call and stuffs the phone in his pocket. I place my hands over my cheeks while I wait for him to say something.

"They wanna do it."

I jump. "Ohmigod! Are you serious?!" I squeal loud enough for the movers upstairs to hear me. He smiles big. "You got the show, baby. He's submitting contracts now."

He steps off the ice and wraps me in his arms. "You're about to be very busy."

"Holy shit!" I giggle. "Sully, I don't know how to ever thank you for doing this."

"I can think of several ways."

CHAPTER FIFTY-TWO

KENDRA

38 weeks pregnant

"Celly Kapowski!!" Delta shouts, slapping Cori on the back when she gets to the bench after a goal.

Cori leans forward, rinses her mouth with water, and sits up again to survey the game. "Twenty-three has a weak spot on the left," she says to the other women, panting.

Sully paces behind the bench. It might as well be porn. Good fucking grief. This is *my* man? *Mine?* Good for me. Maybe it's the hormones, but there's no way I won't jump him the second there isn't a panel of plexiglass between us. I'm supposed to be watching the game, I keep telling myself this, but it's Lee Sullivan. *Whew.*

I cross my thighs, wearing a tight dress that shows off my bump. It's one he loves, though this time with a cute Rogues jacket over top. Sully made sure to outfit me in enough gear, but unfortunately, the jerseys keep riding up my belly. Besides, I like the jacket the team gave me, it's special.

The team is playing like a well-oiled machine.

COACH SULLY

Surrounding me are some of the Lakes WAGs, and their husbands are with them. It's fun being the coach's girlfriend. Normally, I'm in the private box, but every so often, I want to experience the action up close. Besides, the crowd is great. There's so much positivity, more than I've seen at any other hockey game. The rest of our group agrees, it's a different energy.

There's another Lakes player in attendance with us, Shep Wilder. He's yelling as much as the rest of them, though I've noticed he's loudest when it comes to Cori Kapowski.

He smacks the plexiglass behind her. "Atta girl, Cor!" he yells over the fans.

"Can she hear you?" I ask.

"She hears me, but she's not going to turn around. Cori's a pro." He doesn't seem to care about her acknowledgment. He simply continues to cheer loud enough for her to hear through the glass. He talks about her like he knows her well. They must be friends or something off the ice. I don't get to ask because he's back to yelling her name when she jumps on the ice again at shift change.

I wait with our group near the locker room exit. My back is aching more than usual tonight. Week thirty-eight is tearing at every muscle I have. I can't wait to see my man and get him home. Tonight calls for one of his back rubs. The second he walks out, I want to melt into the concrete floor. His cologne, the suit … I've been watching him all night, and finally, he's close enough to touch.

He shakes hands with a few of the players' families before getting to me.

"Congratulations on the win!" I say, pressing my hands to

the lapels of his suit. He looks down at me with a frown. "Hey, I've got to run to my office and grab some paperwork, do you want to join me?"

Oh. Kinda was hoping for a kiss, or some enthusiasm? It's fine. He's got to stay professional and is probably exhausted. It's not like he's getting all the horny hormones I am.

I nod and paste a big smile on my face. "Of course!"

We take a private elevator to the administrative floor.

He stares at me in the elevator, fists tucked in his pockets, looking stressed out.

"Everyone is going to Top Shelf to celebrate after this," I say. "I told them we would join."

He nods. "Yeah."

The door opens, and I follow quietly behind. Did something happen? He's distracted and almost distant. It's not like Sully. They just won their seventh home game, making them undefeated at home, and I can't imagine what would cause him to suddenly be so serious. Is it because the due date is only a couple weeks away? The nursery was finished last week, and we're stocked, fully prepared. I even have our hospital bag packed in the car, right next to the carseat Sully installed.

We turn a corner, the hallway is partially lit, and one or two offices at the end have lights on.

"Here," he says, walking into the dark office. It's been a long time since I've been here. It's backlit by the window that opens into the arena. Bright lights make the ice glow, and fans are still filtering out of tonight's sold-out arena. I'm sure the music is still playing out there, but here, it's eerily quiet. Hard to believe this quiet office is connected to an arena full of screaming fans below.

The silence between us is awkward, so I say the most

obvious thing in the world. "It's been a while since I've seen your offi—"

My words are cut off as Sully yanks me the rest of the way inside the dark room, slams the door, and pins me against it. *Ohmygod.* "Whoa! What—"

"This fucking dress has been driving me out of my mind all night," he growls. The door clicks, I glance down and find him locking it. "Take it off."

"What?" It takes a moment for his words to register, then I smile. *This* is the man I was expecting to see outside the lockers. I pry my fingers off the cold, smooth door to frame his face, and I nip at his bottom lip. He flips on the light switch and lowers his eyes to meet mine. I love it when he does this.

"Kendra, if that dress isn't around your ankles in two seconds, I'll lose my shit."

"Jesus, be patient," I say, laughing.

He loosens his tie, and I shrug off my jacket. My arms slip from the dress straps, and I shove it down until it lands on the floor. Drawing up a knee, I remove the tennis shoes. No way I'm wearing heels this late in the trimester.

He grabs under my ass and picks me up, careful not to squish the bump between us, and sets me on my feet facing the arena.

"Hands on the glass," he says as he fists the back of my thong and rips it down my legs. "Bend over, baby girl."

The anticipation burns through me, climbing up my legs and pooling in my stomach.

"Yes, Daddy."

"That's my good girl." I close my eyes. This man knows all the right things to say.

Behind me, he grips my ass and spreads my cheeks.

Before I know it, his tongue is all over me as he feasts on me from behind.

I cry out, unprepared for the onslaught of pleasure, and bend over farther, pressing my chest to the frigid window, and my nipples harden.

"Sully!"

"That's it, push your pretty tits against the glass for everybody to see."

I gasp. "Can they see us?" I pant out.

"It's tinted … A little."

He tugs my clit between his lips, then cracks a palm across my ass. "*Oh, fuck!*" I whisper. He spits on my pussy, and the noise makes me groan. It's such a filthy sound and gets me every time. Not a second later, he unzips, and before I know it, he's slapping my clit with his cock. My legs are shaking with need.

"I want to feel full."

The head of his dick slicks over me, then pauses at my entrance. He tilts me forward, forcing my elbows to rest on the window ledge when he drives inside. I moan a low sound. "More!"

"This body has been torturing me for hours … Now, be a good girl and take it all." Pulling out, he plunges deep inside, leaving no room to spare. Absolute bliss.

I swallow. "I didn't know you saw me," I say shakily.

"Of course I saw you, I just couldn't focus on you because all I could picture was this … you bent over and taking every inch in your pussy while you watch the fans below." A hand reaches around, and he gropes one of my breasts. "Wondering if anyone is going to look up and see these perfect, full tits against my window. I want everybody to know you're getting railed in my office."

I groan at his words.

"You're going to make such a pretty coach's wife. Everybody already loves you—me most of all."

My heart explodes when I think of our forever.

His wife. I pinch my eyes shut as my orgasm builds. He called me his *wife.*

Sully withdraws and spins me around, picking me up and dropping me on his dick. Leaning back, I brace my arms on the window frame so as to not put pressure on my belly. The way he stuffs me is almost too much. My jaw drops, and he presses his forehead to mine as if the word *wife* is painted across my face. "That's right, baby girl."

Our gazes burn together as he bounces me up and down on him. Everything is so intense. My walls tighten around him, and I know it's about to hit.

"Let Daddy feel you come on his cock …" He smirks at me and nods. "Come for me."

And I do. I cry out with my fingers digging into his muscles.

"Just like that."

With my back to the cold window, the pressure is taken off my arms. He bangs a fist on the glass behind me as his thrusts become more erratic. I gaze up into his fierce eyes.

"Mine," he growls. It's all he says before his climax takes over. I love watching this man come. Seeing his possessive expression fracture into a million pieces is a look that only I will ever know. No other woman has that part of him. He reserves it for me alone. It's mine as much as he is, and I'll never have to share him again.

Suddenly, I feel a warm gush of water.

"Fuck, baby! I love it when you squirt."

This isn't an orgasm.

"No, I'm—I'm not—Oh my god, I think my water just broke."

Sully steps back, and we stare at the pool of water soaking into the floor between us.

"It's too early. I'm only thirty-eight weeks," I mumble.

He takes a deep breath. "Sweetheart, I think Bo is coming early. The emergency bag is still in your car, right?"

I nod, unable to look away from the floor.

"Everything is going to be okay. Let's get you dressed." He grabs my dress, which is thankfully dry, and efficiently drags it over my body as I stand there like a statue. We've attended the classes, read the books, but still nothing has prepared me for the moment of it actually happening. I'm in labor.

"Sully, I'm scared."

He extracts my hair from the back of the dress and slides my jacket over my arms, then cups my face. "Kendra, baby. You are the strongest woman I know. If anyone can do this, it's you. Even if Bo decided to get the drop on us, your body knows what to do. I will be at your side every step of the way. You're not alone."

I exhale. He's right. I'm not alone anymore. I have him. I trust him.

"Remember how we practiced visualizations? Right now, I only want you to think about meeting our baby for the first time. I'll take care of the rest."

I nod, exhaling a slow breath. "I love you."

"I love you too. Time to go."

CHAPTER FIFTY-THREE

SULLY

"It's a girl!" the doctor announces proudly at 8:14 a.m.

A wail rips from Kendra's throat as she collapses back on the inclined hospital bed, and a nurse places our daughter on Kendra's bare chest, covering them both with a pink, blue, and white striped blanket. She's exhausted after spending the last ninety-six minutes pushing. I thought I knew Kendra's strength, but it was only the tip of the iceberg. She's a force of nature. Watching her bring life into this world has me falling even more in love with her.

I'm hypnotized as I take in the mother of my child holding our newborn daughter, who calms as soon as she's placed against Kendra's chest. I've never felt more whole. Hockey has nothing on this. With glassy eyes, Kendra takes my hand and pulls me close. I choke down the lump in my throat and wrap my arms around both of them.

"You're incredible, baby." I press my lips to her forehead. "I'm so proud of you."

Her hand squeezes mine.

"She's so beautiful," she whispers. "I can't believe how beautiful she is."

"Of course she's beautiful, have you seen her mom?"

She smiles with shining eyes. "You and I both know that the last 3D ultrasound photo made her look like a lasagna." She laughs through a sob. "It was a fifty-fifty shot whether we were having a baby or a Stouffer's dinner. I had no idea what was going to come out."

Planting a second kiss to her temple, my shoulders tremble with laughter.

"She looks like you," Kendra says, glancing up at me, then back to our precious baby. "You put me through all that nausea and exhaustion and have the audacity to come out looking like your daddy."

"Those eyes are all yours," I say.

Kendra runs the tip of her finger gently down the center of her tiny nose.

"They remind me of my mom's," she says. "I kind of want to keep the name Bo."

"She'll always be Bo to me." Calling her by any other name would feel weird.

She nods. "Bo Shiloh?"

"Bo Shiloh Ames?" I ask.

"Don't be ridiculous, Sully. Bo Shiloh Sullivan."

My heart clenches. "I love it."

Ever since feeling those little kicks, and now seeing her with our child, our relationship has shifted. Kendra is more than just my girl, more than my future wife, she's the mother of my child—someday children—and there's something profoundly soul-stirring about that. It strengthens our relationship and the bond we share. I always wanted a partner, someone who walks at my side, not behind. My equal. I've never known a love like this.

This is an adventure we'll be on for the rest of our lives, and I can't imagine a better person to do that with.

EPILOGUE

SULLY

8 Weeks Later

Leaning on the doorjamb of the nursery, I stay silent watching Kendra snuggle Bo in her arms while Tina Turner plays softly in the background. The light is low, and it's warm in the room. She glances up and smiles big. I can't believe I get to come home to this every day. This is our home, a place where we will grow and make memories. Kendra and Bo brighten the space, both metaphorically and materially. They are my home.

"My girls," I say.

"She's out like a light," Kendra whispers. I take our daughter into my arms.

I hear the noise before I can stop it, and spit-up covers my suit jacket.

"Aww, look, it's her overwhelming happiness that you're her father!" Kendra coos.

"I'm sure she'll change her tune when she's a teenager."

"She better change her tune within the next four months. Our laundry is seriously out of hand." Miraculously, Bo got none on her onesie—lucky me. She's looking much more comfortable now, and I'm able to gently place her into the crib while Kendra stands and helps me slip off my blazer.

"Is this a bad time to mention I brought home Mexican? It's on the counter."

"Oooh!" Kendra does her little food dance. "Si, papi. I'm going to rinse this off and get it set aside for dry cleaning."

"Thanks, baby."

My fingers brush over Bo's forehead. I could stare at our child for hours. Sometimes I do. Seeing our shared features in the most beautiful baby I've ever seen makes my chest fill with warmth. I give myself a few minutes to stare in wonder at how Bo brought us together much sooner than expected. I always knew I would end up with Kendra, but I'm so glad I didn't miss out on this time together.

"Thank you," I whisper.

Kendra appears behind me and rests her palm on my back. I lean in to give Bo a kiss and then reach around to squeeze Kendra's hand. I have the family I've always dreamed of.

"How was your day today?" she asks as we slink out of the nursery and close the door, leaving it open a small crack.

"Good. The team says they want you to bring Bo by sometime this week." They get to see all the photos Kendra and I share with them, but every player on the team is eager to hold the first Rogues baby.

She chuckles. "I'd love to … but final edits aren't finished on episode four. I'm going to be swamped this week, which means …."

I like the sound of that. Kendra bites her bottom lip and gives me those enchanting light-gray eyes.

The corner of my mouth tips up in a half smile. "What do you need, baby girl?"

"A distraction?"

She's been asking for "distractions" more and more since her sex drive has returned after having Bo. She can't get enough, and neither can I.

"Now?"

"It's been too long since I've felt like myself ... Daddy."

Her eyes find mine, and she nods. I've been waiting to hear that word from her. The one that tells me she's ready for me to take control. We had sex as soon as the doctor gave us the all-clear, but it's been gentle up until now. We've been taking it slow, but she's ready for more.

"Tell me what you want." My jaw clenches at her blinking up at me. She's got the look in her eye I've been craving. The last time I was rough with her was in my office, the night she went into labor.

"I want my daddy."

I can't stop the smile from spreading across my face.

"Take off your clothes." My smile fades as I take a serious tone with her. If she wants to play this game, we will play. "Now."

She raises her eyebrows while her fingers work the waistband of her pants.

"Okay, then."

I grab her chin. "What was that?"

I've gone way too long without seeing that mischievous, sexy grin she's giving me.

"Yes, Daddy."

She shimmies out of her pants, and I reach around to grab a handful of her ass, then slap it. "Good girl." After peeling off her shirt, she turns around, and I brush her hair to the side, giving me access to unclasp her bra. It falls from her shoulders and onto the floor. She bends over to remove her socks, and I slide my hand up her spine, gripping her neck. I want to take her right here in the hallway. She tugs off her socks and stands upright, I snake my fingers to the front of her neck and pull her into my chest. As she rubs her backside against my thigh, I feel up her cheeks, then administer a swat to her ass.

"Bed."

I lean my shoulder against the wall and enjoy the sway of her ass as she saunters to our bedroom, then disappears through the doorway. With blood rushing to my cock, I shove off the wall and follow. When I turn the corner into our room, she's crawling onto the bed, giving me the perfect view of her pussy before she makes herself comfortable, cushioned by pillows and looking every bit the angel she is, then she does something I don't expect.

"Watch," Kendra says, massaging her breasts with her palms, and I smile. Nothing is hotter than seeing this woman take her own pleasure.

"Should I pull up a chair?" I tease.

"Just watch ..." Her eyes are focused. So are mine. I love the sight of her. My cock twitches as I observe her movements. God, she's gorgeous. Kendra adjusts her fingers and gropes again, and this time, the tips bead with milk. *Holy hell.* I haven't touched a drop of her breastmilk, but that doesn't mean I haven't thought about it.

"How long ago?" I don't know when she last nursed, and I'm not about to steal my kid's next meal.

"We've got time."

A drop of milk drips down the underside of her breast, and I groan. It's what I've been waiting for. She parts her thighs, and my hands move to unbuckle my belt. A slow smile creeps onto her face. She knows it drives me crazy, and her eyes are daring me to do something about it.

I will.

I shuck off my pants and unbutton my dress shirt, letting

it fall off my shoulders. I crawl over her, my cock heavy and eager. While cupping her chin, she looks up at me, seeming pleased with herself.

"Are you going to be good for Daddy?" I ask.

Her silver eyes are filled with mirth, and I love her for it.

Seated between her open legs, I get situated, resting my length on her clit. Covering her hands with my own, I guide them up to her breasts again and massage until another bead of milk forms on the tips. With my eyes locked on hers, I dip down and lick her nipple. Holy fuck. The taste explodes on my tongue like honey. She tastes like sugar-coated candy.

My dick hardens even more, and she rolls her hips against me. "That's it, baby girl." I kiss up her breasts and find her neck, biting and sucking. Her small cries fill my ears, and I grind against her. With her hands between us, she continues to knead, and I sit up to watch. As soon as those beads form again, she drags her darkened nipples across my lips, painting them with milk.

"Fuck," I groan, sucking her finger into my mouth. I slurp the breastmilk and spit it on my cock. Then, with my length notched at her entrance, I thrust forward and sink inside the sweetest pussy I've ever known. Leaning forward once again, I suck her hard peak between my lips until I taste her on my tongue. Her legs part wider, giving me more room to work, and I force her to take every inch of me.

"Oh my god," she groans. It's hard not to smile at that, especially when she reaches overhead to use the headboard as leverage to fuck herself on my length. I'll allow her to take what she needs for now.

With my head cocked to the side, I revel in the sight of her rocking against me. The way she showcases her body has me teetering on the edge. "You're doing so well, baby girl.

Keep fucking yourself on me. Use Daddy to make that pretty cunt come." She picks up speed, but it's not enough.

With a hand at the base of her throat, I lean in and whisper, "Harder, Kendra." I growl, "Fuck yourself harder."

Panting and moaning, she's just not getting there. It's been a while since we've been more rough. "Tease your clit, baby." One hand lets go of the headboard and skims the base of my cock when she rubs herself. My palms grip her soft sides as I work her up and down my shaft. Again and again, base to tip. I pause only a second to give a small swat to her cheek. She whimpers—*I know that whimper*. "There you go, baby girl. Don't think."

Her lips roll together as she hums and clamps onto me. Fuck yes. The cry is heaven to my ears. I love listening to my girl get off. "Good fucking girl, there you go, keep going, keep going." I don't change a thing as she comes. My hand stutters as my balls draw up. I can't hold out. I slap the side of her ass, relishing her gasp. Fucking hell. With each pull into me, I release more into her. Kendra's insides are painted with my cum. Nothing gives me a high like watching milk droplets fall from her brown nipples right after I've filled her pussy. I lick the beads of milk, but I need to see the rest.

"Get on your hands and knees, baby girl." She does as she's told, and I spank her a second time. "Turn around."

I glide my palms over her backside, spreading her cheeks, and appreciate my work.

"Push it out for Daddy, let me see how full you are …" My eyes lock onto the cum dripping from her tight pussy. *Damn, I love this woman.* The sight is so erotic I want to start all over again, but instead, I massage the rosy handprint, then swipe the cum with the side of my thumb and push it inside. "Good fucking girl."

Rolling to her side, she sighs with a smile. Her thick

eyelashes flutter closed, and I marvel at how good my life is. I position behind her and bring my knee between her thighs, not wanting a drop to leak out. She groans a second time. "Mmmm ... it's good to be back."

I chuckle into the back of her neck, sweeping her hair aside so I can kiss her shoulder.

It is.

———

After dinner—and a couple helpings of ice cream, we've got about an hour before Bo wakes up again. I love seeing Kendra eat whatever she wants again. No more nausea, and now she can eat full meals because there isn't a baby pressing against her stomach.

I wrap up dishes, and we settle in front of the fireplace. Kendra dug through our board games until she found the *Game of Life* buried in the back of the game cupboard. This has become part of our evening routine. That game is especially appropriate tonight. With my face on MNSports every time I turn around and her working in television, we've decided the best way to unwind is for us to have face-to-face time without screens.

"These fuckin' taxes are killing me," she says, slapping down the pastel paper money to the "bank."

"At least you don't have two cars filled up with kids. Where the hell are the condoms in this game?"

She laughs. "How many kids do you want? In *real* life, I mean."

"Twelve."

She chokes out a laugh and nudges me. "I'm serious."

I shrug. "Two? Three? What about you?"

Kendra nods. "At least two. Being an only child can get

lonely. I want them to have each other when things get tough and we aren't here anymore." Makes sense. "I've been thinking about reversal …"

I glance up. "Yeah?"

"It has a forty- to eighty-five percent success rate."

"Well, I think our odds are pretty good, considering we ended up with Bo after a two percent rate." I chuckle. "But, if not, I'm happy to have another child with you, in whatever form that is. When you're ready to make an appointment with the doctor, let me know and I'll come with you." I spin the wheel on the board and move my two cars the appropriate number of spaces.

"I love you," she says.

When I look at her, she's gazing at me with all the love in the world. *How did I get so lucky?*

"I love you too." With her in my arms, I press my lips to the top of her head. "You are it for me … I will choose you every time, Kendra. You will always be mine."

She sighs and rests her cheek on my chest.

"Will you marry me?"

Ever so slowly, she pushes away from me, and as soon as I see her smile and twinkling eyes, I fish out the box in my pocket and open it. She holds my gaze without even looking at the ring and answers the most beautiful *yes* I've ever heard. I still get a small gasp when she peeks down and sees the diamond sparkling back at her.

I slip it on her finger where it looks even better than I imagined. She climbs to her knees, faces me, and cups my cheeks in her hands.

"And you will always be mine. Yes, baby. My answer is always yes."

I spin her around and hold her to my chest, crossing my

forearms in front so she's pinned against me. "Wanna know how much I love you?"

Her head tilts up to face me. "Yeah."

I point to my phone set up in the corner. "For the aftershow."

Her laugh rings out, and she wiggles free from me, hops up, and snatches my phone from the concealed location. She saunters back, climbing into my arms again. Her finger taps the screen, and the camera adjusts to front-facing. We look at each other on the screen, and she tips up her chin to kiss me.

"I love you enough not to air it. They can see the beginning of our love story, but the happy ending is ours."

ACKNOWLEDGMENTS

There were many days I questioned whether or not this book would even happen, but I'm so happy to finally give you Sully and Kendra's story. Especially since some of you have been asking for his story since Before We Came. I hope it lived up to your expectations!

I need to extend a special thank you to Lorelei, Trish, Rachel, Danielle Baker, and my husband, for helping me work through ideas when this story fell apart and I had to start over with 4 weeks to finish. You carried me through the finish line on this one, everyone who enjoys this story owes their gratitude to you!

As always, thank you to my beta readers: Catie, Emma, Jess, Kailey, Kenz, Lorelei, Nicole, Shannon, and Trish. I love you, mucho.

My copy editor, Dee Houpt, thank you for your patience with me on this one. When you told me you loved it, it was such a weight off my shoulders. Thank you. After the first round of edits, I loved it too, and I can't tell you how much I needed that.

My developmental editor, Bri, who said. "Let's set up a

phone call" after I sent her the manuscript. Timelines are hard, and somehow I make them even harder. After our chat, I finally saw this book come together and I cannot thank you enough for the time you put into these characters and their story. Thank you for believing in this book when I couldn't.

Shoutout to my amazing sensitivity readers, Tione and Teri. Thank you for your emotional energy, thank you for your honest thoughts, and thank you for helping me feel closer to my POC readers.

Thank you Cathryn at Formatting by CC for making these books so beautiful. I appreciate your keen attention to detail and creative vision. Anytime I ask for a change or tweak, the answer is always an enthusiastic yes. You're the best!

To my entire street team, thank you. This was a rocky release, no question, but you made it look smoother than a fresh jar of Skippy. I never imaged to grow big enough to have an entire content team, but wow, do you make releases fun!

I couldn't function without the people on my personal team: Shannon, Rachel, Catie, and Kenz. Shannon, you are my sweet ball of chaos, who somehow keeps my shit straight when I'm totally lost. I don't know how you do it. Thank you for being so understanding of me when I "go dark" and hide. There was a lot of hiding while writing this book, thank you for being patient with me. Rachel, you make the street team happen. I am continuously amazed by your organization skills and creativity. Thank you so much for jumping in and taking control when my head was spinning.

To my social media girlies, Kenz and Catie, for stepping in to run my social media. I got overwhelmed very quickly and you jumped in to help without hesitation. Thank you. You are amazing.

Shout out to my ARC team - yo! Thank you for taking the

time to read this book and leave your reviews. You make every release day so freaking fun!

Thank you to Taryn Delanie Smith for shouting out Stand and Defend (instead of suing me) when I referenced Kendra's likeness to your knockout beauty. Your content is fabulous. Long live the chaos goblin.

Thank you content creators! I have found so many amazing readers through you and I'm so incredibly grateful for your awesome posts!

MORE BOOKS BY SLOANE ST. JAMES

LAKE HOCKEY SERIES

Book 1
Before We Came
Lonan and Birdie

Book 2
Strong and Wild
Rhys and Micky

Book 3
In The Game
Barrett and Raleigh

Book 4
Stand and Defend
Camden and Jordan

WELCOME TO THE SLOANE ZONE

Thank you so much for supporting my writing!
If you enjoyed reading this book, please help spread the word by leaving a review on Amazon, Goodreads, Bookbub, Facebook Reader Groups, Booktok, Bookstagram, or wherever you talk about romance. If you already have, you have my endless gratitude. I hope you sleep well knowing that you are making some woman's mid-life crisis dreams come true!
I love to connect with my readers!
SloaneStJamesWrites@gmail.com
Instagram @SloaneStJames
TikTok @SloaneStJames

Facebook Reader Group:
Sloane's Good Girl Book Club
Interested in being an ARC reader?
www.SloaneStJames.com

Looking for signed paperbacks and other merch?
www.SloaneStJames.com

Printed in Great Britain
by Amazon